"Jim Nesbitt's new novel, *The Fatal Saving Grace,* continues the gritty, hard charging Ed Earl Burch series--as hard-bitten and hard-boiled as its West Texas landscape, serving up a tale of revenge, unfinished business and murder ... Nesbitt's story has twists and surprises, and he excels at tense scenes that put the reader right into the mix--the heat, the quiet menace, the unmistakable smell of blood. His writing is spare and evocative, and like the "the tangy metallic smell of spilled blood hitting the air," it lingers on the senses."

—**James McCrone**, author of *The Faithless Elector, The Bastard Verdict* and *Witness Tree*

I0601304

What Fellow Authors Say About Jim Nesbitt's *The Last Second Chance, The Right Wrong Number, The Best Lousy Choice* and *The Dead Certain Doubt*

"*The Dead Certain Doubt* is a noir gem, peppered with American muscle cars, Kentucky bourbon and universal life lessons. Written in author Jim Nesbitt's powerfully lyrical and staccato prose, the hunt for a troubled young woman who is marked for death by gunrunners and a Mexican drug cartel puts Dallas private detective Ed Earl Burch—and the reader—through the wringer. The pace is swift, the action is raw and the characters are intense and visual. The compelling power of remorse drives the page-turning pace even as the glorious phrasing makes you want to stop and savor the work of a master wordsmith. Nesbitt's prose, characters and gritty authenticity make him one of today's most talented and stylish noir writers."

> —**Carmen Amato**, author of the Emilia Cruz and Galliano Club mystery series

"Dallas has plenty of bottomless pits, and Ed Earl Burch, the washed-up detective in Jim Nesbitt's Texas crime thriller series, has managed to fall into most of them. Usually trying to do the right thing, as if that exists in Nesbitt's extra-hard-boiled tales. And when the attempted good deeds run bad, as always, they quickly move to West Texas, where Burch's rough days and harsh nights seem like paradise before it's all over."

> —**Rod Davis**, author of the Southern noir novels, *South, America* and *East of Texas, West of Hell*

"If you're looking for gritty, *The Right Wrong Number* is as gritty as Number 36 sandpaper."

 —**Bill Crider**, author of the Sheriff Dan Rhodes mysteries

"If Chandler's noir was a neon sign in the LA sunset, Nesbitt's noir is the Shiner Bock sign buzzing outside the last honky-tonk you'll hit before the long drive to the next one. On the way you'll pass towns with names like Crumley and Portis. Roll down the window; it's a hot night. It's a fast ride."

 —**James Lileks**, author of *The Casablanca Tango*, columnist for the *National Review* and *Star Tribune* of Minneapolis, creator of LILEKS.com

"In *The Right Wrong Number*, Jim Nesbitt writes like an angel about devilish deals, bloody murder and nasty sex. His beat is Dallas—not the glitzy spires of J.R. Ewing, but the back alley bars and brothels of Jack Ruby and Candy Barr. His PI, Ed Earl Burch, is steeped in Coke-chased bourbon; cured in the smoke of Zippo-lit Luckies; and longing for hard-bitten girls who got away. Nesbitt channels the lyricism of James Crumley, the twisted kick of Jim Thompson and the cold, dark heart of Mickey Spillane."

 —**Jayne Loader**, author of *Between Pictures* and *Wild America*, director of *The Atomic Café*

"In *The Last Second Chance*, Jim Nesbitt gives readers a splendid first opportunity to meet Ed Earl Burch, as flawed a Luckies-smoking, whiskey-drinking, serial-married hero as ever walked the scarred earth of Dirty Texas ... In Burch, Nesbitt has created a more angst-ridden and bad-ass version of Michael Connelly's Harry Bosch and a Tex-Mex landscape much meaner than the streets of L.A. Add hate-worthy lowlifes and a diminutive dame,

Carla Sue Cantrell, who cracks wiser than the guys, and you've got a book with gumption."

—**Bob Morris**, Edgar finalist, author of *Baja Florida* and *A Deadly Silver Sea*

"If you like to read, if you appreciate words and the people who run them brilliantly through their paces, give Jim Nesbitt's *The Last Second Chance* a read. And his next one, and the one after that. You'll be enthralled, like I was."

—**Cheryl Pellerin**, author of *Trips: How Hallucinogens Work in Your Brain* and *Healing With Cannabis*

"Jim Nesbitt's latest hard-boiled Texas thriller is another masterpiece. *The Right Wrong Number* has everything to keep the reader turning the page—vivid characters, stark Texas landscape, non-stop action and a classic American anti-hero in Ed Earl Burch, Nesbitt's battered but dogged Dallas PI. Buckle up and brace yourself for another wild ride."

—**Paul Finebaum**, ESPN college football analyst, author, host of *The Paul Finebaum Show*

"Cowboy noir for the cartel era ... *The Last Second Chance* is a gripping read with a cathartic ending, and it takes you places you've likely never been."

—**Jeannette Cooperman**, author of *A Circumstance of Blood*

JIM NESBITT

An Ed Earl Burch Novel

THE FATAL SAVING GRACE

THE FATAL SAVING GRACE
An Ed Earl Burch Novel

Published by SPOTTED MULE PRESS

Paperback
ISBN 13: 978-0-9983294-7-5

E-Book
ISBN 13: 978-0-9983294-8-2

Cover design by Momir Borocki
momir.borocki@gmail.com

Copyediting, proofreading
and formatting by Ashley Hagan
ashley@inkwellwriters.com

Author photograph by Pam Nesbitt
Used with exclusive permission.

Jim Nesbitt Web site: https://jimnesbittbooks.com

Author's Note

I have an abiding love for the harsh, stark beauty of the border country of West Texas and northern Mexico, where the mountains rise from the sun-scorched desert like the bones of the earth ripped open for all to see. The primordial power of that land first hooked me in the late 1980s and early 1990s when I was out there chasing stories as a roving correspondent for various news outfits. What I heard, saw, smelled and felt forms the backbone of all five of my Ed Earl Burch novels -- partly because I'm a firm believer in creating a keen sense of place, but mostly because the land is so evocative that it becomes a character unto itself, the perfect player in bloody, gritty stories of revenge and redemption. And while there is no Faver, Texas, and Cuervo County is also a figment of my imagination, my descriptions of those fictitious places are rooted in what I saw in real towns like Sanderson, Marathon, Marfa, Alpine, Valentine and Fort Davis.

Writing a novel is both a lonely road and a collaborative effort and I'd like to thank the people who helped keep me on track, gave wise counsel, kicked me in the butt when needed and helped shape and polish the finished product. Special thanks to Cheryl Pellerin, a damn good writer in her own right, for giving me a tough but fair edit on all five Ed Earl books. And to Ashley Hagan for her peerless copyediting, proofreading and formatting skills.

Thanks and a tip o' the Resistol to my semi-irregular cadre of reviewers, fellow writers, beta readers, and smart-ass buddies who didn't sugarcoat their opinions. The crew includes writers Dick Belsky, Baron R. Birtcher, Rich Zahradnik, John Davis, Dana King, Bruce Coffin, Carmen Amato, Michael Ludden, Mike Seely, and my nephew, Patrick Lee. Thanks also to ace Texas reviewer Kevin Tipple; Dallas crime fiction impresario Sweet Johnny Wesner; my old friend Richard Beene, once the Czar of Bakersfield and now in the midst of all the craziness that is Florida; North Carolina political operative Ray Martin, who is a graphics, marketing and social media wizard; and fellow whisky-slinger and history buff Stanley Hitchins, who ceaselessly touts my work to our Delco high school pals.

Most of all, many thanks and much love to my wife, Pam, who believes in me even when I don't.

For Pam and The Panther

One

When a man gets hit by a .45 ACP Flying Ashtray or three, by all that's ballistically holy, he ought to get dead and stay dead.

All manner of official paperwork swore he *was* dead. All of it based on a bogus death certificate filed by parties unknown in the Cuervo County Coroner's Office, with copies popping up like blowflies on a cow carcass. Even the *federales* had him playing poker with the Devil, his prison mugshot tucked away in ATF and DEA files, DECEASED stamped across his face in bold, black letters.

The con was slick and easy. Money changed hands, files were swapped or ditched, reports were shredded or faked. Somebody else's corpse became him. The relentless power of bureaucratic incompetence and inertia did the rest.

Yessir. According to all that yellowing, lawdog paper, he was nobody they had to worry about no more. *Finito*. A shade. A ghost who said *adios*. A good thug now that he was a dead thug. *Muerto*.

Not hardly.

That's what John Wayne said to all those *hombres* who thought he was dead in *Big Jake*. With a growl and a scowl.

Not hardly.

He liked that. Matter of fact, he just trotted out the Duke's line to a guy he used to be tight with. Caught up to him climbing the three cinder block steps to the front door of his desert double wide.

Tapped him on the shoulder, saw the wild-eyed fear when the dude turned and saw who the finger belonged to. Blurted out: "You're supposed to be dead!"

Not hardly. Said it with a growl but no scowl. Then grabbed him by a greasy hank of raven black hair, yanking his head back and cutting a crimson smile across his throat from ear to ear. With a bone-handled straight razor. His favorite.

Threw the guy into the sand at the side of the steps. Listened to the choking gurgle and death rattle. Then licked the blood off the blade.

Not hardly. He tilted his head back and laughed. Savored the kill. Alone and alive. An endless dome of stars glittering in the midnight sky above the rocky desert outback near Radium Springs, New Mexico. No moon. A dead man at his feet. Used to be a member of his crew. Frankie Sheridan.

Met him at Pelican Bay. An Alice Baker brother doing a long stretch for bank robbery. Had a shamrock tattooed on his chest with the initials AB in capital letters—Alice Baker, Aryan Brotherhood. Blood in, blood out. Ex-Army. Knew his way around diesels, alarm systems, and weapons.

Sent him a ticket to Texas when he got out. Made him a member of his crew, smuggling guns and drugs out of a ranch north of Faver, the Cuervo County seat, a bent outfit that ran cattle for cover and fleeced bitter and gullible white trash while promising them the return of the Republic of Texas for Caucasian Christians only, a New Zion based on God, guns, guts, and the Good Book. Niggers, Jews, Arabs, and Spics need not apply.

Bad move. Frankie was a ratfuck snitch. *Uno chivato.* Not to the lawdogs. Just as bad, though. Frankie sold him out to a rival outfit of gunrunners and drug smugglers. Kept them one step ahead of him as they chased a third outfit that held a cache of stolen military hardware everybody wanted.

Rockets, bloopers, mortars, and full-auto carbines and rifles. Bang-bangs that could tip the scales on both sides of the river. All in the hands of a crew fronted by a flashy woman in jeans, tall boots, a bolero jacket, and a blonde wig. A wet dream for the *pendejos* she hustled.

La Güera. Just the thought of her caused his molars to grind. He wanted her dead. No, he *needed* her dead. She and her lover were the reason his life got flushed into the sewer, his crew dead, his stash of guns and drugs long gone. Had him climbing out of the shitter, clawing to the top of the dung heap. Again.

He caught the lover. Sliced off his manhood. Slit his throat. Then chopped off his head and butchered his body to stuff into a giant barbecue smoker. Tucked the man's jewels into his mouth as the crowning touch to a cannibal's mesquite-smoked delight.

Not the same. Didn't have her. She still needed to feel his blade, feel his eyes boring holes into hers as he gave her that crimson smile. He needed to lick *her* blood off that sharp stainless steel. Taste it. And grin. Only then would the circle be complete. He'd be whole again.

Well, not completely whole.

His right eye was gone, blown out by a glancing hit from one of those .45 ACP slugs that also shattered the orbital bones. Nothing extensive plastic surgery, bone implants and a new glass eye couldn't cure. Had to stack plenty of cash up front to repair damage that severe.

Gave that part of his face a waxy texture straight out of Madame Tussauds. But it sure beat wearing an eye patch and the lopsided face of a Dick Tracy cartoon villain.

His left knee was also shattered, replaced with a titanium joint that allowed him to walk with only a slight limp. Another five-figure hit to his stash of greenbacks.

The man who fired those rounds was also on his payback list. An ex-cop. Big-ass older fucker with a gray beard. Said to be a washed-up Dallas P. I..

Beg to differ, sir. Sumbitch sure kept him from getting to her during that clusterfuck in the West Texas desert. A real Wild West shootout between rival drug gangs wanting the blonde bitch's bang-bangs.

He was oh-so-close to grabbing her up, dodging bullets and bodies, closing the gap between him and Ol' Dude, who was carrying the bitch draped over his right shoulder. He screamed her name and leveled an M-16A1 at the both of them.

"La Güeraaaaaaa! I got you, bitch! Got you now! Gonna slice you wide open and watch you bleeeeeeed!"

Ol' Dude spun on his heel and emptied a 1911 mag at him offhand. Yelled this: *"Not today, you cockbite motherfucker. Not in this lifetime or the next."* A lefty. On target without dropping the bitch. Only thing that kept him alive was a Kevlar vest that caught the Flying Ashtrays that would have shredded his chest.

Washed-up, my ass. The man wrecked me. His time was coming, though. Count on a reckoning. Soon. But not now. He was working his way up the ladder of a list he kept in his head. One body at a time.

Frankie was the bottom rung. *La Güera* was at the top with Ol' Dude second. Five other rungs between Frankie and them.

Time to get gone. And get busy.

Two

A flash of light caught his eye, a chance reflection from the setting sun, bouncing off glass or chrome to his right, a warning from a pile of rocks about fifty yards from his north-bound pickup.

Gave Burch just enough time to tap the brakes and throw off the shot before high-velocity lead punched through the sheet metal of the cab roof just above his head and shattered the windshield, raining glass on the hood, the dash and his lap.

Sweet Jesus. He flicked the old Dodge out of overdrive and jammed her into third, fishtailing on the smooth tarmac of the farm-to-market road, a long stretch of nowhere between Presidio and Faver.

Get the fuck out of the kill zone. Bang her into second. Let the lower gear bleed the speed to a trot. Crank the manual steering hard left, crossing the road in front of an on-rushing cattle truck.

Ignore the horn blast, willing the old girl to stay upright as she lurched over a cattle guard and onto a caliche ranch road guaranteed to rattle his teeth and test the truck's shocks and springs.

Popdick motherfucker. A second slug smacked into the rear of the cab, ripping through the top of the padded seatback a few inches from his right shoulder before smashing the useless AM radio embedded in the dashboard, original equipment he had meant to swap out for something that worked.

He slammed on the brakes, muscling the steering wheel to the right, feeling the back end start to slew to the left until the truck stopped in the middle of the trail, presenting the passenger side to a sniper now 100 yards and a black ribbon of tarmac away.

A rising cloud of dirty-white caliche dust enveloped the truck, screening him from view. He flinched and ducked down below the dash as a third round slapped sheet metal. Couldn't tell where.

Chinga tu madre, cabron. He grabbed the mic of his cop radio. The box was lit up but lifeless. No squelch, no static, no nothin'. Round must have hit the coax cable. He was on his own.

He popped open the door and slipped out of the cab. In a crouch with boots on stones and grit, he eased an M1 Garand from behind the seat, slinging a cloth bandolier that carried six, eight-round *en bloc* clips across his chest.

Fourth round flattened the right rear tire. *Well, fuck me runnin.' 'Bout had enough of this shit.* There was already a clip in the M1. He worked the bolt to put a .30-06 round in the pipe.

Fuckin' American caliber. Won your basic WWI and WWII with it. Fought the slopes to a draw in Korea. Let's see if I can get you to suck on one of these, Mister Man.

Closest cover was two steps to his left. Behind the engine block and surrounding sheet metal. *Not ideal. Fucker's in the catbird seat on top of those damn rocks. Can see right over the truck. Got the height and the angle.*

He needed to even the odds. Behind him was a brush-choked rise with rocks at the naked summit. *That'll work.* He slung the M1 across his back and crawled toward the tailgate, gritting his teeth as his surgery-savaged knees delivered instant payback.

Fifth round clipped the top of the bed rail above his head. He bet his life the shooter was using a bolt-action hunting rifle and had just emptied his magazine. He shoved himself off the ground and into a crouch, unslinging the M1 and lumbering toward a shallow ditch flanking the ranch track.

His knees screamed. The pins and rods holding his left leg together joined the protest. He tucked his shoulder to roll through the ditch, then crashed through the brush on the other side. Lost his hat, a brand-new Resistol straw.

A sixth round *zizzzzzed* past, high and over his bare, bald head. *Angry hornet. Rushed your reload, Jack. Fuck you.* He stayed low and worked his way to the rocks above, ears cocked for a rattler's warning, sweating like a mule in the late afternoon heat.

At the top, he kept the rocks between him and the shooter as he clambered up the back side of the pile toward a flat-top crown, sweat darkening his forest green shirt and khaki whipcord slacks.

Helluva spot. Where's that fucker at? Got the height on you now, pinche chupaverga.

He saw the shooter's rocky perch, his Ray-Bans dulling the glare of the setting sun. Shucking the bandolier then wrapping the web rifle sling around his left arm, he slipped into a prone position. He ignored the sharp rebuke from his knees and rebuilt leg. Tried not to think about the sun lighting him up more than it did the other guy.

Wipe the slate clean. Keep the mind blank. Settle in behind a rifle you love to shoot, and hold it close like a lover, cheek welded to the stock tight and right. Breathe easy. Scan the other guy's rocky perch. Was he still there?

Flash to his left. Roll that way twice and reset. A slug sent rock chips flying from the spot he just vacated. Ricochet whine upon departure. Movement where the flash came from. Settled down and lined up the iron sights on a small, dark shape. It moved then moved again. He let out his breath and squeezed the trigger four times, rocking with the recoil.

The shape fell away, disappearing. He heard something clatter down the rocks. Sounded like rattling antlers. A decoy a hunter would use. Hard to tell from this distance. Could have been a rifle. Couldn't see it to be sure. Way too wily to rise up. Stay still and wait, eyes on the target zone.

Without moving his head, he reached for the Levi Garrett pouch in the right rear pocket of his slacks. Fished out a stringy ball with two fingers and settled it between cheek and gum.

For real tobacco pleasure. Just like Walt Garrison used to say about that nasty-ass Skoal. Tried it once. Never again. Wasn't even snuff, really. Sure wasn't the powdery stuff his granny dipped with a teaspoon. More like candied coffee grounds. He stuck to real tobacco leaf you could chew when you couldn't light up a Lucky Strike.

Stay still, wait and chew. Wait and chew, stay still. The smart play as the sun set. Gave Ed Earl Burch plenty of time to wonder who wanted to get him dead.

This time.

"Found a blood trail on them rocks but no body. Led the boys to some tread marks on a track through the brush. Jeep maybe. They also found a rifle at the bottom of them rocks, a Remington 700 with the stock splintered and the scope all busted up from the fall."

"What caliber?"

"Not that it matters, but .30-06. Same as you. We'll dust the gun and rounds for prints. See where that leads us."

"Probably nowhere. Fucker struck me as just pro enough to wear gloves."

Cuervo County Sheriff Sudden Doggett poked a sharp stick at Burch, a favorite and more frequent pastime:

"Can't have been that good a hand to let an old man like you outgun him."

Burch hollered like a hit dog.

"Bite my ass, Sheriff. Like I said, he was just good enough but wasn't no Carlos Hathcock. If I hadn't seen the sun flashing off his scope, you'd have my body in the morgue with a toe tag."

"He didn't expect you to turn and fight, did he?"

"Nope."

"Why'd you do that instead of punching the pedal to the floor?"

"That old Dodge wouldn't have gotten me out of his kill zone quick enough. Built to haul horses and cows, not haul ass. And I didn't know if he had friends waitin' up the road. Besides, he pissed me off."

"How'd he get up on you so fast? And who sent his ass after you?"

"The first question is pretty easy to answer. I was nosing around Presidio, trying to get a line on our friend Dalrymple. Made the rounds. Talked to the usual suspects. Somebody put me on the spot. Called somebody who called the shooter. Easy to figure which way I'd go to come back to Faver. Plenty of prime spots along the way."

"You goin' back down there?"

"Not until I stop by the Lonesome Y to buy me a new hat."

Burch tugged the bill of a midnight blue ball cap with CCSO embossed across the crown.

"Lost my straw rollin' around in the ocotillo, tryin' not to get dead. Looked around some after the smoke cleared, but it was too dark. Coyotes run off with it by now."

"Too bad. You almost looked like one of us."

"Yeah, without it, your deputies look at me like I stepped in horse plop."

"They're keen-eyed law enforcement officers particular about the company they keep. How you gettin' down there with your truck all shot to shit?"

"I can take that dog-ass Blazer you made me buy."

"Take the Olds your girlfriend gave you."

"Too pretty a car to wind up in an Ojinaga chop shop. Blazer is the ticket. Got a good idea who made those calls. Need to pay them a visit. Get an answer to your second question."

"Talked to that puke of a sheriff they got over there. Álvarez. He's pissed you didn't bother to check in with him before bracing the solid citizens of his county."

"Well I damn sure wasn't going to drive up to Marfa to kiss his ass then tool all the way down to Presidio. Besides, I'm buddies with the police chief down there. He was okay with it."

"Lado Sandoval? Don't know who's worse. That lardass or Álvarez."

"The High Sheriff of Presidio County by a country mile. Now that I study on it, I only talked to scumbags, whores, and snitches down there. Álvarez must feel left out."

"He's sensitive. Little dick syndrome. Still sweepin' up Rick Thompson's mess. Getting eyed for doin' some of the same shit."

"Want me to call him?"

"Oh, hell no. He'd just call whoever sicced that shooter on you. Just know he's on the prod and try not to give him an excuse to put you in jail or shoot you."

"I'll be *extry* nice."

"Don't want you down there on your lonesome again. Take Bobby with you."

"Nah. I'll be fine."

"That wasn't a suggestion."

Burch locked eyes with Doggett, noting the deeper crow's feet and furrows to his brow along with the new crop of wiry silver in the man's Zapata moustache.

Started to say something sharp and rude to the ex-calf roper, the county's first sheriff with both Mexican and Black blood coursing through his veins and dark skin the locals called *moreno*.

Thought better of it. For once.

"Okay. Bobby's good company."

Burch wandered down to the bullpen looking for Bobby Quintero, the deputy Doggett wanted him to drag back to Presidio to watch his back. He wasn't at his desk, so Burch left a note and went outside to burn a Lucky.

Parked it on a bench under the covered walkway between the Sheriff's Office and the courthouse, a weathered, two-story, turn-of-the-century brick building anchored by four huge, granite blocks at each corner and topped by a tin mansard roof with fresh silver paint.

Used to be green, sun-blasted and peeling a decade or so ago when he first came to this town as a shamus. Now it reflected the fierce desert sun like an airport beacon at night. Glad to be out of that glare, Burch snapped open a Zippo and fired up some unfiltered tobacco. Then started to brood.

Overkill bringing Bobby to babysit. Kinda like killing a fly with a shotgun given the deputy's skills as an ex-Ranger with plenty of black ops experience in nasty places like Nicaragua, Mexico, Columbia, Somalia and the Middle East. Still sharp and stealthy, deadly with knife, gun or bare hands, able to slip into a target's backyard or bedroom without a trace.

A serious hombre. Count your blessings. Besides, he liked Bobby. He was good company. Only spoke when he had something to say. Best listen when he did. The man also knew how to enjoy the comfortable silence of a long ride with nothing to do but count cactus, rocks, coyote, and cattle, a crucial survival skill in West Texas.

Doggett's insistence on him having a babysitter still rankled, though. Burch was a loner by nature and necessity, accustomed to working by himself, relying on nobody's wits and skills but his own. Long years as a Dallas P.I. after he lost his detective's shield made him this way, a stubbornly independent operator with the mindset of a semi-outlaw.

Badges? We don't need no stinkin' badges. No rules, neither. Did what he thought *needed* to be done to *get* the job done.

That changed when Doggett gave him a gold shield and made him the one and only investigator for the Cuervo County District Attorney's Office. Technically, that made the DA, Sam Boelcke, his boss. As in: Santiago Quinones Boelcke, the blue-eyed, black haired son of a Mexican mother and a father with pure *Texasdeutsche* ancestry.

But in the stark and dusty real world of the West Texas town of Faver, named for Milton Faver, the pioneer cattle king of the Big Bend Country, he answered to Doggett. And a retired Texas Ranger up in Austin named Dub McKee, an *eminence grise* who had the ear of the governor, the more powerful lieutenant governor, and all the state legislators and county judges that mattered.

McKee and Doggett were the two honchos who cooked up a way to give a cashiered Dallas murder cop a badge again, returning him to the blue brotherhood from which he was banished nearly twenty years ago, quenching the longing for that sense of higher calling and purpose he had before he got the chop.

Only one problem with that. He wasn't housebroke no more. Had to re-learn how to take orders, work with fellow officers, and not be a round-the-clock hard case. One of his Dallas buddies had a black biker T-shirt with a logo inked on the back in bold white letters—Warning: Does Not Play Well With Others.

Words he lived by. For a long, long time. But if he was going to keep this badge, he had to throttle that impulse. Had to quit being an asshole for no reason.

Truth be told, he liked being a semi-outlaw with a boot in both camps. It was one of the barbwire virtues that gave Doggett and McKee the notion that he was just the man to bring to Cuervo County as a reborn lawdog. Not just Cuervo County—McKee wired it up so he could cross the jurisdictional lines of the five adjacent counties. Pretty broad patch to roam.

Didn't have to interview for this tailor-made job. They'd already seen how he handled himself when hired as a P.I. nearly a decade ago to investigate the grisly murder of a war hero and head of a powerful ranching family, trapped in his own barn and burned to death. Nobody wanted to touch it but him.

Burch also dug up the dirt that helped bring down Doggett's predecessor, an ex-Ranger named Blue Willingham, a big law-and-order blowhard in bed with the Garza family cartel who lived just across the river. Blue saved the county the expense of a trial by using his grandfather's break-top Smith & Wesson to blow off the top of his skull as the hounds closed in.

McKee was also impressed by undercover work Burch did four years or so back while trying to rescue the granddaughter of a dying old woman. Triggered a brain fart, too: Let's give Burch a badge and turn him loose to deliver his style of rude justice to the cartel killers, smugglers, rapists, and garden-variety thugs and assholes wandering around this harsh, dry country.

McKee had to sell it hard to Doggett, an ex-Army MP and CID special agent who thought Burch was too much of a loose cannon, but the old Ranger finally coaxed Sheriff Sudden into the corral.

After that, Doggett became a true believer in the particular skills and virtues of Ed Earl Burch and stepped up as the scheme's leading evangelist.

Sounded almost too good to be true when Doggett made the initial pitch over deep whiskies at his ranch house in the desert outback. Then tossed that glittering gold shield in Burch's lap like an angler flicking a lure at a hungry bass.

Living his new gig day-to-day forced him to change his free-wheeling ways to fit in.

Sure, he had that shield clipped to the russet leather gun belt where his Colt 1911 was parked in a cross-draw holster with a basket weave stamp. Proud to wear one again, despite his doubts and fears.

Gotta look the part to play the part, though. He stocked up on the white and forest green speed-snap shirts and tan whipcord slacks Doggett's deputies wore. Sported the same Ray-Ban shooter's sunglasses with smoky-dark green lenses.

For courtroom appearances, there were khakis and a Circle S blue blazer with cowboy piping bordering the yoke and pockets on a hanger hooked to the back of his office door.

Hadn't been this clean cut in decades. His beard and moustache were clipped close like an old-time boxer's, providing less camouflage for his jowls. So was the fringe of salt-and-pepper hair that circled his bald pate. Until he lost it while dodging that sniper, he even had a size eight Resistol straw with a cattleman's crease to the crown and come-and-go dip to the lightly curled brim.

Real Western, now. Sho'nuff. Yew bet.

But he felt rootless and unmoored, stranded in dreaded fake-it-till-you-make-it territory. Some of that would pass as he put in the hours and worked side-by-side with his new *compadres.*

Not all of it, though. There was tension riding under his relationship with Doggett, a live wire that could pop to the surface at any time and shock them both. And there was more to it than a clash between by-the-book and chuck-the-book out the window.

He once saved Doggett's life down in a little piece-of-shit mountain *pueblito* two slow hours south of the river, blowing down Blue Willingham's chief enforcer, Needle

Burnet, just as he was about to fire *coup de grace* hollow-points into Sudden's brainpan.

Never brought it up. Neither did Doggett, who thanked him the night it happened but never mentioned it again. Wasn't an issue when time and 500 miles of Texas kept them apart.

Now it was. He wasn't in and out of the sheriff's life anymore. He was right here in Faver, rolling into the sheriff's fiefdom nearly every day, a walking, talking reminder of that night he sent eight Flying Ashtrays down the narrow hallway of a Mexican shack to wax Burnet.

Some men didn't like to be reminded of a saving grace. The thought they owed their life to another man's actions rankled their soul and curdled their pride, turning grace into something rancid and poisonous.

Might could be fatal. Maybe for both of them. Burch couldn't tell how deep Doggett's resentment ran. But he knew it was there and would have to be dealt with. A boil that needed to be lanced. Sooner rather than later.

Didn't help that the son of Doggett's cousin also got killed that night while leading them to Burnet's hideaway. He knew Doggett felt a ton of guilt about the kid's death. Funny thing about guilt, though—never knew how a man might twist it to avoid blaming himself. Burch didn't know if Doggett hung a hunk of the rap on him, but figured he was a handy surrogate.

He also knew that having a badge again didn't mean as much to him as he thought it would during those decades of longing for the gold shield he lost in Dallas. Couldn't hide this sorry truth from his badass lover, Carla Sue Cantrell, a petite and deadly woman with a lethal taste for the high-wire double-cross of terminally dangerous people.

Carla Sue thought he should ditch his lawdog fantasy and fully commit to the outlaw life. With her by his side. Well, leading the way was more like it. Her previous stings of drug lords, bankers, and bent politicians had netted her a huge pile of money and a standing million dollar contract for any swinging dick who got her dead.

That put her on the run and out of his life until several weeks after Doggett made his gold shield offer. What changed? All the players who wanted her dead had uttered the Big Adios.

Nobody left to honor the contract. Carla Sue could share a bed with Burch without ducking bullets. No more love on the run. Free to take a shot at love in one place, his adobe-walled home at the head of a box canyon twenty miles west of Faver. Out where the coyotes howled and the snakes rattled.

Burch knew she was marking time, hanging around, betting he'd see his second tour as a lawdog wasn't all he hoped it would be. Then she'd pounce and make him a full-blown outlaw. And a partner in both love and money.

Unless she got too restless, an action junkie jonesing too hard for her next high-wire target. Needed that rush. Needed it now. Needed it more than she needed him.

Left him with an empty bed, the echo of her presence and a faint whiff of perfume two months ago. Rocketing for points unknown in that resale red Cutlass drop top, trailing a ton of caliche dust, on the scout for fresh meat and easy money.

"I'll call you when I get to Houston, baby. Might go up to Tennessee. Be back soon."

Pissed Burch right the hell off. But he didn't know whether to feel relieved or depressed. *How do you like wearing that badge all by your lonesome, Big Boy? Not exactly what you saw as your future, is it? What are you going to do now,* pendejo?

He spotted Quintero heading his way, eyes hidden by shades and the brim of his hat, boots clicking on the tiles of the walkway to the time of the deputy's rolling, weight-lifter's gait, a smile lighting up the brown skin of his sharp-angled face.

Burch smiled back, stood up, and crushed the Lucky under his boot heel. Today, he was a lone lawdog, not an outlaw. Today, he and Doggett were *simpatico,* and everything between them was *tranquilo.* Let tomorrow worry about itself.

That went double ditto for Carla Sue.

"Heard it got a little sporty out there."

"Just a bit."

"Also heard tell you drew blood with iron sights from 100 yards away. Not bad for a senior citizen."

"I prefer the term vintage American. Didn't nail the sumbitch though. Bastard shot up my truck."

"The old one with the ugly green paint? He did you a favor. Put it out of its misery."

"That was my stealth vehicle. Nobody looks for a lawdog driving a dented old Dodge. Lost my damn hat, too."

"That's the real tragedy. Good lookin' hats that fit are hard to come by."

"Particularly if you got a bucket head like mine."

Burch lit another Lucky and offered the pack to Quintero. Bobby shook his head and pulled a pouch of Red Man from his back pocket. They sat and watched the courthouse foot traffic head for their cars and trucks and the return ride home.

"Doggett wants you to help me brace some *pendejos* down Presidio way who might have sicced that shooter on me."

"This have somethin' to do with the Burdette murder?"

"Yeah, we're on the trail of a shitbird named Lonny Dalrymple. Fresh meat."

"Thought we had this wrapped up—three killers, two of 'em dead, one of them on Death Row. How did Dalrymple pop up?"

"Credit ol' Bright Eyes for making it a quartet. Matched some more latents from the vic's Airstream. Dogged them 'til she found a match. Also found DNA on a Styrofoam cup from a garbage bag under the sink. A fuckin' spit cup. How stupid is that? Bingo again."

Bright Eyes was Burch's nickname for the county's ace crime tech, Katie Navarro, the scientific powerhouse who kept the long-serving elected coroner, J.B. "Doc" Battles, a veterinarian more familiar with a bottle of Old Crow than a microscope, from fucking up too much and letting murderers get away with their evil deeds.

Short and skinny, with long, silky black hair always in a ponytail tucked through the back of her CCSO baseball cap, she was smart, sharp-tongued and fearless. Her olive-toned face was dominated by big brown eyes that telegraphed her emotions, lighting up when she laughed, flashing daggers when she was pissed.

She was just out of her twenties and loved to flirt with Doggett, who shied away from her like Tommy Lee Jones playing Woodrow F. Call.

"Good deal. I could use the exercise. You okay with me riding along? Don't want to crowd your play."

"Glad to have you along, Bobby. Feel kinda funny about dragging you away from more important work, though."

"Nah, it'll be fun. Serious fun. We'll make their livers quiver. Then have dinner at my cousin's house. He's whipping up some *cabrito* for tomorrow night."

"Pick you up in the morning."

"Civvies or formal wear?"

"Real Western. Badges, boots, and hats. Guns, too."

"Oh, yeah. We'll have some hardware. Bring your Garand. And a shotgun. I'll take care of the rest."

"Done deal. Pick you up around five. Gotta scoot now and get me a new hat."

Bobby made it easy. Could have made a fuss about a babysitting gig but didn't. No wonder I like the sumbitch.

Three

In the cool just before dawn fully broke, Burch and Quintero sipped hot coffee while standing at the counter window of a taco truck on Alvarez Street run by Carmen Cortez, who flirted with both of them while ladling scrambled eggs with chopped chile *pequeño*, diced onions, and a savory brown sauce onto flour tortillas.

"Which of you *hombres* are going to show up at my house tonight to rub my aching back? Both of you? Won't get any sleep with two *machos* knocking on my door," she said, rolling her eyes and fanning herself with a paper plate.

"Carmen, you know my wife has claim to all my back rubs and keeps a frying pan handy in case I forget," Quintero said with a grin.

"*Te creo*, Bobby. *Sé que tu esposa tiene tu pene bajo llave,*" she said with a laugh.

Burch had never seen a man of Mexican descent blush before. Quintero's brown skin lightened with a reddish tint as embarrassment rushed blood to his face.

"Damn, Carmen. We're in public here, and you're making me blush like a schoolboy."

"Nobody here yet but you two. Nice to see I haven't lost my touch."

She shifted her gaze to Burch, arching her eyebrows and slapping a palm on her meaty right hip.

"What about your friend here? See anything you like?"

Burch smiled and took in the ample curves of a mature woman with deeply bronze skin, black curls shot with a few streaks of white, and dark eyes that flashed with her smile and a hint of carnal fun.

"Plenty. And none of me is locked down."

"Hah. I like a challenge. And I like a man with some meat on his bones and white in his beard. I think I'll call you *Oso Blanco*."

"White Bear, right? I like it."

"Beats calling you *El Gringo Nuevo*. Have to be careful around you. You know some Spanish."

"Just enough to get me in trouble."

"You have no idea, *hombre*."

Burch paid the breakfast tab then lifted and resettled his stiff, new Resistol to sit lower on his head. Carmen gave him a receipt and a business card with a number hastily scrawled on the back.

"Call me. Make it soon." It was a command punctuated with a tap of the red-lacquered nail of her index finger on his nose.

"Yes, m'am."

Burch touched two fingers to the front of his hat brim, smiling and keeping his eyes locked on hers. Quintero grabbed his elbow.

"Let's get you out of here before she drags you to a motel room. Might lose your hat again."

"Only if I let her wear it."

Carmen's throaty laugh trailed them as they walked to the Blazer and fired it up for the run down to Presidio.

Straight from the street cop's bible: Somebody needed to pay the freight for dropping dime on him. Siccing a shooter on a cop demanded an immediate response. Pain with interest. Something brutal but short of a bullet to the brain. Bruises and broken bones would do.

Burch had an old friend stuffed down the shaft of the Justin he wore on his left foot that was just the ticket. Black Betty. A ten-inch leather sap with twenty ounces of No. 9 lead shot packed in the head, a lovely piece of nastiness that turned a hardened thug into a motor-mouthed true believer with just a tap or three.

Bought it when he still wore blues in Dallas. Always took good care of Betty. Treated her right. Because she took care of him. Almost as much as the Colt riding on his right hip.

Kept Betty in his gun safe when he was a P.I. to avoid any legal hassles. Used a braided leather blackjack and a hand-held coin sap instead. Easier to keep hidden. Brought Betty out of retirement when he got a Cuervo County gold shield.

"Why are you grinning?"

"Just looking forward to seeing our buddy Mauricio Velázquez and introducing him to an old friend of mine."

"That old friend wouldn't be stuffed down your boot, would it?"

Burch glanced at Quintero and saw him grin.

"Maybe so."

"What's the plan?"

"Scarin' the shit out of Mauricio to get his attention and loosen up his tongue. He's a dealer. Weed, mostly. Some

Mexican brown, on occasion. And he's a half-ass pimp. Sees himself as a lover not a fighter. But his true talent is he's one of those guys nobody pays much attention to but hears everything everybody says. Folks get careless around him and flap their jaws. And he will tell everything he hears for a ten spot or a twenty."

"How much did he set you back?"

"A double sawbuck. But I'm betting he doubled or tripled that by puttin' the crosshairs on me. Either he did or another cockbite named Luis Perez. Runs a chop shop just outside of town. Another fringe player with a talent for fading into the woodwork when the big dogs get drunk and start braggin' about their next score."

"Did you get a line on Dalrymple from these *pendejos?*"

"Not sure what I got. Too busy dodging bullets to check out what they told me. By now, ol' Lonny got word from somebody and has moved on. Don't know why he was anywhere near here, regardless, since he's the only suspect who's still loose and walkin' the sunny side of the dirt."

Thinking about Dalrymple revived the guilt he felt about Leighanna Burdette's torture and violent death at the hands of four of the crew running drugs and guns out of the Bar L R ranch.

The spread was also a haven for rage-filled rednecks, Kluxers, white separatists, and Texas secessionists angry and bitter about the loss of the American Dream they thought they'd been promised as a birthright.

They were primed to be fleeced by the ranch owner, oil heir and former state Sen. Thomas "T For Texas" Bondurant, a race war evangelist now serving forty years and change on a string of drug and weapons charges.

Chain-smoking Luckies while brooding darkened the mood in the Blazer as it rolled down FM2410 toward the junction with U.S. 67 near the ghost town of Shafter, once a thriving little burg for silver mining.

Forecast: Moody. Fifty Percent Chance of Homicide. Or a serious ass-whuppin'.

Quintero broke the silence.

"Out with it, son. You got a black cloud over your head and the look on your face says you want to kill somebody."

Burch stubbed a Lucky in the Blazer's ashtray but kept his eyes on the road.

"Somethin' you should know about this case. I was close to Leigh Burdette. Liked her a lot. Had a roll in the hay with her just before she was killed. Right there in her trailer. Her killers were lookin' for me and found her. Thought she knew where I was. She didn't, and they tortured and killed her."

"And?"

"She'd still be alive if she'd never met me."

"You didn't kill her. Those scumbags did. We're trackin' the last guy who had something to do with this. We'll get him. It's what we do."

Didn't make Burch feel a damn bit better. Quintero kept his own counsel as they rolled closer to the sharp-edged desert mountains cutting the sky. Slate and umber against deep blue. Burch dove deeper into his black hole.

About ten miles northeast of the junction with U.S. 67, still on the Cuervo side of the county line, they rolled up on the ambush site. That put a leash on Burch's black dog reverie and put the heads of both men on swivels.

Quintero reached behind him to pull a FN FAL para carbine with a folding stock out of a fleece-lined canvas bag. He racked a .308 round into the chamber and scanned both sides of the road, his eyes on the rocks looming above the trees and brush.

Burch slowed the Blazer and pointed to skid marks that crossed the road leading to a cattle guard across the gravelly right shoulder.

"That's where I got the hell off the road when that motherfucker's first round hit."

"How'd you keep from flippin' over?"

"Experience and clean livin'."

Quintero snorted a laugh.

"Well, look at you, climbin' up out of the basement and into the naked light of day."

"Shut the hell up and keep your eyes peeled."

Gunfire didn't ruin their day, but Quintero kept the Belgium-made battle rifle up front with the safety on and a round still in the chamber, muzzle pointed toward the cab roof. The junction with U.S. 67 was dead ahead, backdropped by the sharp peaks of the Sierra Vieja and Chinati Mountains lancing in from the northwest.

"Lonny got any kin around here?"

"Only the graybar kind. And most of them are dead. If I recall correctly, you had a hand in that goat ropin'. Or a gun."

Quintero chuckled.

"That got a little messy. Them boys didn't want to give up. Had to plant most of 'em."

"They were all Alice Baker, right? Straight out of Pelican Bay?"

"That's right. All Cali motherfuckers, hard-core Aryan Brotherhood."

"That ain't Lonny Dalrymple. He's a Texas boy. Did a stretch in Huntsville. Got hooked up with the ABT."

"That explains the connection. Aryan Brotherhood is Aryan Brotherhood, right?"

"Not really. Normally, Alice Baker won't have a damn thing to do with the Aryan Brotherhood of Texas. They look down on them peckerwoods as white trailer trash too stupid to live. Unless they need extra bodies or the deal is too sweet to stand on class differences."

"Sounds like a bunch of Baptists."

"I was thinkin' Church of Christ."

"You think Lonny's still hangin' around, hoping for another gig? Maybe hooked himself up with a crew that's all ABT peckerwoods?"

"Lonny'd either have to be mighty lonely or got his nose stuck in a mighty big pile of long green. Why risk it, otherwise?"

"A question we'll be askin' these two scumbags in the very near future."

"You bet."

"By the way—new hat looks good. Didn't think you'd find one as big as your noggin' overnight. Not at the Lonesome Y."

"When they ordered the one I lost, they bought four more size eights with open crowns."

"Boy, they really saw you comin', didn't they?"

"Oh, yeah—saw a city slicker from Dallas and thought they'd cash in. I'm hard on hats."

Four

Mauricio Velázquez's first clue that Ed Earl Burch was very much alive and just two feet away was twenty ounces of leather-wrapped No. 9 shot shattering his favorite stoneware mug, jetting scalding, cinnamon-laced coffee into his face and digging a divot of pine splinters into his girlfriend's kitchen table.

He barely had time to feel the pain from his scorched face when the second clue came whistling in—Black Betty's lead head slamming into his right wrist, shattering bones and tearing ligaments and tendons. His screams started climbing the higher octaves of the pain concerto when an unseen hand grabbed his thick, wiry hair and smacked his face into the tabletop, the hot coffee, the pine splinters and the sharp shards of stoneware.

That was his third clue. By this time, he was adding puke and blood to the mix. The puke cut off his screams but only because he couldn't vomit and holler at the same time. He stopped both long enough to drag a ragged breath, then felt the hand yank his hair upwards, slamming him upright in his chair before slapping his head into the wall.

A wet, rancid dish towel smacked across his face.

"You're a mess, son. Clean yourself up a little so we can have a chat now that I have your attention."

Velázquez, a short, swarthy man whose broad, flat-nosed face was pocked with splinters, shards and chunks of puke, clawed the rag from his face with his left hand, spat on the floor and locked eyes with Burch.

"*Te voy a matar, maldito chupavergas.*"

"Afraid not, Mauricio. You ain't in a position to kill nobody. And homey don't swing that way. Heard suckin' a dick was more your style."

Black Betty's next target was a bended knee. The left one. Velázquez screamed and tried to curl his body over his legs. All he managed to do was cause the chair legs to kick out from underneath, spilling him to the floor and into a puddle of coffee, blood and stomach contents.

Burch righted the chair then yanked Velázquez by the hair, forcing him into the seat.

"Mauricio, I can do this all day. Or until I kill you. Haven't decided yet. Depends on you. You give me three things, son, and this will all be over."

"I already told you what I know, *cabron.*"

"I kindly doubt that. *Muchacho* tried to kill me not too long after I left that back alley you met me in the other day. I want his name and the name of the man you called to sic him on me."

"Come mierda, hijo de puta."

Black Betty cracked across the right knee. Velázquez howled and bellowed more Mexican profanity at Burch, belittling his manhood, his sexual preferences, his mother's profession, and his family lineage. Each was met with a sharp tap on another body part—shoulders, arms, chest, head. Then Burch clamped Velázquez's cock and balls with his right hand and gave them a counter-clockwise twist.

"Two names, Mauricio. Then I want to know where Lonny Dalrymple is hidin' out."

Velázquez went two for three, giving up the shot caller and the shooter. He said Dalrymple was riding an ABT ratline to parts unknown. Left as soon as Burch showed up in Presidio. Burch semi-believed him and knew no self-respecting Aryan Brotherhood of Texas swingin' dick would say shit to a lowlife beaner weed dealer and pimp. He and Quintero would have to work the phones and snitches to come up with a lead on the ratline and likely hideouts for Dalrymple.

The two names were a different story. He and Bobby could work those right away. He vaguely knew who the shooter was—Juan Bracho, wounded and holed up *otra lado.* Bracho was an orphaned *sicario* from the shattered crew of the late Ojinaga drug lord known as *El Duque,* chopped into dog meat during that desert shootout where Burch rescued

La Güera, also known as Rhonda Mae Mutscher, granddaughter of an old family friend now dead.

The name of the shot caller sent a tingle down Burch's spine and almost gave him a chubby—Santiago Cruz, once the second-deadliest hitter in Malo Garza's organization, which ran guns south and drugs north from *Los Tres Picos,* the family's sprawling *rancho* an hour south of the river. Garza land included one of the old smuggling trails that crossed the river and ran straight to Faver. Very appropriate since Big Bend cattle baron Milton Faver got his start hauling freight on the old Chihuahua Trail out of Mexico and, some said, smuggling guns south and silver north before acquiring enough wealth to start his own *rancho.*

When Malo Garza got blown up by a car bomb courtesy of younger rivals from Monterrey about six years back, his empire collapsed, his routes and customers taken by the gang that killed him, his lieutenants and gunsels either bought off or killed outright.

After ducking a hail of bullets at a Piedras Negras whorehouse, Cruz got himself arrested on chump change car theft charges and locked up in the Dolph Briscoe Unit State Prison near Dilley, Texas, where he was protected by *La Eme,* the Mexican prison gang with close ties to the old Garza organization. When Cruz got out, he eventually showed up at *Los Tres Picos* again, working for Valentina Garza, the dead drug lord's daughter, who inherited his ruthless cunning and was seeking to rebuild the family empire.

Quintero spotted Cruz sneaking into Bondurant's Bar L R ranch before it was raided, indicating an interesting interracial link between the Garzas and the crew of Alice Baker ex-cons running guns and drugs out of that isolated Cuervo County spread.

How 'bout that? Money did trump ideology and racial animosity. Might still be the case if Cruz was shielding Lonny Dalrymple.

Let's ask him. Right now. Velázquez said Cruz was still in town. His name wasn't on any paper, but he owned a piece of a bar two doors down from Luis Perez's chop shop on Sierra Street off Rio Grande. Had a cot in the back. They'd have to move fast.

Burch damn near forgot Quintero was leaning on the door frame that led to the dining room and was startled when he spoke.

"Remind me to never piss you off."

"Excessive?"

"The man sicced a sniper on you. I'd say he got off easy."

Burch started using zip ties to bind Velázquez to the chair.

"Where's the girlfriend?"

"Zip-tied and gagged on the couch. She was cussin' a blue streak at me until you started whalin' on Mauricio. That shut her up. Quick."

Quintero held up an old pump shotgun with the bluing worn off and the barrel sawed down and a nickel-plated Colt 1911.

"We sure that's all the firepower he's got?"

"Pretty sure. Did a quick sweep while you were getting your workout in."

"We'll bring those with us, then turn 'em in when we leave town."

"Oh, I don't know—I kinda like this Colt. Never have owned a pimp gun before."

"Have at it, Bobby."

Burch cocked his head at a phone hanging on the kitchen wall. He fished Chief Lado Sandoval's business card out of his shirt pocket and started twirling the numbers on the phone's rotary dial.

"I'll get a bus to haul handsome here to the local Doc-In-A-Box."

"While you're doin' that, I'll keep an eye on these two. Then we can get gone."

"Sounds like a plan."

Five

Presidio is flat, dusty, ugly, and poor. Not all that different from the sprawling town just across the river, Ojinaga. Not as prosperous, though. Not as much *narcotraficante* money. Not as many people. And not nearly as deadly.

Not much to see for two tourists with badges. Besides, Sandoval told Burch to hurry up. Had a dead body they might be interested in. Yeah, yeah, Lado said, he'd send a cruiser and a meat wagon to take care of Velázquez and his girlfriend. *But get your asses in gear, hombre.*

Burch slapped a spinning red flasher with a magnetic base on the roof of the Blazer, made sure Quintero was strapped in, and gunned it. As they wheeled away from the girlfriend's home on Juarez Street, small, concrete block houses flashed by in a pastel whirl, some painted in bright colors like magenta and canary yellow, others covered with stucco in lime or pink. Most were one-story affairs with flat or angled roofs without a peak. Some housed a small *tienda* or barber shop. Others a small-engine mechanic or welder with a shop facing the ever-present back alley.

Rickety fences or low concrete walls were the rule, with chained mutts of some persuasion sniffing and barking through the narrow gaps. So was that back alley where the cars were parked, some still mobile, others awaiting *la resurrección* which was forever promised *para el mañana*.

Heading east on O'Reilly Street, one of the town's main drags, the commercial and government buildings were a tad grander, but not by much. Some were two stories. Most were one. City Hall had some streamline curves and stacked discs that gave it the look of a collapsable camp cup partly opened. Some had a raised, concrete sidewalk with a metal cover extending from the building—a nod to the wooden boardwalks of the Old West. Most were plain storefronts with a display window and maybe a tattered awning to shield customers from the sun.

Burch almost T-boned a rust-ridden flatbed GMC pulling out of a side street, knocking over a trash can and a curbside sign advertising a cafe's daily specials as he cut in front of the truck, scaring a pot-bellied customer picking his teeth as he exited the eatery.

"Easy, boss. Let's get us there in one piece."

"Just wanted to make sure you were awake."

"Am now."

Skidding south onto Rio Grande Street, they spotted the strobing emergency lights of Crown Vic cruisers, an ambulance, and a crime scene Suburban stacked at the corner where Sierra Street angled in from the east. Closer, they could see a Presidio County deputy directing traffic, blocking the turn at Sierra and waving them to the edge of the asphalt. As they pulled over, Burch could see EMTs roll a gurney to the door of a flat-roofed bar on the northeast corner facing the side street.

Its adobe walls were a gaudy mix of purple and orange with LA FINCA in white-bordered electric green capital letters arching above the tin overhang covering the front steps and the longer flank running north along Rio Grande. Dead neon signs advertising Carta Blanca and Negra Modelo hung in the darkened windows.

Burch stopped the Blazer, peeled off his Ray-Bans and leaned out the window.

"Burch and Quintero, Cuervo County SO—lookin' for Chief Sandoval. He's expecting us."

"Kinda out of your jurisdiction, ain'tcha fellas?"

"Workin' a murder case, Deputy. Chasin' a person of interest."

"You might be a little late. Chief's inside. So's my boss, Chief Deputy Cortés. So's a vic with his throat cut from ear to ear. Park it where you can."

45

Burch hooked a U-turn and parked a few yards north on Rio Grande. Quintero whistled low and said: "That was a little bit frosty with a 'fuck you' cherry on top. We're lucky it's only Cortés inside. Álvarez would try to tear us a new asshole and create an international incident."

"Pretty sure Cortés will have a few choice words. Play it cool with Lado—don't want to make it any more unpleasant for him than it already is. Won't be surprised if he's chilly with us. Just eyeball the scene now. We'll get a rundown from him later."

Ducking under the crime scene tape and stepping inside, they paused to let their eyes adjust to the semi-dark. A plain, rough-hewn pine plank stretched halfway down the wall to their right with warped plywood tacked on top. Had all the style of a packing crate.

A patinaed brass cash register with the hand crank and scroll filigree guarded the corner nearest the door. No stools. A long, lead pipe served as the bar rail, held in place by cast iron supports bolted into the concrete floor.

On a shelf behind the bar was a short, thin line of bottles—well brands, mostly. Cheap, but got the job done. Flanking the shelf were two sombreros hanging on the wall, one gray, the other black.

Four mismatched particle board and plywood tables lined the opposite wall, each with an uneven number of equally random and rickety chairs, some metal others wood or plastic. Slow-moving ceiling fans stirred the dust motes floating through the feeble rays of single-bulb lamps mounted high in each corner of the room and the harsher illumination sputtering from a rust-scaled fluorescent fixture above the bar.

A cluster of lawdogs and techs stood or crouched at the back of the room, attention focused on the body face-up on the floor at their center, feet angling toward Burch and Quintero, head shadowed in a darker corner hiding the blood pooling from a slashed throat that was also masked by the gloom.

To an old murder cop like Burch, there was a soothing reverence and ritual to this process, be it the flash of the evidence tech's camera, the careful hunt for a wallet, the lifting of a jacket or shirt with a pencil to get a better look at a wound, or the slow, silent stare of a cop clocking all the details while trying to commune with the dead to get a vibe about how they got that way.

Cops might exchange crude remarks, quips about the horrible things one human could do to another. Black humor was a shield against that horror, an insulation as comfortably lethal as asbestos wrapped around a steam pipe.

Good for now. A saving grace. Later? A slow death with your innards eaten away. Made some cops eat their gun. A saving grace turned fatal.

There was also a rough-edged respect paid the dead, even a stone-cold killer like Santiago Cruz. Unless his master, Valentina Garza, wanted to give him a full-blown Catholic funeral mass, this was as close to a requiem as he was going to get. At the hands of strangers who hated him and his kind.

Sure, his homies would spill some tequila on the ground, get drunk, and toast him on his way to Hell, but it wouldn't be the cold, solemn rite these cops were giving him.

In a heartbeat, the shadows and gloom disappeared, banished by two portable lights the techs telescoped toward the ceiling. No doubt now who the body used to be—Cruz's death grimace seconded by the bloody slash cutting across his throat, a bib of blood sliding over his chest and shoulders to the concrete floor.

Quiet like a bear lumbering through thick brush, Burch stepped into a vacant space of the sacred cop arc, nodding to Chief Sandoval and Chief Deputy Cortés, meeting their dead-eyed stares with one of his own, holding his until Cortés broke then nodding at Sandoval. He heard Quintero say, "*Permiso, por favor,*" to a tech as he sidled next to Burch's left shoulder and whispered.

"I've seen our friend there look a whole lot better."

"You bet. Hard to see how somebody slipped up behind the man unless he was blind drunk or stoned. Had to be a friend or associate."

"Friends are the ones they send when they want you dead."

"*Claro que sí.*"

"Your Spanish is getting much better."

"Couldn't get much worse."

"Ears are gone."

"I saw that. Failed to listen to a warning from somebody. Looks like his throat's slashed, too. Remind you of anybody?"

"Leigh Burdette."

"Bingo. Guy leading the AB assholes who killed her was Cleve Chizik, a Big Stripe at Pelican Bay in Cali. A hitter. Just loved using a blade. Might fit him up for this except for one thing."

"You blew him away already."

"You been doin' your homework."

"See that skinny guy talking to the crime scene tech? The guy in the jeans and loud shirt? He's the detective. Jaime Magdaleno. Good guy. Not a particular buddy of Álvarez or Cortés."

"Good deal. Means we don't have to beg to examine the body if you think Magdaleno will talk to us."

"He will. He's married to my cousin's sister. I'll make sure he comes to dinner tonight."

"The border *menudo*. The ties that bind."

"*Claro. ¿Pero qué más esperabas?* I'm taking off the training wheels since your Spanish is getting better. *Mierda.* Here comes Cortés. He don't look happy."

"Fuck him."

Burch kept his eyes on the body, continuing to clock the details. Long-sleeve flannel shirt in blue, black, and dark gray plaid open over a black tee. Both darkened with blood. From that slashed throat. Bloody bumps where the ears used to be.

Who the hell did you ignore, Cruz? The Garzas? The Monterrey boys? Pistol on the floor next to Cruz's right hand. Looked like a Beretta 92s. Black work boots.

'Banger threads instead of the *Tejano* look. Interesting sartorial choice, given the border surroundings. Curious and worth a question or two. Burch knew he was stalling, pausing before studying the blood darkening the unzipped crotch of Cruz's black jeans, knowing what *that* meant.

A severed cock. A cartel cliche. Right on cue, one of the techs opened Cruz's mouth with a gloved hand and used long-nosed forceps to pull out a wrinkled tube of dark brown meat. Burch winced but remembered Doggett telling him of a similar MO in the murder of Rhonda Mae's lover, Tommy Juan Jaeckel. Filed that nugget away for a future chin wag. Felt a tap on his right shoulder. Cortés.

"Need a word."

"Sure thing."

"Follow me."

"Stay here, Bobby. Keep watching. I'll be right back."

Burch followed Cortés toward the front of the bar. Middle of the room. Cortés turned on his heel and tried to get in Burch's face. It was a stretch since Burch was about four inches taller. Cortés poked a finger in the middle of Burch's chest. Hard.

"I want to know what the fuck you two clowns are doing in my county. You don't have any jurisdiction down here."

Burch took a loud, theatrical sniff. Onions, stale coffee, and dead cigarettes. He let loose a long, low whistle.

"Damn, Cortés—your breath could knock over a Missouri mule. Here, have a stick of this. Might cut the stink some."

Burch offered a pack of Big Red. Cortés swatted his hand away.

"Quit bein' a fuckin' clown and answer my question."

"Quit bein' an asshole and I will."

About a half minute of stare-down followed, as nose-to-nose as Cortés could get. Cortés broke again. Burch reached for the Levi Garrett pouch in his back pocket and forked a string of leaf into his jaw. Slowly.

"Here's the deal. We're workin' a murder case and on the trail of a suspect said to be hidin' out down here. Word is your vic here was protectin' him. We know that because your vic sicced a sniper on me when I was askin' questions about the suspect three days back."

"That makes it twice you've been in our jurisdiction without so much as a courtesy call. Won't warn you again. Next time, you'll get the cuffs and some time to study the inside of our fine jail."

Burch spat a thick jet of tobacco juice at Cortés' feet. The shorter man stepped back.

"Let me disabuse you of that fantasy, Deputy. Under Texas law, I can pursue a lead in a murder case pretty much anywhere in this state. You know that, so quit fuckin' with me like your dick ain't an inny instead of an outty."

"I know all about you, Burch. You're a crooked cop who got tossed off the force in Dallas for bein' on the pad of a drug lord up there. Been workin' as a peephole creeper ever since. Muscle and a hired gun, too, peddlin' your ass to the highest bidder."

"You might want to get your facts straight, asshole. Then ask yourself this—if I'm such a scumbag, who gave me a badge again? Answer might surprise you."

"Sudden Doggett and Sam Boelcke don't scare nobody in this county, least of all the sheriff and me. Them givin' you a badge makes them bigger fools and fuckups than we already thought they were."

"Wasn't talkin' about them. Might want to set your sights a little further up the food chain."

Quintero stepped up beside Burch and aimed his words at Cortés.

"No eres un hombre de verdad, bastardo. Eres un cobarde que abofetea a las putas y besa el culo a unos cabrones como tu víctima de allí."

Cortés' light brown face showed all the signs of a man about to blow his top. His skin turned brick red, darkening his sharp nose and high cheekbones. His thin eyebrows furrowed. He bared his teeth like he was going to bite Quintero. He also clenched his fists.

"Before you say or do anything stupid, we're going to leave you now so your folks can finish their work without a sideshow."

Burch stepped around Cortés and headed toward the door. Cortés grabbed Burch's left shirt sleeve.

"You wait a goddam minute, Burch. I ain't through with you."

Burch broke free and growled: "Yes—you are." He slowly walked to the door, showing his back to Cortés. Over his shoulder, he growled again: "Until next time, Deputy. Happy trails."

Quintero stood his ground until Burch stepped through the door. He eyed Cortés and stuck a finger in his face.

"Don't ever poke a finger at *Oso Blanco* again."

"What the hell did you say to him?"

"I told him he was a coward who beats up whores and kisses the ass of scumbags like Cruz."

"Must have struck a nerve. I thought his heart was going to explode. What did you say to him after I went through the door?"

"You mean after you did your John Wayne slow walk?"

"I thought you'd like that. What did you say?"

"Told him 'Never poke your finger at *Oso Blanco* again.'"

Burch almost swallowed his chaw. Then he tilted his head back and roared, slapping Quintero on the shoulder.

"Bobby, you might just be my favorite Mexican-American."

"Let's see what you say after Carmen gets through with you."

Burch cranked up the Blazer with a smile on his face that disappeared after two blocks. He knew he needed to find a phone and call Doggett and Dub McKee to warn them of the blowback headed their way. He also needed intel on the ratline that was sheltering Lonny Dalrymple and the whereabouts of Juan Bracho, the wounded sniper who couldn't shoot straight. Luckily.

His belly rumbled. It was quarter past seven. Well past the starting gun for beer o'clock. About time to think about dinner. With beer. Or whisky. Maybe both.

"What the hell was that noise?"

"Never mind that. Where's your cousin live? My belly thinks my throat's been cut."

"*Dios mío,* can't believe you said that."

Quintero made the sign of the cross. Burch shook his head.

"Damn, Bobby, don't get spooked. Nothin' I say can make Cruz any more dead."

"Never a good idea to piss off the dead. Specially one who just got dead. They tend to hang around for a day or two."

Burch held up his hand.

"Okay, Bobby. I'll keep my yap zipped about the late and unlamented Santiago Cruz."

"Might have to find you a *curandero* to take the hex off you if you don't."

Six

Burch was on his fourth Negra Modelo, his belly full of tender, milk-fed *cabrito* in a savory *salsa roja*, *tamales* stuffed with pork, and grilled *nopales*, the meaty pads of the prickly pear. He was sitting at a rough plank table on the patio behind the concrete block home of Eddie Arcilla, Quintero's cousin, enjoying the descending dusk. He took another swig of the dark beer and belched loudly.

"Damn. Pardon the hell out of me."

"No need to apologize, *hombre*. Every chef wants to hear that note of praise for his cooking," Arcilla said. "Better save room for the *flan*. My Gabriela made it. Made the tamales, too."

On cue, Gabriela swept onto the slate patio carrying a serving plate with a big wheel of the pale yellow custard glazed with a gleaming caramel sauce that reflected the low flames of the candles and lanterns scattered about.

"Señor Burch ate four of my *tamales* and had two helpings of your *cabrito*, so I know he has room for my *flan, mi amor*."

"I've already been a pig, m'am. Might as well go for being a hog."

"Just don't burp at me when you do."

"No, m'am. This has been an outstanding meal. My thanks to you both."

"Bobby, help me serve the *flan*."

"Sí, Jefina. Será un placer."

Quintero and Burch went back to the patio after helping Eddie and Gabriela clear the plates and bowls and pick up about a case of empty beer bottles. They blew out the candles and lanterns then returned to the table, both facing the back alley and sipping *cafe de olla,* strong and sweet Mexican coffee brewed with cinnamon and sugar cane.

Their pistols were drawn, Burch's Colt 1911 and Quintero's Beretta 92s, sitting flat on the rough pine. They watched the night and the double gate that split the back wooden fence. Both were thinking about the dinner guest who didn't show up—Jaime Magdaleno—and the nasty potentials that could explain his absence.

Burch wasn't a praying man but hoped they weren't already sitting a death watch. He didn't say that out loud, not wanting to spook Quintero again by mentioning the dead. But the night felt heavy, peddling dread instead of joy, fear not comfort.

They had already called the usual people and places— his wife, his office, the duty sergeant, his partner, his girlfriend. Even took a flyer on Chief Lado Sandoval. Nothing. Eddie Arcilla came out with a carafe, refilled their cups, then sat at the table with a steaming cup of his own, tapping Burch on the shoulder.

"You expect trouble?"

"I always expect it but am ready to be pleasantly surprised if it doesn't show up."

Arcilla laughed. Quintero didn't.

"You're a funny man, Señor Burch."

"Don't encourage him."

"Why not? I'm a witty guy. Already the mood is lightened by my joyful spirit."

"See what you did, Eddie? He'll be cracking bad jokes all the way home. Like somebody's dad. Shoot me now, please."

They heard the house phone ring, loud and insistent, like a tomcat yowling for breakfast at five in the morning. Arcilla jumped up to answer it.

"Go with him, Bobby."

Burch fired up a Lucky, sipped his coffee, and waited, watching the night and hearing the muffled voices on this side of the telephone line.

Death took a time out. Jaime Magdaleno showed up a few minutes after ten, creeping down the alley behind Arcilla's house and slipping through the back gate.

Quintero stepped up and greeted the detective with a tight *abrazo*, clapping his hands on the man's shoulders as he broke the embrace.

"We were worried about you, brother. Thought the wolves might have got you."

"*Mis disculpas, mi hermano. Vi algunos lobos por ahí pero se les escapó. Aunque tomó algo de tiempo.*"

"*En inglés, por favor.* My partner here knows only enough Spanish to get drunk and get laid."

"Bite me, Bobby. I know enough to know a champion wolf hunter when I hear one. And a man who knows how to dodge a pack when he needs to."

"*Gracias.* Took a while but I gave them the slip."

Burch offered his name and right hand to Magdaleno, ready for a *macho* grip in return. Got a bone-crusher. Good thing he shot, drank, and jacked off with his left.

He gestured toward a seat across the table from he and Quintero. They moved their guns so the barrels weren't pointed the detective's way. He tapped Quintero on the leg with his boot, signaling him to take the lead, pure murder cop reflex rising up from Burch's past, treating Magdaleno like a perp. Or a witness they didn't know if they could trust.

"Tell us about these wolves chasing you. Think you dodged them for good, or do we need to help you get out of here?"

"Who can say for sure, but I don't think so. They seem more interested in watching me, seeing where I go and who I talk to. They're from across the river. The wolves on this side don't like them very much. Been bad blood ever since *El Duque* and most of his crew got killed and these newcomers showed up to take over."

"Bodies startin' to stack up?"

"You better believe it. More over there than here so far."

"How does the Cruz killing fit in?"

"Still tryin' to figure that out. When Cruz first got out of prison, he bought a piece of that bar and kept a pretty low profile, under *El Duque*'s protection. Might have done some wet work for him. But not around here. Smart move considerin' Malo Garza was dead. Then he pops up workin' for Garza's daughter."

Burch leaned in.

"Yeah, he was the go-between for Valentina Garza and that Alice Baker crew runnin' guns and drugs out of a Kluxer ranch up our way. Kind of disappeared after we raided the place just before *El Duque* got chopped up in that desert shootout. Nasty deal with *El Duque*. I was there. Saw his brains get blown out. Barely got away my own 'sef."

"Those two deals fucked everything up. Big win for the good guys. Wiped out the natural order of things around here. The Garzas have been trying to muscle in and fill the vacuum, but they're getting pushback from the other gangs. And the wolves on this side of the river."

Quintero again. A flat natural. Smooth and easy with the lead change. Like they'd been partners for years.

"So how does Cruz wind up with his throat cut from ear to ear and his family jewels sliced off and stuffed in his mouth? Was he leading the Garza charge here?"

"We don't think so. That's being handled by the two senior guys in the Garza outfit—Gustavo Portales and

Francisco Sanchez. *El Tiburon* and *Azul*. Their *sicarios* are duking it out with hitters from the other gangs. Cruz wasn't in on that."

"Did he get clipped just because he was a Garza *hombre*? Because of the killer he used to be?"

"If that were the case, they'd have stripped him naked and hung him by the heels from the *Puente Internacional* to advertise the kill. No, we're hearing he might have got dead because he switched sides one too many times. Made him hard to trust."

Burch was listening with half his brain engaged. The other half kept replaying the details Doggett gave him during a testy phone call before dinner of Tommy Juan Jaeckel's gory death—throat slashed open, head cut off and stuffed into a giant smoker, pride and both joys stuffed into his mouth. A revenge killing for betraying the Aryan Brotherhood crew running guns and drugs at a spread twenty miles north of that Kluxer ranch owned by Thomas "T-For-Texas" Bondurant.

Common denominator: the honcho running both Alice Baker crews, a nasty piece of work named Cleve Chizik who loved to use a razor to slash a throat and sever a cock. Or slice the nipples off a woman's breasts. He killed Tommy Juan and Leigh Burdette.

Cruz also looked like his gruesome handiwork. The two men knew each other. Cruz was Chizik's contact with the Garzas on a big gunrunning deal before that sledgehammer raid on Bondurant's ranch that smashed a lot of sweet setups and dreams of an *imperio narco,* resurrected Aztec glory with a poppy and coca leaf foundation.

Only one problem with this line of thinking—Burch shot Chizik at the end of that desert firefight between rival drug gangs, blowing him down with eight Flying Ashtrays from his Colt 1911 before the thug could kill the object of his obsession, Rhonda Mae Mutscher. *La Güera.*

He could still hear Doggett growl during their chin wag. His boss didn't like the replay of the confrontation with Cortés and was even less pleased with the details of the Cruz murder and the possibility of Chizik's resurrection.

"Thought you nailed that cocksucker."

"I did. Hit him with eight Flying Ashtrays."

"Files say he's dead. Wouldn't be the first time that paper lied, though. Or that Doc Battles fucked up. Could be you just missed."

"Not hardly."

The conversation with his *El Jefe Ultimo,* ex-Ranger Dub McKee, was a shade less terse. Dub said he'd unleash a firehose of shit on anybody from Presidio who gave him noise about rude visitors from Cuervo County. And he'd start working on intel about that AB ratline and Lonny Dalrymple's whereabouts.

"Quit stepping on your dick down there and get back to Faver, cabron."

"Sí, Jefe. We'll be pullin' out shortly."

"It's gettin' late. Try not to shoot anybody. Try not to get ambushed again."

"Didn't know you cared."

Like slamming a book closed, Burch clapped both sides of his brain together and refocused on the back and forth between Quintero and Magdaleno. He waited for a lull, then leaned back in.

"We think Cruz might have been working on something else before he got clipped. I was down here the other day, trying to get a line on a murder suspect we heard was hidin' out down here. Dirtbag named Lonny Dalrymple. On my way home, a sniper tried to nail me just over the Cuervo County line. Came back down here with Bobby to talk to some of the scumbags I button-holed the other day."

"No wonder Cortés got in your face today."

"Fuck him. Here's the deal—one of these assholes told us Cruz was the shot-caller who sicced the sniper on me. Had to bang him up a little bit to get him to talk, but he'll live. Might not play the piano again, though. Mauricio Velázquez."

"¡No manches, I know that asshole! He's a CI for us."

"Yeah, but he'll peddle his ass to anybody who'll give him a double sawbuck."

Quintero's turn:

"Here's one other factoid for you to chew on. Our suspect is a Texas boy, an ex-con who belongs to the Aryan Brotherhood of Texas. So, you've got a member of the Garza organization protecting an ABT asshole. Normally, the two would rather shiv each other than be buddies."

"Unless there's a lot of money on the table, right?"

"Bingo. We think Cruz was protecting Dalrymple because the Garzas are doing another deal with the Aryans. Either Alice Baker or ABT. Or both."

"Got a line on Dalrymple?"

"Mauricio said he jumped on an Aryan ratline the first time I came down here lookin' for him. He didn't know where."

"I know a guy ..."

"Always a promising line of patter. We know a guy, too. When we get back to Faver, we'll send you everything we've got on the ranch raid and that shootout. Anything we dig up, you get. One last thing—Juan Bracho, the shooter who tried to take me out. Think you can get us across the river quiet-like to pay him a visit?"

"You won't have to. He's got a girlfriend over here he won't be able to stay away from for long."

"Might be better to grab him over there."

"For long-term parking?"

Burch didn't answer. Just locked eyes with the younger detective.

"Got it."

Quintero held his hand up, like a point man on a jungle trail signaling a halt. They heard a muffler rumbling in the alley and ducked into the darkest corner of the short concrete wall dividing the patio and the rest of the backyard.

The silhouette of a low-rider crept into view. Looked like an Impala. '63 or '64. Chopped and lowered.

The three lawmen tracked the car with their pistols until the Coke-bottle-bottom taillights slid out of sight. They heard the engine rev up and the tires squeal when the car exited the alley and hit the street.

"We need to get you the hell out of here, Jaime."

"You need to take your own advice and *vamanos*. I'll make sure Eddie and Gabriela are safe. Anything happens to them, and it's my wife who'll shoot me, not these *pinche chupavergas*."

Seven

Cortez, Colorado, bored the shit out of her. Too many tree-hugging granola eaters. Too much Rocky Mountain high. Just a little weed and wine. No speedball freaks or codeine guzzlers.

Too many mountain bikers, hikers, and kayakers.

Not enough cattle and cowboys. Not enough natural-born killers.

The country was stunning, though, with wide-open valleys and a horizon broken by mountains and mesas. On clear nights, the sky was a black velvet blanket cushioning a dazzling spray of stars and planets, reminding her of West Texas and Cuervo County.

But it was also a haunted place, marked by the ancient cliffside ruins of too many dead Puebloans whose spirits still walked the land. She felt their presence, and it flipped her out. So did those quick-frozen moments on the street when somebody stared at her too hard and too long, trying to figure out where they'd seen her before.

Happened again two days ago as she was walking out of a bank on Main. Dude across the street pinning her with his eyes. Five-alarm panic. Code Red alert. That's when she slowly slid a hand into her purse to touch the soothing cold of a Colt Python .357 Magnum. A carbon steel pacifier with a four-inch barrel and deep, dark bluing.

Get a grip, girl. He's just a tourist. Can't remember where he parked. See? He found his car, has his keys in hand and is walking up the street.

Calm down. Breathe easy. Walk away slow. And go about your business like you don't have a single care or worry. Even though your heart is doing the Jackhammer Boogie.

Check your six in the reflection of a dress shop display window. He's gone. Check it again seven doors down. Still gone.

Just another groovy day in East Bumfuck, Colorado.

The Feds stuck her out here in Four Corners Country after the big blowup in the West Texas desert, the one where all the major players got arrested, got away, or got dead. She testified against those who got busted that night as well as the other drug gangs that bought stolen assault rifles, machine guns, and military bang-bangs smuggled across the Texas border by herself and her dead lover, Tommy Juan Jaeckel.

It was the last act of *La Güera*, the flashy cowgirl in the blonde wig, tight designer jeans, tall boots, and spangly bolero jacket who beguiled the drug gang bosses and seduced them into buying her goods for a premium price. They were high-grade goods, not junk, and she smiled and flirted until she got top dollar.

Then she took the Judas package the Feds put together. New town, new name, new ID, new backstory, new dead-end job. All under the ever-watchful eyes of her new best friends, the U.S. Marshals Service.

This also meant the final curtain call for Rhonda Mae Mutscher, the name she was given at birth but one she hadn't used for a very long time. She'd lived under so many different names the past fifteen years that Rhonda Mae was almost a total stranger to her, living only in a small chamber of her heart and a file cabinet tucked into the back of her brain.

Memories of the woman who raised her, her grandmother, Juanita Mutscher, now dead. And nightmares of her father, a Dixie Mafia drug runner who paid a crooked Dallas judge to give him custody of her.

My ever-lovin' daddy.

Motherfucker is still after me. Happy for the Feds to make me disappear.

Poof.

Gone.

Adios.

Not even a ghost. Nor a trace of the Cheshire cat's smile.

Her name was Claire Doyle now, Claire Anna Doyle. After years of going by a first and middle name—Rhonda Mae, Rita Gail, Carla June—she was just plain Claire.

Repeat after me, Claire Doyle. You're from Enid, Oklahoma. D.O.B. 7/9/1966. Means you're thirty now instead of your true age—thirty-five.

Daddy named Charlie. Mama named Ruth. Both dead. Oil field trash. High school dropout. GED and accounting certificate from Autry Technology Center.

Learn it. Live it. You're Claire Doyle.

Says so on your Social Security card, your Colorado driver's license, and the title for a rust-pocked '76 Malibu Classic you nicknamed Big Russet for its sun-faded red paint.

Big Russet had a thick brick of ill-gotten hundred dollar bills tucked behind the coils of the back seat. Three hundred grand and change.

Rainy day money. Laundered. Wrapped and duct taped. Held in trust by the Bank of Chevy. No interest. No passbook. No free toaster.

For walkaround cash, she did the bookkeeping for a couple who owned a Mom-and-Pop office supply store.

Chester Bumgarner and his wife Lucille. Call me Chet, he said. Call me Lucy. He was a retired state trooper, born and raised in Cortez. She was once a county court clerk on his patrol beat.

Pretty soon, Claire was handling the books for Chet and Lucy's friends. A couple of farmers. A bar owner. Owners of a bookstore, a souvenir shop and a place that proudly proclaimed: "We buy junk and sell antiques."

Chet and Lucy let her bring her four-year-old son to the store. They didn't have kids of their own but doted on hers like he was a grandson. *Oh, yeah. Forgot to mention that. I've got a kid. Named him Charlie. After his make-believe grandfather.*

Couldn't name him for his real father, Armando Ruiz, the fierce and wily lieutenant with Lipan Apache blood who protected her after the love of her life was murdered, butchered and stuffed into a giant smoker. That would be a dead giveaway.

Same reason she couldn't name him for her dead lover, Tommy Juan. Which Armando wouldn't have minded since they were cousins. Didn't matter now. Both men were dead. Made her feel a little less guilty about naming her son Charlie.

He was a good looking kid, with jet black hair, reddish brown skin, big dark eyes that dominated a face with a sharp nose and chin. His father's son.

She saw very little of herself in Charlie but considered that a blessing. He didn't have her wolfish amber eyes, a striking feature she inherited from her mother and kept hidden behind contact lenses with a dark brown tint. She kept her hair dyed black and let it grow to shoulder length, pulling it back into a tight ponytail that accentuated her sharp facial features, giving her a stern, severe look a librarian might envy. Wireframe cheaters dangled from a chain around her neck when they weren't perched on her nose.

She wore very little makeup—some lip gloss and eyeliner, maybe. Favored loose slacks, bib overalls, jeans, and oversized shirts and tees that hid her curves. Scuffed Justin shit kickers or Danner hiking boots, a dark green parka, and a stained gray Stetson fedora completed the look that was anything but a fashion statement.

She looked dowdy. Frumpy. Drab. Almost mannish. Everything *La Güera* was not. Her Fed handlers approved. What they didn't know about the laundered cash, the pistol, and another full-auto bang-bang from her gunrunning days wouldn't hurt them.

Most days, it was just her and Charlie and her circle of clients. Nights out were early dinners at Chet and Lucy's or the home of one of the others. Maybe a dinner at one of the Mexican restaurants on Main. A weekend jaunt to the BurroFest in Mancos or the hot-air balloon rally in the Parque de Vida in Cortez would jazz Charlie so much he'd sleep through most of the next day.

Bless his little heart. Had a Big Day. Had Big Fun. Now have your Big Dreams. Not me, kiddo. Can't relax. Don't sleep that much. And when I do, I dream of dead lovers and cartel killers.

Charlie was a big hit at Pippo's Cafe on Main, her breakfast spot. The waitresses and regulars would pick him up and walk him around while she wolfed down *migas* and *chorizo* for breakfast, washing it down with a big mug of Mexican coffee.

One of the waitresses, usually Wanda, filled Charlie's sippy cup with milk and fed him from a small dish of scrambled eggs. He liked ketchup and pepper and would point to the shaker and the bottle, which made Wanda smile.

"Little man likes his eggs and knows what he wants on them," she said.

"He'll start asking for *huevos ranchero* next with the *salsa verde.*"

"And the *chorizo,* just like his mama."

"Just so long as he lays off the refried beans. He farts like a bull already."

Wanda laughed, fed Charlie the last teaspoon, then wiped his mouth and chin. She kissed the boy on the head, ruffled his hair, then winked at Claire.

"Gotta scoot. Gotta serve them ol' waddies at the back table."

"Thanks for feeding him."

"Highlight of my day."

Claire scooped up Charlie, cradled him against her right hip, and felt him wrap his arms around her neck. She left a ten-spot on the table for Wanda to pick up and slung her purse over her left shoulder.

When she looked up to start heading for the front door, she saw a tall man with shaggy gray hair headed her way, his ruddy face lit with a smile like he'd spotted a long-lost friend.

He was big across the shoulders and chest with biceps that stretched the sleeves of his denim jacket, muscles that came from swinging a sledgehammer, cracking rocks, or pumping iron in a prison yard with nothing but time and sweat to lose. Narrow hips with long, thin legs gave him the out-of-kilter look of a beer barrel on toothpicks.

She stood to the side, giving him room to pass, hoping that smile was meant for somebody else. No such luck. He stopped, barring her way, his smile still bright but his blue eyes narrowed, cold and locked on her face.

"Good to see you again, Rita. Been a while. Let me buy you a cup of coffee."

She felt a blade of ice knife into her heart. Rita was the everyday name she used in Texas when she wasn't prancing around as the gun-hustling *La Güera*.

"I don't know you, mister. And my name's not Rita."

"Sure it is, Rita. And you've got a beautiful kid now. Didn't have that down in Texas. Is Tommy Juan the father?"

He leaned toward her, close enough for the stench of stale cigarettes and coffee to roll into her face. She got a glimpse of a tattoo on his neck, an SS lightning rune. He gripped her left arm, hard and tight, trying to steer her back to the table she just left.

"Let go of me! Right now, motherfucker!"

Loud and brassy. So the whole room could hear.

She turned inside of him and slammed her left heel onto the vamp of his left biker boot, above the steel toe box, right where the metatarsal bones started to rise toward the ankle joint. His smile disappeared, replaced by a red-faced grimace of pain and anger. She broke free and shuffled away, protecting Charlie by keeping her body between him and the big man.

"You bitch! You just broke my foot! All I wanted to do was buy you a cup of coffee for old time's sake! And you broke my foot!"

He was playing to the crowd starting to gather, the coots from the back table, some hard-knuckled cowboys from the counter and Carlos, the day cook. They weren't buying what he was selling.

Wanda slipped up to her side, took Charlie and hustled him into the kitchen. Carlos leveled a sawed-off shotgun at the big man's head.

"You best leave while you're still breathin,' *pendejo*. She's our friend, and we don't like you puttin' your paws on her."

The big man raised his hands and backed away.

"I'm goin', I'm goin'. But this ain't over, Rita. We'll meet again. Real soon."

He flashed that big smile and lasered menace and hate at her with those blue eyes. In a heartbeat, the smile disappeared, his eyes widened and he threw his hands in front of his body as a feeble shield.

Had just enough time to scream: "Noooooooo!" Six hollow-point slugs from her Colt Python shut him up forever, filling the diner with a staccato roar and the smell of freshly burnt gunpowder.

"Won't ever have to see you again, motherfucker."

Not true, hon. You'll see this bastard in your dreams. Every night. For the rest of your natural-born life.

Wind-driven rain hammered Big Russet as she guided the big Chevy through the night, south out of Farmington, sticking to the two-lane blacktop of State Road 371 that would leave the Colorado Plateau for the Zuni Mountains and the vestigial blacktop of storied Route 66, where she would turn east-southeast to avoid Albuquerque.

The wipers worked, the headlights were bright, and the tires were fair. Big Russet was no Hot Rod Lincoln but was a sturdy, if aged, American machine designed for the open road, stout enough to bull through the storm and get her long gone from Cortez.

Trust old GM iron and roll straight through the night. She didn't have to worry about falling asleep because unexpected wind gusts would slap the car at irregular intervals, causing an adrenaline rush that kept her wide awake. Charlie, cocooned in blankets in the back seat, snored softly.

Jesus, that went south all of a sudden. Like a damn roller coaster dropping into the first deep plunge. You got complacent, dumbass. Fat, dumb and bored in East Bumfuck in spite of the occasional fright if somebody stared too long.

Went about your business like you were invisible. Didn't check your backtrail. Didn't change directions on the street to catch a tail. Quit putting wedges in the door frame. Didn't watch the street from your flat, looking for exhaust from a parked car or a match flare from a darkened doorway.

Thought touching that Python when you got startled kept you safe. Got a quick reminder that what a gun really does is keep you from getting dead. But only if you use it before the other guy.

Blocked El Diablo Ultimo clean out of your mind. Your ever-lovin' daddy, Danny Ray. Dixie Mafia badass. Rich enough to buy the judges who let him yank me away from Granny, get me hooked on 'ludes and coke, and sell me to older men.

Even tried to fuck me himself. Until I jammed the barrel of that very Python against his balls. Hammer cocked. Finger on the trigger. Your choice, daddy. Keep your dick to yourself. Or die with a bloody hole in your crotch.

Been on the run ever since. Knowin' Danny Ray was on my trail. Fearing his long reach and perverted obsession. Until there were so many hombres who wanted her dead that dear daddy became just one of the crowd.

Get sharp again, girl. Or you'll be joining Tommy Juan and Armando in the Big Adios.

Once the gunfire echoes faded at Pippo's, Carlos hustled her and Charlie out the back door and into his dark blue '65 Chevy panel truck. As they drove toward her apartment, she told him she needed a new set of tags for Big Russet and registration that matched.

He nodded and took a detour to his cousin's garage, ducking inside, then returning with just what she needed. For a grand. Which she could pay Carlos.

"*Mi primo* runs a chop shop out of his garage at night. Days, he's just another wetback who fixes cars. He keeps some tags and registration from wrecked cars current and handy for emergencies. Strictly for friends and family. Got a set for a Chevy like yours. A year older but close enough until you get wherever you're going and get a new set."

"Good thing I got the sister-in-law discount. Don't think I could afford full freight."

Carlos chuckled, then looked her in the eye.

"You're on the run now, *guapa*. With a little one. Everything will cost you more."

They waited at Carlos' house until dark then drove to her place. When they got close to her side street, Carlos doused the lights and let the truck glide to a stop with the front bumper flush with the corner. They sat still and watched, clocking the parked cars and trucks. She noted a jacked-up truck with off-road tires she'd never seen before and pointed it out to Carlos.

"Anything in your apartment you can't walk away from?"

"Nothing that can't be replaced. All I need is my car. We can slip down the alley and get it."

Inside the garage, she handed Charlie to Carlos, who spoke to him in Spanish, telling him what a handsome boy he was. She opened the trunk and dug out the brick of cash, breaking it to get three grand, then taping it back together. She handed the cash to Carlos and took Charlie off his hands.

"This is too much."

"No, it's for you and your cousin. You got me out of a tight. And I know you would have blown that fucker's head off if I hadn't killed him first."

"Would have done that with much pleasure. It's sad that I didn't."

"You don't need blood on your hands."

"Wouldn't be the first I've spilled."

"Thought not. All the more reason to keep the money."

Carlos changed the plates while she kept Charlie amused. When he was done, she gave him a hug while he mussed Charlie's hair.

"Get Charlie settled. When you're ready, start the car and I'll lift the door. I sprayed WD-40 on the hinges. Maybe they won't squeak so damn bad. Be safe and be well, *guapa*."

"*Y tu, amigo.*"

That was three hours ago. Only ten more to go.

Trust Big Russet to get her and Charlie to the only place where she might feel safe and amongst friends. West Texas. Where the graves of her two lovers were.

One still held her heart. The other was Charlie's dad.

Eight

Juana Blas dreaded making the thirty-mile drive north of Faver that led to the dead end of a gravel road and a double-wide squatting behind the sagging gate of a barbed wire fence.

It wasn't the distance that bothered her. She was a *Tejana,* born and raised in Faver and accustomed to racking up long miles to get almost anywhere in the wide-open wasteland of West Texas.

The frequency of her trips out here wasn't that bad, either. Twice a month. Early in the evening, just after sundown. Home before midnight. Two hundred dollars richer for her carnal labors.

Sessions with most of her clients didn't seem like work. She loved to suck, fuck and explore the deeper kink of some of her more twisted regulars. As long as it didn't involve latex, *el pipi,* or *la cagada.*

Juana savored the buffet of cocks and occasional pussies she got to taste and feel. She kept herself clean and fit, made the *machos* wear *el profiláctico* and got tested regularly for *VIH, El Gálico* and *El Drip*. She came once or twice a day with clients and rarely had to use her vibrator.

Nothing tasty about this *pendejo,* though. He was a bald-headed pig with a fringe of reddish-blonde hair, a big belly and a little dick. Liked to slap her around, spank her and twist her nipples hard while they fucked.

Enjoyed punishing her with a big, black dildo. Grunted, snorted, and pawed the sheets when she fucked him in the ass with a strap-on. Didn't like to shower that much. Smelled like piss, sweat and cigarette smoke.

Used to be a Cuervo County deputy. Busted her for soliciting back in the day. Made her give him freebies in the back seat of his cruiser. Before her cousin, Tony the Blade, became her pimp. Then the pig became a paying customer. Deputy Brad Settles.

"Be nice to this *cabrón*, Juana. He's bent. Works for the Garzas and some *gringo* gunrunners on this side of the river. They pick up the tab for you. Keep him sweet, and we got no worries. He'll tell you things I need to know. Pillow talk."

That's how it worked as long as Blue Willingham was sheriff. Despite all his bold talk about waging a Texas Tough war on drugs, Blue was in bed with the Garzas. Settles was one of his boys, on the Garza pad. He was also a double-dipper, taking an extra hundred dollars of Garza juice on the quiet to spy on his boss.

Servicing Settles equaled easy but disgusting *pesos*. She'd do his favorite nasties, half-listen to him brag and gossip, then pay attention when he gave her some intel on the Garzas or the courthouse and Sheriff's Office. Who was in with Blue, what he was angling to do, who else was paying him off, who was on the outs. Passed it to Tony as soon as she could.

Settles had a seat at the table, saw and heard a lot. Remembered everything and told all. For the right price.

That changed when Blue sucked on his graddaddy's break-top Smith & Wesson .44 and splattered blood and brains all over his office. With Doggett as interim sheriff, Settles was no longer part of the inner circle but could still earn his keep as a spy for the Garzas.

When Doggett twice got elected to full terms, Settles got pushed to the far edges. Lots of night shifts, lots of jail duty. Lots of *night* jail duty. Harder to dig up dirt even though his buddies tried to keep him in the loop.

"What's with this *pendejo,* Juana? He ain't tellin' you shit I'm not hearin' from somebody else."

"I know, Tony. I'm hearing some of the same shit from my other regulars. It's like somebody turned the faucet off on his ass."

"Somebody has. *Pinche* Doggett. Garzas are pissed because they don't have a pipeline to him and his top deputies. Got ears in the jail and the courthouse, but nobody in Doggett's inner circle. And Doggett knows Settles is a Garza spy and hates him a whole lot."

"That mean I can stop fuckin' this guy? He's a pig."

"Long as his money's green, you keep giving him a twirl. Garzas got other jobs for him. Heard they're usin' him as a hitter."

"That tub of guts? He's no killer."

"You'd be surprised, *guapa*. Heard he does good work. Blew away some of those Monterrey fucks he caught on this side of the river. The Garzas want to keep him happy."

"*Mierda*."

Settles finally lost his badge when he beat the shit out of a prisoner named Gustavo Montáñez, a day laborer from across the river arrested for drunk and disorderly on a freezing Friday night just before Christmas. Broke the prisoner's jaw, dislocated a knee, bruised a kidney, and busted enough ribs to puncture a lung. With a nightstick. Man was pissing and spitting up blood when they got him to the hospital.

Settles claimed Montáñez took a swing at him while being escorted to his cell. Nobody else saw it that way, deputies, drunks or skels. Neither did the video camera focused on the main jail hallway. That unblinking eye showed Settles whaling on a drunk and staggering prisoner with no provocation.

Doggett took his badge and gun. Sam Boelcke charged him with aggravated battery. The district court judge, one of the few old-school Anglos left on the bench, bumped the charge down to simple assault and fined Settles three hundred dollars. They both belonged to the same hunt club. *Pinche gringos.*

Juana was surprised to see the pipe metal gate closed. He usually left it open for her. She got out of her car, rattled the chain loose, and swung the gate clear of the gravel and dirt track to the doublewide.

No porch light, so she angled her headlamps toward the door and kept them lit when she parked. Only one light on inside, its dim glow framed by the front window to the right of the door.

She climbed the rickety wooden steps then knocked but got no answer. She twisted the doorknob. It was open. That wasn't unusual. But everything else was. A chill ran up her spine and made her shiver. She reached into her purse and pulled out a Charter Arms snub-nosed revolver with five rounds of .38 Special jacketed hollow points in the cylinder.

She didn't want to walk through that door. She knew something bad was inside. But she wanted her money. She crossed herself with her free hand then stepped over the threshold, the stubby pistol leading the way.

The trailer was hot and stuffy, the air slowly stirred by a wobbly ceiling fan at the center of the living room ceiling. Two more steps in, and a strong coppery smell hit her nostrils, sharp and cutting. She sniffed twice and remembered the smell. Another step added a bass note stench straight from the septic tank. No memory needed for that.

Her dead father was a butcher, so Juana knew the tangy, metallic smell came from the iron content of spilled blood hitting the air. Told her either Settles was bleeding out in the master bedroom or was butchering a cow back there. She knew she was fooling herself with the thought of choice cuts of beef, but it resurrected an image of her father that gave her comfort and the strength to keep her feet moving toward Settles' bedroom.

The septic tank smell grew stronger, causing her to gag. She pulled a bandana out of her purse and held it to her nose with her free left hand. The bedroom door was ajar, and she tapped it open with her right foot. She groped for the light switch on the wall just inside the door, gagging again. Harsh light flooded the room from a naked bulb screwed into the ceiling fan. An arc of jagged glass from the shattered light globe looked like shark's teeth ready to take a bite.

Juana screamed then puked her dinner on the carpet and over her new Nocona lizard skin boots. She retched a second time, drawing only bile. She felt dizzy and kept her head down, wiping her mouth and taking short breaths to recover. Seconds felt like minutes before she finally risked standing straight. She crossed herself once more and again faced what had made her scream.

Settles' blood-spattered body was face-up on the bed, spread-eagled, feet toward the headboard, ankles and wrists bound to the posts at each corner with the ropes and handcuffs he liked to use while fucking her with that big, black dildo. His head lolled over the foot of the bed at an unnatural angle, its weight pulling at the edges of a yawning throat wound razored from ear to ear, giving the body a second saw-toothed mouth far larger and bloodier than the one he was born with.

Slashing arterial blood jets climbed the walls to the right of the bed, cutting a diagonal across an oversized framed print of Frederic Remington's painting of a cowboy trailing a column of Texas longhorns. Blood flooded the carpet beneath the head, the ceiling light glinting ruby red off the liquid surface. The mattress below the body's crotch was also soaked with flow from a wound that marked where Settle's tiny dick and pendulous balls used to be. Those severed parts sat on his chest, matting the red hair with residual blood.

"¡Santo dios!" Crossing herself a third time, staring at the body and all that blood.

There's the good and merciful God above and the greed of we sinful mortals down here. You're a sinner, Juana, but you are in the hands of God. He would want you to have what you need to stay alive. It's not greed. It's survival. You will light a candle for this man and leave an offering at the church. He was a pig but he didn't deserve to die like this.

That's what Juana told herself as she turned away from the gore and put her eyes to work looking for Settles' wallet. Wasn't on the cheap dresser or rickety night table. She spotted his jeans looped over the top rail of an oak armchair. Wallet in the back pocket. Two crisp hundred dollar bills inside. Parked next to another eighty dollars in tens and twenties. God was good. Gave her a bonus to soften the horror she found. Tequila and a fat twist of *la mota* would also ease the pain. After she got home.

The floor creaked. An electric jolt sparked her nerves. She spun around. A short, muscular man with a shaved head and an unblinking right eye walked through the door. She spotted a long scar running along his left cheek and jawline and saw he favored his left leg.

"You could have walked away and lived, but you didn't. I could tell you recognized the blood smell but kept coming anyway."

"I wanted my money."

"Even though you didn't fuck this pig."

"Even though. I deserved this money for all the times I did fuck him. For all the times they made me fuck him. It was degrading. It always made me feel like I defiled myself."

"But you're a whore. Comes with the territory."

"None of my other regulars make me feel this way. Some are sad men who sleep in a very cold bed. I give them a release, some warmth, and a smile. Others are more like me.

90

They like to fuck and like being with a woman who knows what she's doing in bed and gives them something they're not getting at home."

"So you're a therapist with benefits."

He smiled when he said this and took a step closer. She threw her purse at him and raised her revolver. She managed to fire once before he grabbed her by the neck. She heard him grunt as the bullet smacked flesh.

It was the last sound Juana ever heard. He snapped her neck then let her drop to the floor. He picked up her pistol and purse and used her bandana to put pressure on the bullet wound to his right side.

Not too bad. Looked like a through-and-through. Hurt like a bastard. Knew a vet in Marfa who would patch him up and keep his mouth shut. For some long green. And three or four twists of Mexican brown.

"Crazy bitch. I liked you. I might have let you live."

Not hardly. There's the Duke again. Love using his line after I kill somebody. Terse and final. Hard as a tombstone.

Perfect benediction for Settles. Motherfucker was supposed to shepherd three of his crew to a safe hideout after the ranch raid. Ratted them out to the Garzas instead. All three got dead.

He shook his head then looked at her body. Then looked at Settles. An image floated into his brain, and he started to laugh.

Stop the bleeding. Strip the whore. Everything but her puke-streaked boots.

Put her in bed with Settles. Stuff his cock and balls in her mouth. Slice her nipples off. Put them in that dead prick's mouth. Lick the blade.

"This'll drive the cops nuts. Make 'em think they've got a real psycho on their hands."

He laughed again.

"Yeah, baby. I'm Sweeney Todd."

Nine

He called before they left Presidio. She was sitting in a rocker on his front porch when he drove up. He pulled her to her feet and kissed her hard and long, tongue probing her mouth. She kissed him back and let her tongue dance with his. He broke the embrace, unlocked the front door, then grabbed her hand to pull her inside. They linked fingers as they strolled to his bedroom. Just like long-time lovers with all the time in the world.

Overdrive once they stepped through the bedroom door. Fast and hot. Clothes flew every which way. Hat and bandana head scarf. Gunbelt and boots. Boxers, bra, panties, and jeans. Socks—two white, two lime green. Sneakers.

Tongues stabbing, hands sliding and gripping, fingers grasping and thrusting, mouths biting and sucking, they plowed into his bed. Two fleshy lovers taking up every inch of mattress.

She was thick and curvy with a big ass and heavy breasts. He was bald, broad-shouldered and skinny-legged, with a belly that covered the muscles of an ex-jock gone to seed. Her rich, dark curls carried stray strands of gray and white and the scent of sandalwood and fried onions. She licked his chest, tasting a mix of leather, tobacco, sweat, and Old Spice.

He spread her legs wide and forced his head between her meaty thighs, sucking and tonguing her pussy, lapping up her sweet and salty musk. She licked his cock and balls then took him deep in her mouth. She shuddered then came up for air.

"*Dame tu verga*. Fuck me hard, *hombre*."

"That's the only way I know how to fuck, *espléndida*."

That drew a throaty and muffled laugh.

"Listen to *Oso Blanco* with the fancy Spanish. You can't turn my head with words, *hombre*. But you can with *El Gallo*."

"*Sí, mi linda*."

"Less talk. More cock."

Burch spun around and forced himself between her thighs, plunging his cock into her pussy, leaning forward to bite her hard-cherry nipples, sucking them into his mouth and buzzing them with his tongue.

She arched her back and hissed, then bit him hard on the shoulder. Her legs wrapped around his hips and pulled his cock deeper. Bellies, hot and sweaty, slapped together. Their bodies bucked and spasmed.

She bit his ear then shouted.

"Faster, *hombre!* Harder! Fuck meeeeee! Harder! Make me cum!"

He found a higher gear. The bedsprings screeched. Sweat dripped from his face onto her heavy breasts. She licked his bearded chin. Then pulled his head down so she could stab his mouth with her tongue. He felt her spasm in long waves, her pussy gripping his cock. That cued his balls to jet cum. He heard growling and howling. From her mouth. And his. One more deep thrust made her scream.

"¡Dios mío, tu gallo me volvió loco! ¡Dame más!"

Another thrust. She drew in a sharp, ragged breath. Then stuck her tongue in his ear.

"Reload time for John Henry, Carmen."

"John Henry? Such a cute name for *El Gallo*. Don't take too long, *Oso Blanco*. Gotta meet my cousin and open the food truck in an hour or two."

She reached down and stroked his wilted penis. He felt John Henry start to stir.

"Where's your girlfriend, baby?"

"Not here."

"Gone for good?"

"Hard to tell."

"Don't matter to me. See me as often as you can, *Oso Blanco*. If she's dumb enough to leave a good fuck behind maybe she's too stupid to come back."

The loud, rude jangle of the bedside phone rocketed him from the depths of a deeply therapeutic, post-carnal snooze, rattling his eyeballs and popping the lids wide open.

Burch thought he heard a floorboard creak. Faint but deeper than the non-stop ringing. He reached across his body, ripped open the night table drawer, and pulled out a snub-nosed .357 Magnum. A nickel-plated Taurus five-shot he seized from a pimp who pulled a switchblade on him in Dallas years back.

He scanned his bedroom, heart hammering, hand tracing the warm but empty space in his bed. Nobody there. He waited. No more phantom noises.

Then he answered the fuckin' phone.

"Goddamit, this better be good."

"Mornin' to you, too, handsome. Must not have had your coffee, yet."

"Might need a whisky before breakfast, Bobby."

"You sound hungover."

"Nope. Fuck frazzled."

"Carmen?"

"The same. My sheets smell like pussy, perfume, and fried onions."

"I'm guessing I'm no longer your favorite wetback."

"I'm not that fickle, but you definitely need to regard her as a threat."

"Here's the deal—you got thirty minutes to shit, shave, and shower before I pick you up to meet Doggett at a murder scene on some ranch road north of town."

"Coffee. Black. Two *el grandes*. And two packs of Luckies. I'm out."

"Anything else, your highness?"

"Fuck you, Bobby. We'll take the Blazer when you get here and bang the hell out of that piece of shit. No sense fuckin' up your ride."

When Burch and Quintero rolled up on the battered and forlorn doublewide of the late and unlamented Brad Settles, whore-hopper and defrocked deputy, they spotted Sheriff Sudden Doggett standing next to a Cuervo County meat wagon, staring them down while jamming Red Man into his jaw.

"Motherfuckin' dawg, he's already got his mad face on. Gonna be a whole lot of fun dealin' with him."

"Always looks like that lately. What gives?"

He's mad at me for saving his life. Doesn't like the daily reminder. Six-to-five pick 'em whether he fires me. Or shoots me. Maybe both.

Burch handed Quintero a squat blue jar of Vicks' VapoRub.

"Them bodies been cookin' for two days."

He watched Quintero finger ointment into each nostril, then did the same when handed the jar. Got instant memories of childhood fevers and head-clogged misery as he inhaled the triple team of menthol, camphor, and eucalyptus oil. Beats the gagging stench of sun-broiled death all to hell and back.

Burch swung out of the driver's side of the Blazer, wincing as he put weight on his left leg, and got a warning bite from the surgical rod and pins that held it together. He capped the Vicks jar and tossed it on the dash, then fished out a pouch of Levi Garrett to load chaw into his jaw.

Stalling and poking a stick at Doggett at the same time, one of his special talents.

"Took you sumbitches long enough to get here."

"Got in way late from Presidio, Sheriff."

"Not too late to have a visitor, I hear. You best not try one of your drive-by fucks on Carmen Cortez. That woman will cut the liver and lights out of you."

Burch didn't much care for Doggett broadcasting his carnal misadventures across the sand and gravel drive of a dead man's doublewide. In front of Quintero, a couple of crime scene techs, and a deputy he recognized but couldn't name.

"A little louder, Sheriff. Let them stiffs in on the latest gossip."

He could hear Quintero choke down a laugh. One of the techs snorted. Deputy No-Name looked like he bit his tongue in half as he turned away.

With three choppy steps, Doggett was chest-to-chest with Burch, his head tilted back to lock eyeballs with the taller man.

"Listen to me, you sumbitch. Your badge is hangin' by a thread right now. By a fuckin' thread. Say one more smartass word and you're gone."

Quintero shouldered a sliver of space between them. Didn't break the laser staredown, though.

"C'mon, Sheriff. Let me put asshole here to work doin' what you hired him for."

"Do that, Bobby. Get him the fuck out of my sight. Tell him to put a leash on that cock of his, too."

Burch let Quintero lead him by the arm toward the yawning front door, his jaw sore from clenching his teeth and grinding his molars. He spat his chaw into the dust.

"Forgot to tell you Carmen is his second cousin."

"Thanks for nothin', Bobby, but fuckin' his kin ain't what gives him the red ass about me."

"Wanna tell me what does?"

"No."

Katie Navarro met them at the door, letting them step fully inside the trailer before saying a word, her big, dark eyes glittering with curiosity as she gave Burch a couple of silent up-and-down glances. Like sizing up a customer for a suit. Or a casket.

"How many times did you piss in Doggett's Cheerios this morning?"

"Not gonna talk about it, Katie."

"He lit you up like a Christmas tree, and you're not gonna say why?"

"Nope. Not interested in committing career suicide today."

"Word of warning, Burch. He's partial to his cousin Carmen."

"So Bobby told me."

"And Carmen's fuckin' nuts, so watch your ass."

"Much obliged for the warning. Can we talk about those two stiffs in the bedroom?"

"Let me give you the grand tour. You're gonna like this one, Burch. Kind of a *déjà vu* all over again thing. All that's missin' is an ashtray full of Lucky Strike butts and an empty pack."

Katie, a short, wiry, and intense senior crime tech, was Cuervo County's *de facto* coroner, given the incompetence and whisky-loving nature of Doc Battles, a veterinarian first elected to the office when LBJ was still known as Landslide Lyndon. That was a jab at the 87-vote margin of his 1948 Democratic primary win over former Texas Gov. Coke Stevenson, an extraordinarily vicious campaign marked by voter fraud on both sides.

She was standing in the middle of the living room, a left fist on cocked left hip, head tilted in the same direction, her long black hair pulled back in a ponytail tucked through the back end of her dark blue ballcap with CCSO stitched in white above the bill. She was eyeing Burch like an angler waiting for a hawg of a large-mouthed bass to come boiling up from its lily-pad lair to hit her top-water lure.

Burch pulled out a fresh pack of Luckies, one of two Quintero bought for him with the double order of black coffee. He held it up, rocking it back and forth in his hand.

"Luckies like these, you mean? Luckies like the ones I smoke? Luckies like the butts you found in Leigh Burdette's Airstream with my DNA? Right next to her corpse with the throat slashed wide open and the nipples cut off? These kind of Luckies?"

Burch felt Quintero's hand on his shoulder.

"Easy, partner. Katie's just yankin' your chain."

Burch pocketed the Luckies.

"Seems to be everybody's favorite sport this mornin', Bobby—'cept yours. I'm waiting for her to mention the three Coney Island whitefish she found in the wastebasket with my manly essence inside. Heard you told Doggett you wished your boyfriend could pull a trifecta like that, Katie."

"Jesus, partner. Dial it down."

Katie was up in his grill with two long strides, eyes flashing, head back for the laser lock look. Your basic small-and-tall standoff. When she spoke, it was in a harsh, husky whisper.

"Listen here, asshole. I'm teasing you about *déjà vu* because the crime scene you're about to look at reminds me a helluva lot of Leigh Burdette's trailer. Not for nothin', Burch, but that Burdette kill could have taken a whole 'nother turn for you if Blue Willingham had still been sheriff."

"You're not tellin' me nothin' I don't already know, Katie."

"That right? Well, clearly, you need to be reminded. With a two-by-four upside your hard head. There're only two reasons you weren't railroaded for Leigh Burdette's murder. You're lookin' at one. The other is that man right behind you."

Burch turned in the direction Katie was pointing. Sudden Doggett, leaning his back against the front door jamb, sunglasses still on, a grim smile underneath his salt-and-pepper Zapata moustache.

"She's right, you know. And you know Blue would have just shot your ass and claimed you were tryin' to escape. Not a totally bad idea, come to think on it."

Doggett took a long pause, spit in a Dixie cup, loaded his jaw with more Red Man, then pointed at Burch.

"As much as I've enjoyed Katie putting you in your place, do us all a big damn favor—can the drama queen act and get to work. Daylight's burnin', and we need to get them bodies in the cool confines of the morgue right quick."

"Yes, sir."

"Wow. I like the sound of that. Say it more often, why don't you?"

Burch eyed the impromptu artistry of a killer who enjoyed his gory obsession.

Settles' blood-streaked body was the foundation of this creation, head lolling over the foot of the bed, widening the maw of the slashed throat with the weight of the body's bald head, ankles bound to the headboard with ropes and scarves.

The hooker was perched atop Settle's mountainous belly, her boots splayed over his shoulders, her money-maker close and centered on the yawning throat wound. Her head curved downward, face turned to the left and buried in the shallow, bloody vee of her trick's razored crotch, his pride and joy stuffed in her red-rimmed mouth to suggest her teeth did the butchery.

"He had fun posing this scene. Just for us. Knows we know it's all post-mortem. Knows we know he killed Settles first, then the hooker."

"Was she even here when Settles got it?"

"Doubtful, Bobby. She walked in after the fact, I'd bet, and puked on the floor. Does that track for you, Katie?"

"Yup. She surprised him, and he broke her neck. That's the only anomaly. Everything else tracks the Burdette killing. Killer here loves to use a blade. Straight razor, just like Burdette's killer. Throat sliced open deep and wide. Likes to slice the nipples off a woman's titties. Snapped her neck on this one but still cut those damn nipples off. Put 'em in Settles' mouth. Some folks might call that a signature move."

"Have to be the signature of a dead man," Burch said. "I blew away the cocksucker who killed Leigh Burdette during that goat ropin' out in the desert goin' on four years back. Cleve Chizik, an Alice Baker hitter straight out of Pelican Bay."

"Yeah, and the records all show he's dead and buried in a pauper's grave. I know that. But I found a couple of other things that might give you a chubby. First, the killer's left-handed, just like Leigh Burdette's."

"Lots of lefty psycho-killers out there, Katie."

"Don't interrupt. Second, he's a short guy. Had to reach around and up to cut Settles' throat so the wound is a little sloppy on the right side. Chizik's a short guy. And he's left-handed."

He eyed the arterial spray that jetted across the oversized cowboy print before climbing the wall and anointing the ceiling. *Damn, Settles' blood pressure must have been off the charts. Getting murdered saved him from strokin' out.*

"That's a Remington print."

"Good eye, Bobby. Blood spray makes it look more like a Jackson Pollock."

Bobby chuckled. "This is West Texas, not the MoMA, partner."

"Maybe so, but Donald Judd and his little colony of artsy-fartsy folk are just up the road in Marfa."

"Think our killer might be hidin' out up there, sharpening his razor when he ain't paintin' abstract nudes?"

"I kindly doubt it, but he's close, Bobby. Real close. He's on a mission and ain't goin' nowhere until he's through."

Katie cleared her throat.

"If you boys are done playin' Bob Ross, I'll tell you what else I found. Guarantee it will make one of you want to give me a love child."

"Can you give us a second, Katie? I want to add a couple of fluffy clouds and some nice little birds to the ceiling. In Bob's memory."

"Quit fuckin' around and pay attention, Burch. Here's the prize. Found some blood splatter on the carpet that ain't part of the kill pattern. Also got a faint whiff of burnt gunpowder when I walked in the room. I think our gal here shot the killer before he snapped her neck."

Five seconds of silence passed. Burch broke it by clapping his hands, stomping his boots and doing a real shitty version of an Apache war whoop, sounding more like a crow with black lung.

"How to be, Katie. Hello, DNA match. We got you now, motherfucker. Chizik rising from the dead or his copycat. Call your mama, Katie. Tell her she's about to be a grandmother."

"You'll never get that lucky, Burch."

"What about Bobby?"

"Him I like, but he's married. No sale with you."

Burch pulled a single Lucky out of the pack, licked one end, and placed it on the edge of the dresser.

"That's for you, Katie. Thanks for the memories."

"You're an asshole, Burch."

"So I'm told."

The phone rang as soon as Burch stepped into his office. Dub McKee on the other side of the line. The salty ex-Ranger wasted no time on pleasantries.

"What the hell's wrong with you two? At each other's throats like Frank and Ava."

"Sinatra and Gabor?"

"No, dumbass. Sinatra and Ava Gardner. Care to answer my question?"

Burch said to himself: *Truth is, Dub, some men just can't stand the light of a saving grace. Having me walk through the door every day is a constant reminder that another man almost blew out his candle, and I'm the reason that didn't happen.*

"Nope. It's between me and him," Burch said aloud to McKee

"Maybe so, but we need to clear the air between you two. I'm getting calls from the county judge and half the commission. I'll be down there in a day or so. Gonna put the two of you in a room until we get this settled."

"Bring the Maker's."

Ten

Burch reached the count of ten-Mississippi in a whisper only he could hear, nodding to the deputy with the battering ram to breach the front door of a lonely adobe shack sitting on the barren crest of a brushy hill forty miles east of Faver.

It took two swings to splinter the door. Burch finished the job with his boots then stepped over the wrecked plywood, sweeping the living room with a Winchester Model 12 pump he picked up in a Mesquite pawn shop shortly before he left Dallas, bellowing the obligatory "Cuervo Sheriff's Office! Hands up and show yourself!"

He heard Quintero and his wingman slamming through the back door, yelling the same phrase with a Spanish twist: *"¡Sheriff de Cuervo! ¡Manos arriba!"*

Nobody in the living room. Just a dog-turd-brown couch with yellowed stuffing spilling out of rips in the cushions, a portable TV with rabbit-ear antennae, stacked milk crates serving as an end table, and a wobbly ceiling fan with a dim globe light fighting a losing battle against the dusty gloom.

Empty beer bottles were scattered on the floor. Pearl and Lone Star. The air smelled like the business end of a giant blunt.

"Clear!" Quintero's voice.

"Clear!" Burch's wingman, battering ram on the floor, cocked Colt 1911 in hand.

That left a bedroom at the end of a long, narrow hallway to Burch's front left. He spotted Quintero peeking around the refrigerator in the kitchen, cradling his .308 FN FAL with the folded stock.

Burch pointed at his own chest and nodded toward the hallway. He turned the corner, leveling his twelve-gauge at the bedroom door, ready to turn plywood to sawdust with buckshot. Distance about twenty-five feet.

"Lonny Dalrymple!! Show yourself with them hands empty, motherfucker! Or I start blastin'!"

"Go fuck yourself, Deputy Dawg. Got me a sweet piece of ass in here with me. Rancher's daughter. Pretty lil' thing. I'll blow her brains out in a heartbeat if you don't let me go."

"Horseshit, Lonny. You ain't got nobody in there but Rosie Palm."

"Thas' where you're wrong, Deputy Dawg. Say hello to the man, honey. Tell him how you been in here suckin' and fuckin' ol' Lonny the past two days. Can't get enough of my sweet stick, can you Sugar?"

Burch flashed some hand signs at Quintero. Translation: *Scoot 'round the corner and see if you can peek into that bedroom.* Subtext: *Blast that bastard if you got a clean shot.* Bobby nodded and was gone. His wingman stepped up to help cover Burch.

"Time's up, motherfucker."

"Wait! Don't shoot, mister. Don't shoot."

Well, shit. Lonny wasn't lyin'. Young girl's voice. Twangy with jitters.

"What'd I tell yew, Deputy Dawg? Sweet thang here's my hostage. My get-out-of-jail card. Let's talk about how you gonna let me and her waltz out of here scot-free."

"Not gonna happen, Lonny. You murdered Leigh Burdette. You gotta pay for that."

"I didn't kill that fat cow. That was Chizik, Eveready, and Sledge. They're the ones what carved her up, shoved candles up her cunt, and burned her with cigarettes."

"Bullshit, Lonny. Your fingerprints are all over that trailer. Left your spit cup in a trash can under the sink, dumbass."

"That don't mean shit. I was their driver. All I did was watch. It was Chizik, Sledge, and Eveready done all that nasty shit. Made me want to puke."

"Law don't see it that way. You were right there and went along with her killin'. Got off on it, didn't you? Gave you a big chubby, I bet. You'll get the needle for that thrill. Just like Sledge. Just like Chizik and Eveready if they weren't already dead."

Loud, gravely laughter from behind the door. Ending with the sound of Dalrymple hacking up a lungful of tar and phlegm.

"All you cops is the same—dumber than a box of rocks. Chizik ain't dead. He's alive and well. Runnin' loose. Slicin' and dicin'. Dealin' payback to all them cocksuckers what fucked us up the ass on our last deal."

"Horseshit again, Lonny. Chizik's dead. Know how I know that? Shot his sorry ass myself. With the .45 I've got ridin' on my hip right now. Flyin' Ashtrays don't lie, *pendejo*. They kill you quick and true."

"So you're *THAT* asshole. Know all about you, Burch, you fat-ass motherfucker. Chizik's got big plans for you. Gonna use that razor of his to give you a second smile right underneath your beard and them double chins. You and that blonde bitch are *REAL* high on his payback list."

"You talk too much, Lonny. Just like every other punk-ass bitch who takes it up the ass to stay alive. Bet you miss all that cock, Lonny. Bet you made sweet thang work you over with a dildo so you could get it up."

From behind the door, a low-pitched growl started rumbling, growing in volume and rising in pitch until it became a screaming string of profanity mixed with word-like noise not catalogued in Webster's.

Gave Burch just enough time to drop to one surgery-scarred knee before the door flew open with a bang. Lonny Dalrymple, all six-foot-five and 290 pounds of red-headed, red-bearded, buck-nekkid rage came roaring out of the bedroom like a Viking berserker, banging wildly with a .44 Magnum hand cannon, sending slugs flying over Burch's head, blasting huge hunks out of the adobe wall at the opposite end of the shack.

Burch steadied up and aimed slow. Fired three rounds of buckshot, slamming Dalrymple to a sudden and very dead stop. Pistol flew from the dead man's right hand, clattering toward Burch. Body hit the hallway's linoleum floor face first, shaking the whole shack, head bouncing twice before stopping about two feet from Burch's bended knee.

Shucking the last empty shell from the Winchester, Burch stood up, anticipating a bite from the pins and rods in his left leg that didn't happen. He leaned over Dalrymple's body, pressing two fingers into the side of his neck.

No pulse. *Finito y adios, pendejo.*

He picked up the dead man's pistol. A Smith & Wesson Model 29. Dirty Harry's gun.

Did you feel lucky, punk? Guess so. You guessed wrong. Made my day, you cockbite motherfucker. Bit of payback for Leigh. A downpayment until I catch up with Chizik. Then the bill gets paid in full. With Flying Ashtrays.

A naked girl stood in the bedroom doorway, her eyes wide with fear and horror as she stared at her dead lover's body. She was tall, thin, and pale with small breasts, dark red nipples, and reddish blonde hair that reminded Burch of Sissy Spacek in *Carrie*.

He clicked the safety on his shotgun and handed it to his wingman then stepped up to the girl and took her by the hand.

"It's over now, Miss. He can't hurt you no more. Let's get some clothes on you and get you home. What's your name?"

Her face reddened. Her features collapsed, twisted with pain as she burst into tears and started to howl. She jerked her hand away from Burch.

"But I loved him ... I LOVED HIM ... I LOVED HIM, AND YOU KILLED HIM ... YOU KILLED HIM, AND I'LL HATE YOU FOREVER ... I WISH IT WAS YOU WHO WAS DEAD!"

Get in line, kid.

"Damn, partner. You sure goaded the shit out of this guy."

"Tried to keep him focused on me so he wouldn't shoot the girl. And give you a chance to spot him through the window and take him down."

"Let's just say you went one-for-two."

"That's a five-hundred average in baseball. Better than Teddy Ballgame his own'sef."

Quintero snorted. They were on either side of the dead man's head, backs leaning against opposite hallway sheetrock. Eyes on the corpse. Not each other.

"We pushed our luck on this one, partner. Should have had more than four of us up here. Should have spotted that girl on my scout. Could've went sideways worse than it did."

"No argument from me, Bobby. But don't go blamin' yourself. We didn't have a whole lot of choice. Didn't want to give him time to get long gone. Something made him leave that Aryan ratline and strike out on his own."

"Think he knew Cruz got sliced up?"

"That'd be my guess. Lost his connection to the Garzas and figured the ratline was blown."

They fell silent. Waiting on the evidence techs and the meat wagon. Waiting on Doggett or Chief Deputy Roger D'Angelo to show up for the post-shoot interview and the ass-chewing for not doing this one by the book.

Watching Jill Banks, one of two female deputies on the Cuervo County Sheriff's Office roster, escort the fully clothed young woman to a dusty cruiser out front.

Lonny hadn't lied; she was a rancher's daughter. Dottie O'Malley. They had her fingerprints and statement. It was true love, not a kidnapping. And she was seventeen, the age of consent in the Great State of Texas. Which was no guarantee of wisdom.

Burch could feel the post-kill jitters coming on. Always turned him into a blabbermouth—out loud and in his head. Needed to shut up and do something with his hands. Keep them from starting to shake. That's why the Good Lord made Lucky Strikes and a Zippo lighter. He fired up a nail and sucked the smoke down deep.

Quintero broke the quiet: "He sure was a Chatty Cathy. Thought those Aryan Brotherhood boys took a blood oath of silence. The skinhead *omertà*."

"*Omertà,* my ass. Not even the greaseballs believe in that shit anymore. Look at Sammy the Bull—just ratted out Gotti. And he ain't the first. Those assholes have been singing like birds ever since Joe Valachi."

"You believe what he said about Chizik not being dead?"

"I believe he believed Chizik is still above ground, but he didn't say he had beers with the guy. That said, my gut tells me 'yes' even though I emptied a mag of Flying Ashtrays into his sorry ass. Blame it on Kevlar and put Chizik at the top of our list. And he stays there unless those DNA results tell us something different."

"Gonna stir up a lot of stink if Chizik IS still alive. Egg on Doggett's face."

"Yup. Means the boss has another rotten apple he's gonna have to dig up. Also proves how incompetent Doc Battles is. Which is no surprise. Means we'll be combing through all his files to make sure there hasn't been another switcheroo covering the tracks of another felon who's supposed to be dead but ain't."

"You know, it doesn't have to be a bent deputy making that switcheroo."

"I know. But that leads to a dark thought we need to keep between just you and me."

Katie Navarro. They both spooked when they heard her familiar voice hailing them as she stepped through the splintered front door.

"You boys both look like the cat that just swallowed the canary. Talkin' about me behind my back again, fellas?"

"Nah, Katie. Too much fun doggin' you to your face. You just interrupted a solemn religious moment. Bobby here was takin' my confession for the killin' of a murder suspect who wanted to smoke my ass with a Dirty Harry gun."

"You ain't Catholic, Burch."

"No, but Bobby is and he's very ecumenical. Believes confession is good, even for the soul of a backslud, heathen Baptist."

"Cut the crap and give me the rundown. Daylight's burnin'."

Quintero did the honors, stepping up before Burch punched any more of Navarro's buttons. Introduced her to the naked corpse. Described how Burch got him dead. Pointed out the hand cannon on the floor and the hunks of adobe missing from the far wall.

Burch fetched his shotgun, shucked the final three shells of buckshot, and showed the gun to Katie before leaning it against a living room wall. She nodded.

Thumbing another Lucky to his lips, he said: "One more thing, Katie. Be looking for Chizik's fingerprints. Asshole here said that fucker is still alive before I had to put him down."

"Thought you said you killed his sorry ass."

"Thought I did but apparently not. If he's still walking among us, I get the distinct honor and privilege of killing his ass all over again."

"Lucky you."

Burch fired up the Lucky and squinted at Navarro through the smoke.

"Luck's got nothin' to do with it."

Doggett's office.

The sheriff at his desk with an action shot of him body slamming a calf into the arena dirt looming on the back wall. From his rodeo days. Back when they nicknamed him Sudden for his blurry speed. Before he landed wrong at Pocatello, shattering his left leg. Nobody called him by his given names, Elroy Jesus. He sure didn't. Just plain Sudden, court-approved, and the name that appeared on the ballot every four years.

Burch and Dub McKee sat side-by-side in leather armchairs planted in front of Doggett, looking at his dark-brown hangdog face, noting how much deeper the furrows ran from the corners of his eyes and how much frosting speckled his Zapata moustache and his thick black hair.

All three men had rocks glasses in their hands with three or four fingers of Maker's Mark poured neat in each. They sipped the Kentucky bourbon in silence, eyeing each other, waiting to see who would take the first shot in what was bound to be an unpleasant conversation a diplomat would describe as a "full and frank discussion of the issues."

"You just had to smoke the guy, didn't you? Couldn't get him to give up, or just didn't give a shit if he did or didn't?"

"He dealt the play. Came out of that bedroom blasting away with a .44 Mag."

"Admit it—deep down, you're glad he dealt the play. You wanted to kill his ass."

"You're goddam right I wanted to ice him. I feel personally responsible for Leigh Burdette's death. But I wasn't going to shoot him in cold blood. He had to make the first move. If he'da walked out with his hands up, I'da hooked him right up, and he'd be sitting in one of your jail cells."

"Bullshit. You woulda found another reason to smoke him."

"Are you callin' me a murderer, Sheriff? Is that where we're at?"

Doggett and Burch were out of their chairs, leaning across the desk, almost nose to nose, glaring at each other. Fists clenched. Right on the verge of a punch fest.

But each also looked like a man trying very hard to avoid taking that first swing. Or saying something else they couldn't take back. Words or actions that would terminally sever the ties between them. A black eye or broken nose. A screamed "FUCK YOU!" Badge on the desk. Ass out the door.

Leaning away from both men, McKee sipped his whiskey and sighed.

"Fellas, unless you're going to get to it, I suggest you both sit your ass down and listen to what this old Ranger has to say. You need to quit acting like two bucks in rutting season and focus on hunting down this serial killer we got wanderin' around these parts."

Burch and Doggett broke their stare-down and looked down at McKee. Seconds ticked by like minutes. Then they both did as they were told. McKee topped off their glasses.

"First off, you two are going to come to my hotel room tonight and settle this bad blood over a fresh bottle of Maker's. We either come to a resolution that works for everybody, or I'm going to shut this deal down, *sabe?*"

McKee still had the laser stare of a mankiller with a badge. Used it on Doggett and Burch until both men nodded and said, "Got it."

"Okay, good deal. Burch, the only thing I don't like about this latest guy you killed is we lost a chance to squeeze him about Chizik's whereabouts and who got greased to write that false death declaration."

Doggett: "We're going through Doc Battles' files to make sure there aren't other dead killers wandering around out there. I've got a notion who might have spread the grease and who got greased."

Burch: "I'm splittin' hairs here, but I don't think we can call Chizik a serial killer. He likes killin' but don't fit the classic definition. He's not killing street walkers, bums, or drug addicts at random. He's going after a list of folks who he thinks done him wrong. Including me, if we're to believe the late Lonny Dalrymple."

"And that blonde gunrunner who's in WitSec, right?"

"Top of the list, Dub. Only because he already killed her lover, Tommy Juan Jaeckel, the *hombre* who ratted out Chizik's original gunrunning crew. Chopped him up and stuffed him in a giant smoker just over the Brewster County line."

"Nasty. You got called in on that one, didn't you, Sheriff?"

"Yup. Took me a week to thaw out and get the stink out of my lungs."

"How'd we track down Dalrymple?"

"One of Bobby Quintero's snitches. Biker who likes to hunt. He was on the scout for muley tracks and spotted smoke from the chimney of a shack hunters like to use. Hung around until he spotted Lonny step outside. Recognized him. Called it in. Pocketed a hunnert bucks. Didn't see the girl. Neither did we before we made our move."

"We got damn lucky that girl didn't get caught in the crossfire."

"No argument from me, Dub."

"Why didn't you back off once you found out the girl was there?"

"Time and distance. That shack is way off in the boonies. Backup is an hour away. Figured our best bet was to keep the pressure on Lonny and force him to make a move."

"How'd he wind up in some hunter's shack? Thought you said he was ridin' some kind of Aryan Brotherhood of Texas rat line, hoppin' from safe house to safe house."

"That's what a snitch in Presidio told us. But looks like Lonny got spooked and made other plans. He was part of Chizik's crew at the Bar L R and knew the backcountry around Faver pretty good. Lonny was a Texas boy who knew how to rough it."

"Risky comin' back here, Ed Earl. What's that tell you?"

"Could be he knew those Alice Baker scumbags were getting the band back together, setting up another gunrunning crew. If that's the case, then Chizik will also want to be a part of it. Gives him another reason to be here other than settlin' old scores with his razor blade."

"Let's get him dead this time. Make sure he stays that way. See you boys tonight."

On the top floor of the Cattlemen's Hotel, a squat, three-story limestone and brick block that was the tallest building in Faver, Dub McKee held his come-to-Jesus meeting with Burch and Doggett.

They sat around a makeshift poker table with green baize tightly tucked across the top. A freshly cracked bottle of Maker's Mark sat in the center. An ice bucket sitting on a folded bath towel was on the weathered pine floor near McKee's left boot.

"Spit it out. What's got you two bowed up at each other?"

"He's too much of a loose cannon. Draws trouble like shit draws flies. One of these days, he's gonna go rogue and get one of my deputies killed."

"I thought we agreed that his particular skills are just what we need out here—a guy with experience who isn't afraid to drop the hammer on the bad guys."

"We don't need a damn vigilante who shoots first and asks questions later. Could have got that girl killed takin' that scumbag down. Should have called in backup and outwaited the bastard."

Burch sipped his whiskey, puffed a Lucky, and kept his own counsel, face blank, eyes hooded. Just like he had cards in his hand.

In his mind's eye, his gold badge was already on the table, and he was miles away, roaring down the highway under the starry blanket of the desert night in that big, nocturne blue Olds Four-Four-Two, punching the accelerator to hear that 455 Rocket scream like a tiger.

Fuck this. I'm gone.

McKee looked his way.

"Your turn."

"I pass."

"Bullshit. You'll answer."

Burch folded his imaginary hand and looked hard at each man.

"I'm gonna say this once and then shut up. I think me walkin' into that Sheriff's Office every day reminds him of something he'd rather forget, something that causes him shame even though it shouldn't."

He looked at Doggett and pointed a finger.

"Me blowin' away Needle Burnet before he could finish you off was a stroke of good luck. I'm damn glad I walked into that shack when I did and smoked him before he killed you. About the only good thing that happened that night. Evened up the score for your kid cousin getting killed."

Doggett shook his head and started to interrupt.

"Let me finish, goddamit. Shoe could have been on the other foot that night. Could have just as easily been you savin' my sorry ass. And if it had been, I hope to Christ I would've thanked you and been grateful for the saving grace."

"I thanked you."

"And been mad at me about it ever since."

"You expect me to kiss your ass?"

"Hell, no. But it might be nice if you could forgive yourself for needin' somebody to save your bacon. Be even better if you quit usin' me for a damn punchin' bag."

Burch stopped talking and took a gulp of iced whiskey. Doggett and McKee followed suit. The only sounds were the high desert wind rattling the fake window shutters outside and the creak of floorboards beneath their boots.

McKee finally spoke.

"I want you boys to shake hands and quit pokin' sticks at each other. Think you can do that?"

The three men stood up. Doggett and Burch shook hands under the steely gaze of the old Ranger, a mankiller with a badge. A truce. No telling how long it would last. McKee poured fresh whiskey into all three glasses.

In his mind's eye, Burch hooked a U-turn in the big Olds, burned asphalt back to Faver, and plucked his gold badge off the table's green baize. Before McKee or Doggett made it disappear.

For good.

Eleven

Nancy Jo Quartermain kept a hand on the ancient L.C. Smith ten-gauge leaning against the jamb inside her front door as she watched a tall woman wearing a navy blue ball cap, dark shades, and a canvas barn coat with all the style of a potato sack climb out of a rust-dappled Malibu Classic and hike a toddler higher up on her hip. Loose-fitting jeans and mud-spattered shit-kickers of dubious cowboy lineage rounded out a look that spelled homely in capital letters. Nothing to see here, fellas. No curves. No cleavage. No ass. Black hair cut short and swept under the cap.

Twilight and Nancy Jo's aged eyes helped hide the face behind those flyboy lenses, but there was something in the woman's long-legged stride she found familiar. Confident, purposeful, and athletic in the four-legged sense. Said she could sit a horse and stay there if the animal got unruly. Check a crow hop with legs and reins, then find that mystic middle ground where horse and rider become partners.

Nancy Jo couldn't tell all that just by watching the woman walk. The memory of someone she once knew well was bubbling up, serving the details of someone she had watched working with horses and teaching others to ride. A flat natural horsewoman. Handy with a long gun or pistol, too. Walking back into her life long after the old woman had given up hope of ever seeing her again, trailing the ghost of a dead lover and a string of gunrunners and drug smugglers who were very much alive and wanted to kill her with slow and maximum cruelty and pain.

Rita. Sweet Rita. Smiling at Nancy Jo now that the distance was closed. A ghost. A painful memory. Now flesh made whole. Rita Jane or June some called her at the Bar L R, that bogus ranch and retreat for Kluxers and suckers just north of Faver. Just plain Rita was fine, she told them. So just plain Rita it was for Nancy Jo.

The two became close, almost like mother and daughter, living on what was once a thriving spread owned by Thomas "T For Texas" Bondurant, the racist huckster, oil heir, and former state senator. Nancy Jo ran the kitchen and served as the ranch's de facto quartermaster; a fitting title given her married name. Made sure the place was well stocked in everything from feed and salt blocks to diesel fuel and horse liniment.

Rita kept the books for the ranch's two legitimate income streams—cows and two-legged suckers. Its small cattle operation had a tight cadre of cowpunchers running about two hundred head of mostly Corriente steers, a wily and stringy breed born for the high desert brush and the rodeo arena. Once the essence of any ranch, cowboys and cattle were now window dressing, flesh and blood camouflage for the darker endeavors of this outfit. Bondurant didn't care if they made money just as long as they didn't bleed too much cash and put on a good giddyap show.

The other legal but less savory ranch enterprise was a retreat for white supremacists and Texas secessionists, which featured a year-round schedule of seminars, lectures, and training sessions for the disgruntled, disenfranchised, and disgusted rednecks and racists who had lost jobs, homes, families, and status they viewed as a birthright. Bitter and angry, they were looking for someone to blame. While picking their threadbare pockets, Bondurant was only too happy to point out the scapegoats they already hated—blacks, wetbacks, Jews, Yankees, queers, and the federal government.

He was a gifted orator who gilded the myth of Manifest Destiny, promised them the tools to regain their God-given station in life, and etched the vision of a reborn Republic of Texas, a whites-only paradise severed from the Union and rebuilt on the Bible and bullets. Niggers, spics, and the Children of Abraham need not apply.

Rita did not keep track of the darkest and most lucrative branch of ranch commerce—the gunrunning and drug smuggling camouflaged by cows and Kluxers willing to be fleeced to feel better about themselves and their dead-end lives. While the latter might be considered distastefully predatory hate trafficking, it wasn't illegal. And cowboys and cattle—that was the vital core of the Great American Myth, as patriotic as an American flag made in China.

That didn't mean Rita was blind to the illicit trade those Aryan Brotherhood ex-cons were running from the far north side of the ranch. She shared her bed with Tommy Juan Jaeckel, who was hip deep in running guns, explosives, and stolen military ordnance to the drug gangs south of the Rio Grande, and smuggling weed, heroin, blow, and meth north to feed the ever-ready veins, lungs, and snouts of American drug fiends.

Tommy Juan was a local *Tejano,* a handsome, olive-skinned man with jet black hair, Mexican and Apache blood, and a taste for oversized rodeo belt buckles he never earned and tall boots with loud colors and exotic skins for the broncs he never rode. Born and raised near Faver, he knew every deer trail, cattle path, ranch road, and smugglers' crossing for fifty miles on both sides of the river. Knew every bent sheriff's deputy, Border Patrol officer, *federale,* and cop on either side, too.

Handy for the Alice Baker boys who mostly made their bones in California prisons before getting out and heading east to run guns and drugs from the Bar Triple T, the first ranch Cleve Chizik used as cover. Handy for Tommy Juan, too, a slick operator who was known to cut side deals and double-cross his partners for enough long green. That's how Tommy Juan wound up butchered and stuffed into a giant smoker on a desolate mesa just a few miles west of the

Cuervo County line, his head chopped off and topping his carcass, with the family jewels stuffed in his mouth.

After his tongue was cut out, of course. That for ratting out the Alice Baker boys and what was left of the Garza family, trying to rebuild and claw their way back to the top of the heap after a rival gang from Monterrey triggered a pound of C4 tucked under the driver's seat of Malo Garza's silver Mercedes, turning the patriarch into a pile of smokin' stew meat.

Tommy Juan didn't see himself as a snitch. He was merely a businessman capitalizing on an opportunity to weed out the competition and shorten his prison sentence for gunrunning and trying to stick the high sheriff of Cuervo County with an Arkansas toothpick. Instead of fleeing West Texas, he audaciously started hustling the clients of those he ratted out to start his own gunrunning operation, fronted by Rita, wearing a blonde wig and skin-tight designer jeans and calling herself *La Güera,* the outlaw's cowgirl wet dream.

Tommy Juan's death turned Rita into an avenging angel, burning with a molten desire for payback. She got it, too, but at a very high cost—too many of the men who followed her were killed in that midnight gunfight in the desert between rival drug gangs hungry for her cache of weapons. That included her *segundo* and sometime lover, Armando Ruiz, and his cousins, tight-knit killers, trackers, and smugglers with Lipan Apache blood. Nancy Jo knew a Dallas PI named Burch rescued Rita from that meat grinder before she disappeared like chimney smoke on a blustery day. Knew the same man was now an investigator for the local DA.

Small world. With lots of curious connections and crosscurrents.

She knew of Burch because he came to her for help giving Rita one last chance to see her dying grandmother, a fool's errand that slipped under the hide of her hard-bitten cynicism. Took a lot of sand for him to stand in the front yard of her trim adobe house with the chickens pecking around his boots and the twin barrels of this very shotgun pointed at his chest.

Sand counted for something with Nancy Jo. Burch still smelled like the ex-cop he was, but she decided to put him in touch with the Ruiz cousins protecting Rita. She was blood kin to them. Lived in the same wild and lawless world. Before she married old man Quartermain, she was a whore with big tits and a bigger ass, a brothel madam who knew how to make the cops and pimps leave her girls alone.

She also ran *mota* across the river. With her Ruiz cousins. Small world.

The two women stood just a few feet apart; one tall, young, and bouncing a toddler on her hip, the other short and stout with reddish-brown skin and thick, gray hair. The young one's smile disappeared, shut down by the icy glare of Nancy Jo's eyes.

We followed you. We protected you. We died.

The glare didn't faze Charlie. He squirmed on his mama's hip until he could reach out to Nancy Jo with both arms. The old woman smiled only for Charlie and scooped him up.

"Come here, sweet boy. Let me take a look at you while mama moves that car behind the house before some bad men see her and kill us all."

"His name is Charlie. He's Armando's boy. That makes him, what, a great nephew once removed?"

"Makes him blood kin. A Ruiz."

Noise from the main road grabbed Nancy Jo's attention. A poorly muffled rumble. The slight squeal of tapped brakes. A bobtailed rig with a fading Comanche Propane logo on the tank.

"Park that car quick and get in the house. Charlie, let's you and me go inside and see if I can find them store-bought cookies in the pantry. Maybe a glass of milk to dunk them in."

"Cookie."

"That's right, sweetheart. Ol' Nancy Jo is gonna find you a cookie. And some milk."

The two women sat at a kitchen table made of rough-sawn pine, its bare top gouged and scarred by wayward knives and forks and cigarette burns. Charlie sat on Nancy Jo's lap and dunked Hydrox cookies into a clay tumbler of milk by the smoky light of a kerosine lamp.

"It was crazy for you to come here, Rita. Too close to too many people who want you dead."

"Nowhere else for me to run that wasn't watched by killers. They found me where the Feds stashed me. Had to kill one to get away. This is the only place I feel safe. The only place Charlie will be safe. With kin."

"Didn't take you long to play that card, Missy. If I had a lick of sense, I'd shoot you myself and tell them *pendejos* to pick up the carcass."

"Long as Charlie stays safe, that would be all right by me. I'm sick to death of runnin'."

"Charlie will be safe with us until we get you sorted out. You'll both stay here until then."

"After that, I'm on my own, right?"

"Didn't say that. You're the boy's mother, and he's Armando's son. That counts. A whole lot. If you were by yourself, we'd likely send you on your way."

"I know."

"What do I call you? I know Rita was a fake name, but it suited you."

"The name I was born with is Rhonda Mae—Rhonda Mae Mutscher. The name on my driver's license is Claire—Claire Doyle. Same for the title of that car and a Social Security card."

Nancy Jo snorted and shook her head.

"Goddam Feds. Trust them to hang an ugly name around your neck and make you live with it."

She pulled a pack of Delicados out the pocket of her dress and shook out two of the strong, unfiltered cigarettes, a favorite of Mexicans of a certain vintage and far younger *Tejanos* and *Tejanas* trying to strike a tough, streetwise pose. She lit both nails with the lamp, handing one to the woman with three names.

"Tell you what," she said, squinting from tobacco smoke. "Why don't we go in a whole different direction. You've always looked like an Alejandra to me. Why don't we call you Alejandra Ruiz. Yes? It's a grand and sweeping name."

"How about Ana?"

"No, that was my sister's name. She's dead now, but she was a holier-than-thou piece of shit—*una puta santurrona*. She'd fuck the mayor or police chief then yell at my girls walking down the street and call them whores."

"Maybe I should take that name as a penance for my sins. Ana Ruiz. Short and sweet. No halo, no wings. No holier-than-thou."

"*Tu absuelvo*," Nancy Jo said, making the sign of the cross. "In the name of the Father, the Son, and the Holy Ghost, I baptize you Ana Ruiz. There's a fella I know who can fix you up with the right paperwork. And Texas tags and title for that Chevy."

"No doubt he's a Ruiz."

They both laughed. And for a moment, they shared the warm closeness of those days at the Bar L R ranch. A happier time. Before Tommy Juan's murder. Before that desert nightmare.

Their cigarette smoke had a longer half-life.

Twelve

Chizik was holed up in a ratty motel on the southeast side of Sanderson, slowly going stir crazy from a steady diet of *The Price Is Right*, *Days Of Our Lives* and *Password* and the need to lay low, take it easy, and let the gunshot wound heal.

A bent vet in Marfa patched him up after the whore shot him. Lucky break—a through-and-through just above his right hip. No vitals hit. Doc McClanahan gave him a go-bag full of bandages, tape, syringes, antibiotics, antiseptics—some for horses, some for humans. And pain pills. Darvon, his favorite. Made him dream in Technicolor. Pricey, though. A grand for the bag. Three more for the patch-up. And a balloon of Mex brown for a tip and memory eraser.

Doc was a skin popper, a druggie dabbler skittering along the edge of full-blown mainlining. Good to know. Made him a risk Chizik couldn't ignore. Made Doc a walking dead man. With a ticket to punch. Not now, though. Had to play it smart. Had to put some distance between him and Doc. Just until he was healed up enough to be mobile, agile, and hostile again. Meant he had to eat the pain and nervous tension of a two-hour drive east to Sanderson, the Cactus Capital of Texas, the seat of Terrell County government, a once-rowdy Santa Fe railroad, and cattle town dubbed, "Too Mean For Judge Roy Bean."

Chizik made the run on U.S. Highway 90 in a baby blue '65 Ford Fairlane that needed new shocks and a front-end alignment. Made every bump a clenched-teeth adventure. Hoping he didn't spring a leak. Hoping he didn't get a flat. Hoping a cop didn't pull him over. Got to the Motor Inn on the east edge of town just after dark, shaking with pain and tension.

Owner was an ex-con named Jingles McCoy, a bank robber who spent fifteen years in the infamous Eastham Unit, where Clyde Barrow did time and once broke out five of his buddies. Jingles did his bit and used some buried greenbacks the law never found to buy himself a piece of desert nowhere just south of the Santa Rita Cemetery. Wedged between U.S. 90 and Legion Street. With a roadside view of the world rolling by without him.

For a couple of grand and the right knowing look, Jingles would give you a room for two weeks on the backside of the motel, door facing the rocks, rattlesnakes, and railroad tracks. And a gravel trail that crossed the tracks and led to the unforgiving wasteland only the desperate sought for refuge. Long as you stayed, Jingles made sure you got your breakfast eggs, coffee, chicken-fried steak, and milk gravy from a cafe two blocks away. Made sure you got a tough dinner steak, overcooked green beans, mashed potatoes, and sweet tea from the same place. Got you good Mex beer— Tecate or Carta Blanca—and a bottle of mescal for dessert. Carted your bloody bandages to a burn pit out back. Made sure you saw the fire and smoke.

Didn't have cable, so daytime game shows and afternoon soaps were the main attractions on a black-and-white TV with lousy reception. Nighttime was a broadcast nightmare. Couldn't stand *Murphy Brown, Home Improvement* or *The Cosby Show*. Prayed for *Monday Night Football* and *Matlock*, Andy Griffith's homespun defense lawyer.

Jingles would also dial up a whore for you if you were so inclined. Chizik was in dire need of some carnal healing but didn't indulge. Too risky. Didn't want anybody else to know he was around other than Jingles, who was paid enough to keep his mouth shut. He did take advantage of another nocturnal service—free long-distance dialing. From a phone hanging from the back office wall of a shuttered Shamrock station a mile south of the motel.

Jingles' son drove him there. Unlocked the door, led him to the back office phone, held a flashlight while he dialed, then left him in the dark to wait in the car. Call connected him to an Alice Baker brother who was putting another crew together for the ever-lucrative trade in guns and drugs that crossed the river and demanded secure and secret waystations in rough country.

Chizik wouldn't be the leader. As a head honcho, he was considered damaged goods with two failures under his belt. Like a snakebit head football coach, he was seen as unlucky. But he was still valued for his experience recruiting clients, closing deals, keeping a crew focused, and running the complex logistics of guns headed south and drugs headed north. Long as somebody else was top dog and kept him on a tight leash.

That rankled Chizik, who loved being The Man. But he knew there was only one other option. A bullet to the brain. A hole in the desert. He'd swallow his pride, be somebody's Number Two, and bide his time. Needed the money. Stash he built from freelance wet work and strong-arm robberies needed fresh green blood. And there was no reason he couldn't keep his side project rolling. Needed to scratch that murderous itch. When able.

"Brother Cleve, I want you to scout a couple of ranches we're looking at not far from the river. You know the turf. You know what works and what doesn't. And you know what to avoid, keepin' us runnin' under the radar."

"When and where?"

"The where is Van Horn. You'll meet a brother whose number I'll give you in a second. The when is a little up in the air. Two weeks. Maybe three."

"Why the wait?"

"Gotta find a replacement for Mike Perry, a guy we were gonna bring in on this. Got himself killed up in Colorado late last week. Freaky thing. Got shot dead by a woman with a kid in the middle of a restaurant in a town called Cortez."

Chizik felt an icy finger run up his spine.

"I knew Mike. Did time at Pelican Bay with him. Brought him on board that first crew I put together. The one the ATF busted up. Me and him didn't get popped because he was in Vegas, and I was shacked up with a whore in El Paso when the raid went down."

"Luck of the draw, right? Somebody tip you guys off?"

"Hell, no. Elsewise we'd have had the drugs and guns long gone before that raid went down. Mike was a big fucker nobody messed with. How'd a woman get the drop on him?"

"We're still piecin' it together from cops we own. Woman pulled a Colt Python from her purse and emptied all six slugs into Mike. Brother with him said Mike recognized her from some place. Wanted to talk to her. We're beginning to think she was in WitSec but don't have that nailed down."

The icy finger turned into a high-voltage zap, right to the forebrain.

"What was Mike doin' in Colorado?"

"Workin' for some friends of ours. Like I said, we're still piecin' it together. You know anything?"

143

"Not on this. Mike was a damn righteous brother. I want in on the payback."

"We'll keep it in mind. One other thing. You gotta move. Need to get you somewheres off the beaten track."

"I like it here."

"Ain't safe. Too many people know about that place. And Jingles—well, he's become a problem we want you to solve. For your usual price."

"Happy to do it. Where to after?"

"Bunny ranch outside Valentine is the ticket. Out in the boonies. Brothers run the place. You'll have a tricked-out Airstream all to yourself. Hot and cold runnin' pussy and booze. Or whatever else you fancy. Here's the number. Ask for Benny."

"Sounds restful."

"Just what the doctor ordered. Get there and lay low. We'll be in touch."

Click. *Not a chance I'll show up where you want me to be, cabron.* Chizik would hit the road and stay clear of old friends and lovers. That included all but one or two A-B brothers.

He had more questions. He knew, though. He just knew. Mike's killer was *La Güera*.

Sure didn't want to tip his hand to the guy who just hung up, a numbnuts O.G. named Whitey Mueller. Bucket-mouthed bastard who loved to gossip. Fuckin' squarehead chemist from Oxnard known for his high-grade meth recipe. Popped and sent to Folsom, then Pelican Bay. Made his Alice Baker bones with a homemade garrote. Nicknamed Captain Midnight because most of his kills were guys asleep in their bunks when Whitey made his play.

Piss on workin' for him. Had a sneak-fuck way of killin'. Not eyeball-to-eyeball like Chizik. Not the sharp, quick skills of a murderous barber.

Sweeney Todd, that's me.

Back in his motel room, taking a pull from an icy bottle of Carta Blanca, Chizik tallied his bloody scorecard. Four kills. Three rungs up his Judas Ladder. One entry in the collateral damage column. Not an error or an unearned run. Maybe a Texas Leaguer. A flare. A gork. A dying quail. A ground ball with eyes.

Not a frozen rope but still a hit. *Jesus, stop it. Enough Bull Durham riffs. Love that movie.*

Two of the Judas kills—Frankie Sheridan and Brad Settles—were eye-for-an-eye deals straight out of the Book of

Leviticus. Both betrayed him and his crew. Brothers died because of these two fucks. He only wished he could raise them from the dead and kill them again. Slower, this time. With a lot more agony. Pliers. A blow torch. And a tailor's shears.

Slitting the throat of Santiago Cruz was payback-by-proxy. He actually liked working with Cruz, who was the primary contact between his crew at the Kluxer ranch and the Garza drug gang, rebuilding under the leadership of Valentina Garza, eldest daughter of the late Malo Garza. He worked his ass off to become the Garzas' Number One gunrunner only to face the prospect of a bullet to the brain after the roadside rocket ambush of a black GMC Yukon killed seven Garza *sicarios*. Two of his crew were also riding in that SUV but disappeared, creating suspicion of a double cross.

Chizik crossed the river to plead his case directly to Valentina Garza at the headquarters hacienda of *Los Tres Picos,* the family's sprawling *rancho*. She ridiculed him. Made him grovel. Then let him keep the deal and live. But not before shooting his best friend and second-in-command, Jack Reese, splattering his brains and blood all over Chizik.

When he learned Cruz was Valentina Garza's lover, he added the man's name to the Judas Ladder. As a temporary surrogate for the woman, a sacrifice for her sin. A downpayment. Against that day when he could finally slash *her* throat and avenge Jack's murder. Then lick the blade clean. And cross her name off the next-highest rung of the ladder.

That prospect gave him a chubby. He thought about jacking off. Pity he wasn't showing up at that bunny ranch near Valentine. Won't be taking a taste of some of their hot-and-cold running pussy. Won't be taking that risk. Not now. Not when he was so close to achieving his ultimate goal. Payback. Swift, sure, sharp, and bloody. Against everybody on the Ladder.

Took him a long time to get this far. Can't stop now. Won't. Keep riding this revenge rocket straight to Hell. Enjoy the trip.

Lots of memories. Most bitter. Some sweet. Lots of pain. Mental and spiritual. Not just physical. When Burch left him shot to pieces in the desert rocks and sand, three of his gun hands hustled him away from the midnight chaos of chattering automatic weapons, booming blooper rounds, green and red tracers, and screaming men. They got him to Doc Blevins, a biker from Alpine who stopped the bleeding and put his ruined leg in an air cast. Doc was once a combat medic with the 82nd Airborne, a vet of their 1989 jump into Panama to help grab Manuel Noriega.

Blevins patched him up for a long and bumpy ride across a shallow smugglers crossing in the padded cargo bay of a Jeep Wagoneer. Then a backcountry trek to a surgery clinic in Juarez owned by the cartel that had the strongest grip of the moment on the fiercely contested city, one of the deadliest war zones on the planet.

Chizik didn't need a Blue Cross/Blue Shield card. He was a brother of The Brand, a gunrunner who serviced *narcotraficantes* allied with the Juarez cartel, gold-plated bona fides that got him lined up with the surgeons who could repair his shattered body. All he needed to do was fork over $150,000 from an offshore account, a significant hunk of the pile of greenbacks he once hoped to parlay into a nest egg that would let him leave the life.

Oh fuckin' well.

After the sawbones were done with him, it took a year of ball-busting rehabilitation and strength training to restore muscle to his body and retool his lethal skills to compensate for his limp and his lost right eye. Splitting time between Juarez and Van Horn, with a beard, long hair, and a new identity—Jacob Stephen Carney. Accountant with a trucking outfit running goods between Mexico and the States, a NAFTA creature.

Working out with Buster Wachtel, a Brand brother and muscle freak with a gym off *Avenida Benito Juarez,* where he offered martial arts and weapons training to a select clientele. Stopping by Webb Burgoyne's gym in Van Horn to work the speed and heavy bags and hone his close-quarter blade skills with the ex-Delta Force operator. Meaning more money out the door, offset by chump change earned through scouting, recruiting, and logistical work for others who wore The Brand. The scut work of an office bitch.

Bitter as gall but high-grade fuel that fed his deadly obsession with *La Güera* and hyped his motivation to be an even stronger killer than he used to be, fine tuning his skills with gun, blade, and bare hands as he built his Judas Ladder name by motherfuckin' name.

Another year passed. The Cowboys won the Super Bowl. Slick Willie got reelected. Chizik got more scut work, augmented by occasional calls to snuff out a rival or traitor. The former got a bullet. The latter got the blade. Being officially dead helped. It made him invisible, a ghost, a killer who didn't exist on wanted posters or in active crime files.

The early hits were test runs. Auditions for select honchos. Chizik saw them as opportunities to prove he was deadlier than ever. Didn't take long for the wet work to fill his dance card. No more office bitch. His brothers—those few in the know—saw him for what he willed himself to be. A resurrected life-taker. A rebuilt monster who dealt out death. With a rapidly refilling bank account.

Turn off the memory machine. Time to get gone.

He stuffed his nine-millimeter Smith & Wesson Model 59 behind his back, slipped into his leather jacket, and grabbed his go-bag. As he stepped through the door and into the cold night, he tapped the left pocket of his jacket, smiling as he felt the outline of his straight razor.

Gotta tidy up before I hit the road. Cut away a couple of loose threads.

Feed the blade. Then lick it clean. Just like that murderous London barber, star of stage and screen.

Thirteen

"**W**hat the fuck happened up there?"

"Mike spotted somebody he knew in a diner, braced her, and she shot his ass. Woman had a kid with her."

"I already know all that, fucknuts! Was it my daughter? Remember her, asshole? The one I'm payin' good money for you shitheads to find?"

Silence broken only by static on the long-distance line. Then a nervous, long-winded answer.

"I don't know, sir. Mike told me to drop him off and take a spin around the block while he checked it out. I didn't see the woman. By the time I made the circuit, people were runnin' out of there and you could hear the sirens on the way. Found a good place to plant myself. Watched and waited."

"Lot of fuckin' good that did, Arnie. Cops spotted you and dragged you downtown."

"You're right, sir. Customer saw me drop Mike off and spotted me parked across the street. Sicced the cops on me."

"Sucks to be you. What the fuck were you doin' in Colorado, anyhow? And knock off the sir shit. Never was an officer. Three stripes and a rocker was my highest rank."

"Can the sirs. Got it. We're up here because one of Mike's bent Barneys spotted her. Retired Texas sheriff's deputy living up this way. Left word to call."

"You know this guy? Mike ever introduce you?"

"No. Mike always played his cards close to the vest."

"So you can't check him out 'cause you don't know who he is."

"We could track him down."

"Waste of time at this point. OK, how'd the other guys do?"

"Petey struck paydirt. Braced one of the kitchen crew. Twitchy fucker with a bad coke habit. For a bindle, got the woman's name."

"Petey think to grab the cunt's coffee cup, plate, silverware? Somethin' that might have her fuckin' prints?"

"Nah. Just got the name. Claire Doyle. Got her address from the DMV. Staked it out, but she never showed."

"One step ahead of you clowns. Blew town as fast as she could. Didn't wait around. Didn't hesitate. Adios, she's a ghost. What's that tell you?"

"She's been ready to go at a moment's notice. Been lookin' over her shoulder. Waitin' for somebody like Mike to show up. Never let her guard down."

"Bingo. You're not as dumb as you look. Put Terry on, and go get yourself a drink."

Terry Balaban on the line. Gravel in his voice. Slow talker. Fast thinker.

"Yeah, boss."

"Three things, Terry. With Mike dead, you lead the crew. Two—let's assume the Annie Oakley cunt is my daughter. Get on her trail and track her down. Three—is Arnie out of the room?"

"Slunk out of here like a dog with its tail between its legs."

"He knows he fucked up lettin' Mike go it alone. Not that he could have stopped Mike. What's our exposure with him? With Arnie, that is."

"Cops don't know about the rest of us. So we're in the clear. For now. Don't know how long that'll last, though."

"Tell me the why. Lay it on me."

"They found Mike's backup piece in the glove box. Impounded the car. Goin' over it with a fine-tooth comb, no doubt. There's some cash, a sawed-off shotgun, and a grease gun hidden in the trunk."

"Fuck, a grease gun? A fuckin' M3? My dad carried one of those in Italy. And a sawed-off? How the hell is Arnie still walkin' the streets?"

"We found a damn good lawyer. That and Mike was using one of his aliases. Had a P.I. license and a pistol permit in that name. Cops had no choice but to let Arnie go. He ain't got a record. Only one of us who don't. It'll take them awhile to find out who Mike really was. And find that shit in the trunk. Then it'll hit the fan."

"Arnie needs to disappear before that happens. Permanently. And get the hell out of that bumfuck town."

"Done, boss."

As soon as he broke the connection, Danny Ray Mutscher hurled the phone across the living room, shattering a wall mirror that ran the length of the mahogany-dyed leather couch and ripping the phone plug from the jack. The phone cord whipped through the air, the plug locking like an infrared missile on a line of Swarovski crystal figurines his girlfriend Ava bought—a stag, a bull elephant, a pair of gazelles, and a pair of lovebirds on a tree branch.

Fuck, not the lovebirds. Ava's favorites. "Just like us, honey." That's what she always said. Now just one of five crystal dust bursts on the marble floor. A ragged line. Like an airstrike. Fuck.

Who cares about the goddam lovebirds? Rhonda Mae is what matters. His daughter. His obsession. His fuck fantasy. His flesh and blood.

For fifteen years, she eluded him and the crews he sent to track her down. His life ran on two tracks—his ruthless rise up the ranks of that chicken-fried confederation of drug thugs known as the Dixie Mafia and his obsessive pursuit of Rhonda Mae. The former gave him the money, clout, and manpower to keep the chase alive. And he burned through a lot of cash and manpower. His crews loved the gelt even though they tended to get dead too quick to spend it.

That's because his daughter was not only elusive, she was lethal—on her own nickel as a dead shot and by association with the gunrunners and drug smugglers who shot first and asked questions later. This latest set of gunsels got so close. In the same town. Looking at her through a diner window. In bumfuck Colorado. Where the Feds stuck her and left her to die on the vine.

Have to get her. Have to have her. In MY life again. Under MY control. In MY bed.

He remembered walking into that biker bar out on Harry Hines. He found her in the back room. Barely a teenager. Whacked out on 'ludes. Sprawled across a pool table. Ass in the air. Pullin' a train. He got in line. Gave the conductor a twenty. Dropped trou' and took his turn. Hard as granite. Grabbed her hips. Slammed that hole all the way to the hilt. Tight. Sloppy and slick. Taboo. He came like a geyser.

Pulled out, wiped his cock with a bandana and left. She never knew. Thought the time she stopped him with a gun barrel to his balls was the first time he tried.

Wrong, daughter of mine. I had you more than a few times. I'll have you again.

He felt an iron band of pressure squeezing his forehead. The room started to tilt. He staggered to the bar. Grabbed a bottle of Very Old Barton from the well. Bubbled it down his throat until he gagged.

Need to calm the hell down. Got just the thing. Mexican brown in that blood red and gold benjarong bowl picked up in Bangkok. Along with a bad case of the clap. Grab that glass straw. Snort deep to fill both nostrils. Burn that snout. Hack and gag. Bubble the Barton again. Wait for the hit.

His crotch felt tight. He looked down. A raging boner tented his slacks.

"Jesus Christ, I need to fuck somethin'! Need it right now!"

Where's the phone? Oh, yeah—smashed to pieces scattered on the couch. Gotta walk to the bedroom. Hard to do with this baseball bat in my trousers. Get where you're goin', asshole. Grab the extension. Punch in the numbers.

"Send Dottie over here right now. Whaddya mean she's not there? Find her. What? Oh, for Christ's sake—send me anything with big tits, a big ass, and a Hoover for a mouth! Ava? Don't worry about Ava. She's in Vegas. Get me a cunt to fuck right now."

He slammed the phone down on its cradle. Broke the receiver in half. The heroin kicked in. His cock withered.

Perfect.

Fourteen

Bloque Alvarez winced as the brakes squealed on the old Chevy C60 truck he drove for Comanche Propane, announcing his arrival to top off the silvery hundred-gallon tank sitting in back of Nancy Jo Quartermain's house. If Nancy Jo was home, she'd cuss him out for waking her from a mid-morning nap, then rag him about not bothering to get those brakes fixed since the last time he refilled the tank.

¡Coño! There she was, standing in the front door, wagging a finger. Once he got within earshot, she scolded him—like always—calling him by his given name, Estaban, not the nickname hung on him in grade school because he was short, square, and thick like a concrete block. *El Bloque.* Shortened to just plain *Bloque.*

"Estaban! Why don't you do as I say and get those brakes fixed?" she yelled. "We can hear you a mile away. *Bobo!* Get them fixed before you have a wreck and break your neck!"

He ducked his head and smiled, letting her rant roll over him, knowing she didn't mean it. He turned to his task, unrolling the hose and snaking it over to the tank, making sure the connection was tight, then watching the gauge as the fuel flowed.

The scolding stopped when he was done. She waved him into the house and poured him a hot, perfect cup of her *café de olla,* sweetened with dark brown *piloncillo* and spiced with cinnamon. Even served up a *gorditas de harina,* a sweet griddle cookie also dusted with cinnamon.

He liked the old woman. Called her *abuelita,* which sometimes drew a swat on the butt. Other times a hug. Really wished she was his *abuela.* His true blood kin. His anchor. Far better than the family fate dealt him—the father who beat him then got himself killed in a drive-by on the other side of the river, the mother who was a coke addict and whore who left when he was still a toddler, the grandparents he never met.

But Nancy Jo as his *abuelita* was just a pipe huffer's dream, a warm and blurry image floating up on that first hit. And Bloque wasn't sucking on a pipe right now. He was jittery, a fiend between scores, hunting for a means to feed that endless narcotic need. He just might have something to trade. *Información.* A hunch. Something he saw while driving down the main road near Nancy Jo's house two days ago.

An old Chevy with faded red paint. A tall woman with a toddler on her hip crossing the raked dirt yard out front. Nancy Jo waddling out of the front door.

A flash of recognition. Bloque knew the woman. Maybe. She might be the one who worked with Nancy Jo at the rancho owned by that crazy Kluxer, the one that got raided a few years back. It used to be on his route. Sucked up so much propane he'd have to make two long trips into the scrubby desert nowhere north of Faver.

Nancy Jo always made sure he got fed after that second delivery. He ate in a quiet corner of the big ranch kitchen, watching the hustle of cooks whipping up lunch or dinner for the guests, bitter *gringo* losers with dreams of a whites-only Texas republic. Sometimes, he chatted with the young woman known as Rita, the ranch's auburn-haired business manager and girlfriend of Tommy Juan Jaeckel, who was a Ruiz, like Nancy Jo. A nephew twice removed.

Nobody talked about Tommy Juan these days. Nobody mentioned who he pissed off or the gruesome manner of his death. Not in public. That could get you dead. Too many ears. Too many wagging tongues. Too many hands stuck out for a piece of silver. On both sides of the river. But everybody knew. Head chopped off. *El pito y los heuvos* sliced and stuffed in his mouth. Body quartered. All of it loaded into a giant smoker. A legend too horribly delicious for absolute silence. A grim lesson whispered about behind closed doors.

Part of that legend was the ghost-like disappearance of Tommy Juan's partner in gunrunning crime, the blonde cowgirl hustler known as *La Güera*. Everybody he knew assumed this was Rita in gaudy disguise. She and Tommy Juan disappeared from the ranch within a few months of each other. *La Güera* popped up a few months later, hawking military-grade weapons to the highest bidders.

Turned out, she was a rat. Helped nail drug smugglers, gunrunners, and bent law on both sides of the river. Everybody wanted her dead. But she was gone. Feds had her stashed somewhere. Nobody knew where.

Nobody but Bloque.

They say knowledge is power. And power can be money, if you knew who to call. Bloque knew—his uncle, a dangerous man who made people disappear for Adolfo Medina's crew, a rival to the Garza family. His uncle, Umberto Beltrán, would know what to do with this knowledge. And he'd make sure Bloque was richly rewarded and his name made known to the right people. Maybe Adolfo Medina himself.

The old Chevy was gone for now. No woman. No toddler. But he'd spotted a toy dump truck in the front yard and a child's hoodie and coloring book on the living room couch. That told him they'd be back.

"I saw you had some company earlier this week, *abuelita*," he said. "A woman and a child. That made me happy. I worry you get lonely out here, all by yourself."

"Quite a speech, Estaban. But don't worry about me. Worry about yourself and those brakes, *chico*."

She stood up from the table and started fussing with the pan used to make the coffee, her back to Bloque, her face hidden.

"Are they still here?"

"Who?"

"The woman and her child."

"No, *chico*. That was my sister Ana's daughter and her boy. On their way to Houston for a new job. She decided to take a detour and see me. Been a few years since I saw her."

He could hear the lie in Nancy Jo's voice, nicer than normal, almost loving, tripped by a thin and nervous wire. He sipped her coffee and munched on her griddle cookie, his brain buzzing with images of bricks of cash stacked high on a table, enough to feed his habit forever.

Until it killed him. Not really a scary thought. Bloque could control his habit just enough to keep his job but knew he didn't have the *cojones* to get clean and stay that way.

Never would. That was the sharp, cold truth. It cut through all the bullshit rationales and lies an addict told himself and anyone else who would listen. Bloque ducked the shuck and stuck to that icy fact. Looked it dead in the eye. His habit would kill him. *Ya lo creo, hombre. Y no temo a la muerte.*

No fear and no self-pity. He did regret betraying Nancy Jo, his *abuelita* in heart and narcotic fantasy. And Rita. He knew the two were fast friends. More than that. They were kin in spirit if not blood. Just like he wanted to be to the old woman serving him in her kitchen.

Sad to sell that out.

But business is business, *pendejo*. You'll make that call to your uncle. Because a habit never leaves you alone. Not until you're six feet under.

Fifteen

Valentina Garza took another straight bite of Presidente from a heavy rocks glass while watching her two lieutenants, Tibby and Azul, walk into her office, eyes on her, faces stony and fixed like jadeite Olmec masks.

The bottle of Pedro Domecq's most popular product stood tall on her desk, its level of eighty-proof amber lowered by two earlier four-finger pours. Next to the bottle, closer to her right hand, was her father's nine-millimeter Browning Hi-Power, his favorite killing tool, the gold 'G' inlay in the upright rosewood grip reflecting the hooded light of her desk lamp. A constant companion that kept her father's spirit by her side.

She felt the burn of the brandy as it slid down her throat. But that was it. Nothing more. No numbness. No relief. Nothing from this bite and all the others she poured from the bottle she cracked open this morning.

It will take a lot more than draining a bottle of my country's most popular liquor to quench my rage. Only blood will do. The blood of the man who killed my beloved, my secret lover. The blood of the men who ordered it done.

"Sit, gentlemen. Sit. Can I offer you a *cafecito* or *agua con hielo*? Juan will be only too happy to fetch whatever you want."

Silent Juan, the silver-haired butler she inherited from her father, stepped from a wall-draped corner behind her desk and nodded at the two men.

"Or, perhaps you'd prefer some of this?"

She tapped the neck of the Presidente bottle with a long, blood-red fingernail and arched an eyebrow, looking at each man. Their masks didn't slip. Their eyes told her nothing. No fear. No guilt. Just steely stares.

Tibby, older and built like the squat and heavily-muscled *luchador* he used to be, took the lead.

"*No pero gracias, Madrina.* We're here to tell you what we know about Santiago and what we are already doing to avenge his death."

"First tell me why he was in Presidio with no protection from us."

Azul, younger, taller, and blue-eyed, stepped up.

"He refused our help. We offered him bodyguards. He threatened to kill them. We prepared a safe place to stay. He cursed us and stayed in the back room of that bar he bought."

Tibby picked up the thread.

"Only when he was in town. He had another place somewhere in the desert. We never found it. We kept him out of the fighting, and he threatened to join the other side. He didn't, of course. This was just more of him being an asshole."

She knew why.

He did it for me. To keep an eye on you two, who he never completely trusted. To keep tracking down my father's killers, no matter where they were hiding. And to be free to come to me whenever I could get away.

Santiago had been her insurance policy. She needed Tibby and Azul to rebuild her father's organization and kill those who stood in her way. Those she didn't kill herself. She needed to trust those two far more than she liked.

Her secret lover didn't need either man. He didn't need to temper his suspicion. He could watch her back free of the politics and complications of rebuilding a business, piecing together a family from the shattered remains. He didn't need to cut a deal or ignore a flaw.

And he could continue his ruthless hunt for anyone who played even the slightest role in her father's death. Or the traitors who rushed to profit from the fall of the House of Garza. Those were the hyenas she hated most. Former allies. Former friends. New vassals of the Monterrey *cochinos* who killed her father with a car bomb then wiped out half the outfit.

Comadrejas. Weasels who deserved no mercy.

"Tell me about his murder."

Tibby nodded to Azul.

"It looks like he was jumped by someone he knew, *Madrina.* Someone who got close enough to kill him with a straight razor."

"That takes skill, nerve, and muscle, no? More than just putting two in the back of the skull."

"*Exactamente.* The killer is very skillful with the razor. Very surgical."

"What does that mean?"

"It means he was precise with the cuts he made. No hesitation. No hacking or slashing."

"You're saying the killer cut Santiago's throat with precision and skill. What of it?"

Azul hesitated. Tibby took over.

"He cut more than Santiago's throat, *Madrina.* The killer also sliced off *su pene y sus bolas.* Stuffed them in Santiago's mouth. Cut off both ears as well."

Such a lovely cock. So thick and hard. Riding it felt like flying. Mounted on Pegasus. Soaring above the pressures and demands, the rage and the bloodshed. Losing herself as ripples of pleasure grew stronger and stronger. Until she cried out and heard him growl as his body stiffened, his hands pulling her ass even closer, his cock filling her pussy.

Licking him clean, sucking his balls, coaxing a revival with tongue and mouth. Cock worship. Like never before. Never again.

She stood up, shaking out the long black curls that flowed down her back, rising to the full height she also inherited from her father. Looking down at the two men, she took another bite of Presidente before she spoke.

"Why the ears? The killer has already exacted the traitor's penalty by cutting off his manhood and stuffing it in the mouth. 'This is what we do to traitors.' Message enough, no?"

"The ears send a second message. You do that to someone who doesn't listen, doesn't obey. Someone who was warned not to do something and did it anyway."

"If I didn't know better, I'd say that points the finger at one of you. Santiago was being an asshole, was giving you trouble. And our people knew that. Kill him, cut off his ears, and send a message—'This is what happens to those who don't listen.' Stuff *el pene y los huevos* in his mouth as an exclamation point."

She stared at each man as she said this and swept her father's Hi-Power off the desk with her right hand. Their masks slipped, and she spotted a twitch in the corner of Tibby's mouth and an eyelid flutter on Azul.

Poker tells. And she was holding the winning hand. She kept them on the hook for nearly a minute then placed the pistol back on the desk.

"Relax, both of you. I'm not a schoolgirl, Tibby. Since I don't think either of you did this, my question is why send this second message at all? And who is it for?"

"The message is for you, *Madrina*. The ears were found in an envelope with your name on it. In the cash register behind the bar."

"How do we know this?"

"We own the sheriff. We get everything his investigator finds."

"That *pendejo* sells his ass to the highest bidder. If he tells us something, he tells our enemies."

"Not anymore. He likes smooth young boys. We got pictures. And he's up for re-election."

"You'll keep giving him his bite, no?"

"Of course, *Madrina*. Not as big a bite as before, but he won't go hungry."

"Double it. I want him kept sweet until we find this surgeon of yours."

Azul spoke.

"We think we might know who the killer is. Benito Morales, runs a crew of ours on the Texas side."

"I know Benito Morales. What does that old horse thief have to say?"

"His crew helped those *gringo* gunrunners track down Tommy Juan Jaeckel and get the weapons he stole from them. The head *gringo* tortured him. Used a propane burner and a straight razor. Real skillful with that blade. Sliced his eyelids open. When it was time, he sliced his throat all the way to the neck bone. And cut off his cock and balls."

"Yes, yes, I know this. Then they chopped the man up, cut his head off and stuffed him in a smoker. *Pene y los bolas* in the mouth, of course."

"Benito was impressed. And he's a man who is very skilled with a knife and razor. Never saw any man handle a blade that well, let alone a *gringo*. Said the man truly enjoyed his work. Took his time. Kept his cool. *Intimo. Profundo.* Like a lover. He even licked the blood off the blade."

"You're starting to sound like someone describing a snuff film, Azul. Get to the point."

"The point is, *Madrina*, you know this man. Chizik. We did business with him. You met him in this very room when we thought he might have betrayed us. You heard him out. You let him live."

"Yes, and to make a point, I blew out the brains of his *segundo* with my father's pistol."

"His best friend, *Madrina*."

"He left here wearing the brains and blood of his best friend. I told him he could always buy another."

"*Sí*. Reason enough to hate you. And want you dead."

"Find this Chizik and bring him to me. He'll die right here in this very room. After Benito has his fun with him, of course."

"*Sí, Madrina*. Benito will enjoy that. We'll also double your guard detail when you cross the river to meet our *gringo* bankers."

"No. If Chizik wants to kill me, let him come. I've got my father's gun to keep me warm. And safe. I'll use it to kill this Chizik myself. For Santiago."

Sixteen

It was half past eight, the sun was a faded memory, and Burch was still in his office with a stomach soured by too much coffee and Dr. Pepper, eyes reddened and raw from too much fine print and too many Luckies.

His neck and right shoulder were terminally knotted and in dire need of an ice bag, payback for cradling the handset of a puke green phone with grimy push buttons through two dozen calls. His left hand needed a steroid shot from scrawling notes across the green-tinted paper of a steno pad in his illegible redneck Sanskrit.

Homegrown squiggles and slashes nobody else could read or interpret, noting lots of facts from fellow Texas lawdogs but very little truth about Chizik's whereabouts.

His back and butt demanded disc surgery after hard time in an unpadded oak swivel chair. And it felt like an ex-wife's lawyer had driven an iron spike straight into his forebrain. Made him wince every time he moved his head.

Only one cure for that last complaint—a handful of aspirin and a snort from a bottle of Maker's he kept in the bottom desk drawer. Had to first quench the fire already in his stomach before pouring more fuel down there, though. Grabbed a bottle of Pepto sitting next to the whisky, shook it, and popped the top off its crusty pink neck to take a long pull.

"Damn, that tastes awful. Like a bubblegum jock strap."

Shook out a half dozen or so off-brand aspirins. Crunched them with his teeth. Bubbled the Maker's bottle to wash them down. Swallowed another slug to make sure they stayed there.

Belched a nasty mix of Pepto and bourbon fumes. Dug a pouch of Levi Garrett out of his hip pocket. Popped a stringy wad of tobacco between cheek and gum.

"Much better. Any worse, and somebody would have to shoot me."

He liked talking to himself in the empty quiet of his office. Good company was hard to come by. Propped his Justins on the desk, leaned back in his chair and relaxed for the first time in twelve hours. Riffled the steno pad pages, waiting for a call from Quintero on the road to Sanderson, tracking what could be a bloody calling card from their boy.

They'd flipped a coin that morning, and Burch lost. He'd pull the desk duty, write up reports on this and three other cases, and dial up fellow peace officers across Texas to reheat the cold trail on Chizik. No joy with the phone calls. Of the fifteen murders in the past five days that involved a blade, none had the gory signature of force feeding the vic a schlong-and-nutsack dessert.

Quintero, damn his luck, got to get out of the office, dragging along a young deputy as backup, while he rousted some snitches who knew Chizik, his old crews, and the Alice Baker underground. Most were addicts, burnouts on the edges of outlaw life who would swallow their fear of getting tagged as a rat if enough long green crossed their palms.

Pinche Cabrón Primero was still in the wind. Had been since killing Settles ten days ago. Like he climbed down a hole in the desert and pulled it in after him. But Katie Navarro lessened this frustration when lab results rolled in on the blood sample she took from the ex-deputy's doublewide. Chizik was a match.

Which meant they were riveted on the right guy and weren't chasing a copycat who shared a lethal kink for straight razors. But the DNA results also signaled that Burch wasn't the killer he used to be with Flying Ashtrays and his Colt 1911, once a mortal lock any time he pulled the piece.

Proved what he once heard an old cop say about the patron saint of cops. *Lads, St. Michael is a fickle bastard. He taketh away just as much as he giveth his bedraggled flock.*

True. And the same could be said of Father Time. That relentless asshole waits for no man and betrays us all with failing eyesight, slowed reflexes, and body parts that failed to work.

Not me, old man. I'm still in my prime. Emptied a mag at Chizik. Heard the slugs strike home. Saw the body smack the sand. Done deal. Dead meat. Carve another notch in Old Slabsides.

Must have been a Kevlar miracle. Keep telling yourself that.

Pissed him off thinking about it. He'd double down on his trips to the range. See an eye doc about getting contacts. And a gunsmith about swapping out the sights on his pistol for ones with white dots. Made him feel like a washed-up golf pro forced to trade in his precision blades for a bag of forgiving duffer clubs.

The initial call from Sanderson rang his desk phone at a quarter past two. Double homicide at a fleabag motel on the east side of town. The ex-con owner and his son found dead by one of the Mexican housekeepers, throats slashed, blood soaking the threadbare carpet.

A Straight-Razor Special. That's what a Terrell County sheriff's investigator named Barton called it. Barton remembered the flyer on Chizik and dialed up Burch. Quintero was closer so he rolled that way. *Takin' his sweet fuckin' time about checking in.*

Bobby must have heard that. His call rang Burch's phone two seconds later.

"Miss me, sweetheart?"

"Oh, hell, no. This kid I'm ridin' with don't smoke, don't cuss, don't complain. Pretty much keeps to himself and don't piss off the local badges. Kinda restful. May hit Doggett up for a trade."

"Bastard. You'd eat your gun in two weeks' time from boredom."

"Not a chance. My wife would kill me if I did that. Looks like our boy was here. Their coroner ain't Doc Battles. He's pretty sharp. Pegs the killer as strong, short, and left-handed. Just like Katie called it. Got up close before he did the deed. Nailed the owner in his office, his son in a room down the hall. Between midnight and three in the ayem."

"Got a helluva head start. What the hell was Chizik doin' there?"

"Hidin' out, looks like. And lickin' his wounds. Looks like he's been here a while. Had a room at the back of the motel, away from the highway. Found medical supplies. Boxes of bandages, squeeze bottles of Betadine solution, and syringes. Penicillin vials in the 'fridge. And some Cephalexin capsules for dogs and Wonder Dust powder for horses."

"Sounds like he went to a vet to get that bullet pulled."

"Be my bet."

"Got any dead vets with their throats slashed in the greater Terrell County metroplex?"

"I asked. No such luck. Some empty mescal and beer bottles in the room. They're getting prints they'll send along. He took the owner's car, a green '76 Buick Skylark with Texas plates, so an APB is already out on that. Left an old junker Fairlane."

"He'll swap plates then buy another junker. What about the owner?"

"Named Robert Samuel McCoy—Bobby Sam, but everybody called him Jingles. Always playin' pocket pool with his spare change. Did twelve of a twenty bit for bank robbery. Stayed off the radar screen ever since."

"Clean?"

"Not hardly. Stayed away from anything heavy, but the locals think he used heist money to buy that motel. Offered nice, quiet rooms on the backside for traveling scumbags with the right connections and a fat stack of green."

"Why ice a guy like that? He's not a player. Not really."

"Cain't say. Didn't like the room service? Doesn't make much sense to kill the guy who's hiding you out. Chizik's gettin' erratic. Kill crazy."

"Or he found out McCoy double-crossed him."

"I could buy something like that. Bad blood between scumbags. Feelings get hurt. Somebody gets clipped."

"Got a line on our boy?"

"*Maybe. Two data points. That Skylark was spotted headed west on U.S. 90 early this morning by one of McCoy's buddies. He called it in once word of the murders got out. Second, before we drove here, one of my songbirds told me the AB has set up a bunny ranch in an old RV park near Valentine. Out in the brush. Off the beaten track.*"

"He needs a new ride and a new place to hide. Head on back. We'll hit Valentine *mañana*."

"*OK.*"

Click.

Burch mulled things over as the dial tone buzzed in his ear. They whiffed on Chizik. Again. But at least they knew he was still alive. Not bled out in the desert with a dead whore's bullet in his guts.

His belly rumbled. A vision of chicken-fried steak smothered in peppery milk gravy floated before him. Alma's Cafe served the best in town. Probably closed by now. But the boss, Alma Morales, would fix a plate and let him eat in the kitchen if he talked sweet and low. And promised to drop by her Flying Cloud at the edge of town to wreck the bed sheets.

Make the move. Do the deal. He slid the phone closer to punch up Alma's number. His nostrils twitched, and he could almost taste that first bite—sloppy, crunchy, and spicy. Could almost feel the carnal dessert, too.

Three sharp raps on his door startled him, jarring the needle out of the grooves of his fantasy.

"Door's open. Step the fuck on in."

"Don't mind if I fuckin' do."

Voice sounded like Yankee gravel dipped in swagger and horseshit. Matched by the pocked face, iron-gray handlebar moustache, and tall, big-bellied body of the guy shoving the door open and walking into his office like he owned it.

Dark blue windbreaker with U.S. Marshal in a vertical line of bold, gold letters printed on the sleeves. Dark blue ballcap with the same gold letters stacked above the bill. Told Burch what he already knew.

A fuckin' Fed. The natural antagonist of any self-respecting state or local lawman, until they proved otherwise. By actions, not words.

Not an unexpected visit. He'd been warned one of Uncle Sam's darlings was headed his way. Even had a name. But Burch had hoped he could slip away before his door was darkened.

No such luck. He hung up the phone. So much for the fat man's perfecta. So much for the deal that would have left his belly and ol' John Henry sated and very, very happy.

His name was Gabe Cucinotta. Born in the Bronx. Based in Durango, Colorado. A loud-mouthed fish in a very small pond. Pissed to find himself swimming in Hicksville instead of New York, Chicago, or even Denver, for chrissakes. Bitched about it all the time. Whether you listened or not.

A Yankees fan. Goes without saying. He'd say it anyway. Eventually. Inevitably. Repeatedly.

Burch never was much for the Sherlock Holmes or Philo Vance school of inductive and deductive detecting. Didn't divine the fat Fed's background with a glance. His take was a good and educated hunch, based on years of coply experience dealing with the high-handedness of *federales,* both American and Mexican; the natural and mutual animosity built up by repeated encounters; and, the phone call Dub McKee made to tip him off and give him the lowdown on Cucinotta about thirty minutes before the deputy marshal pounded on his door.

Cucinotta grabbed an aluminum chair, spun it so the ladder back was facing Burch, then plunked it down and straddled it, his arms draped across the top, muscles straining the sleeves of his windbreaker, eyes locked on Burch in a stare meant to menace.

A shopworn move that almost caused Burch to laugh in the man's face. He ignored the stare and fished out another stringy clump of Levi Garrett to stuff in his cheek. Put the Pepto and Maker's back where they belonged. Then met the stare with a smile.

"How can I help you, Marshal?"

"Don't know that you can, but your boss sent me your way. Said you might have a line on a woman I'm tracking down—Rhonda Mae Mutscher."

"You boys lose her? Haven't seen her since she entered WitSec—let's see, was it three years ago, or four? Time flies when you're chasin' the real scumbags."

That drew a twitch of the moustache and turned the glare into a narrow-eyed glower.

"Gimme a break, Detective. I know all about you and Mutscher, tracking her down for her dying grandmother. I know all about her gunrunning with her dead lover and how she ratted out all the drug gangs and bent cops on this stretch of the border."

"Well, son, if you know all that, what the hell makes you think she'd ever come back to West Texas, where every cartel *jefe* wants her dead and every *sicario* wants to be the one who guns her down and claims the reward? She ain't nowhere near that stupid."

"Maybe not, but she's got a kid now and needs to find family and friends to keep him safe."

"The only family that ever mattered to her was her grandmother. And she's dead. Her father's a raging Dixie Mafia asshole who wants to find her and fuck her. And a lot of the people who followed her and protected her during those gunrunning days got themselves dead."

"What about the boy's father? What about his family?"

"If the father is who I think it is, the man's dead. So's a lot of his family. They're the ones who followed her. No love lost among their survivors."

"Not even for the son of one of their own? Gotta be somebody who'd take her in, for the boy's sake, if not her's."

An instant answer flashed across Burch's brainpan, an image of Nancy Jo Quartermain pointing that ancient L.C. Smith ten-gauge at him. She was the only one who might help Rhonda Mae. In memory of the boy's father, Armando Ruiz.

Burch kept Nancy Jo's name to himself. *Not gonna give her name to a fuckin' Fed. This fuckin' Fed in particular, a Yankee blowhard and would-be tough guy.* He shifted gears.

"Marshal, you still haven't told me why you guys think she headed this way. If she was seen anywhere within a hunnert miles of here, our string of CIs would'a lit up like a fuckin' Christmas tree. Scumbags don't keep quiet about something that radioactive."

"Let's just say we have reason to believe she thinks this is the only place she and her son are safe."

"Not good enough, Marshal. Either somebody told you she said that to them, or you're just guessing. Either somebody told you she's here, or you're takin' a flier."

"I need some cooperation here, Detective. I've got two men with me, and we need some names of folks she'd likely contact. Names of the boy's family."

"Won't do you a damn bit of good. If that boy is the son of Armando Ruiz, he's got Lipan Apache blood in him. Those people are fierce. You walk up on them without an introduction, and they'll either stonewall you or shoot you."

"Half my family is mobbed up or made guys, Detective, so stone-cold killers don't scare me. I need an in, and you're just the man who can give me one."

"Not likely, Marshal. Not on my own nickel."

"You're forcing me to go over your head."

"Be my guest. But let me pull out my crystal ball and do a little prognosticatin' for you. It's unlikely my boss will force me to fork over any names and addresses and let you run loose in his county. He *might*—just might, mind you—order me to nose around on your behalf."

"Doggett ain't the only one I can call, Detective."

"And you ain't the only one who knows how to use a phone, Marshal. I've got a few friends I can dial up. One of them's the U.S. attorney for these parts. I'm more than happy to dial him up to let him know to expect your call."

"You're gonna regret the day I walked through your door."

"I already do."

Chizik switched rides just west of Marathon, spotting a '79 Chevy Blazer four-by-four with a cardboard For Sale sign taped inside the front window parked next to a mustard-colored roadside bar called The Bitter End. Said so in blocky black letters on the white background of a hand-painted wooden sign hanging over the chopped Harleys sitting out front. Chizik tucked the Skylark out back, slipped the pistol into his belt, and strolled into the weak yellow light inside.

"What'll it be?"

"Shot of Jack with a Pearl bottle back."

"Don't got Pearl. Lone Star?"

"That'll do."

Chizik slid a twenty across the bar while the tender served up his order.

Older guy with white hair raked back from a widow's peak and dark, hooded eyes that didn't miss a trick. Thin, but muscular, wearing a black leather vest with a small Lone Wolf patch on the left chest panel over a gray t-shirt, looking like he still rode, pumped iron, and hit the speed bag.

When the man put the beaded Lone Star bottle on the bar, Chizik realized it was his lucky day. He spotted small, faded black letters tattooed on the web of the tender's right hand in Old English script—A.B. Alice Baker. The Brand.

He smiled and slowly placed his hand across his chest with the thumb of his right interlocking with the pinky of his left—the A.B. sign. The tender looked him in the eye and nodded.

Chizik's reply: "Brother."

"What do you need?"

"Who owns that Blazer with the For Sale sign on it?"

"My brother-in-law."

"How's it run?"

"Like a champ.

"How much?"

"He's asking seven K. For a brother, make it five-and-a-half."

"How much to lose a Skylark sitting out back? It's hot and needs to get lost."

"Not a thing. We'll take that across the border and make some change parting it out."

"Done."

Chizik handed the man his Texas driver's license with the latest alias he was using—Charles Robert Macklin from

Fort Stockton, a name plucked from a dead infant's birth certificate.

"Be right back with a bill of sale."

"Be right back with the jack."

Chizik slid off his stool and eyed three day-drinkers at the bar and two playing pool on the other side of the room. Bikers minding their own business but well aware of the stranger in their playhouse. Nobody lamped him with bad intent, though.

He turned toward the back door and the Skylark waiting outside. Popped the trunk, reached in for money stuffed in the go-bag sitting on top of the spare tire. Thumbed through a pack of Ben Franklins, counting out the sale price and slipping the bills in his pocket.

The bill of sale and his driver's license were waiting for him on the bar. He swapped them for the greenbacks in his pocket.

Bye-bye, Buick, dark green and dusty. Hello, Blazer, faded red with a white top and side panels.

"Need to use your phone."

Tender jerked his head to a door behind the bar. Led to a cramped, stuffy room with a grimy linoleum floor, stacked cases of bottled beer, and a metal desk with a phone. Chizik dialed up the bunny ranch number and asked for Benny, using Whitey Mueller's name for a bona fide.

"Where the fuck you been? Whitey told us to expect you here two days ago."

"Been busy, tyin' up loose ends for Whitey."

"Don't wanna know about that. You're hotter than a Saturday Night Special, brother. Too hot for that gunrunnin' crew Whitey wanted you for."

"Whitey needs to blame himself for that. He's the one who asked me to do the job that heated me up. Good news, though. Tired of a honcho's headaches. Kind of like staying focused on these lone wolf jobs. Just have to worry about myself, not everybody else."

"Welcome sign's still out for you on those kind of jobs. Get your ass here as soon as you can. Money for that business you done for Whitey is waitin'. Also got some intel that might interest you."

"Spill it."

"First off, we know where Valentina Garza will be three days from now."

"More good news. Where?"

"El Paso. At the Paso del Norte, meeting her American bankers."

"Can you get me in?"

"We can get you close."

"What else?"

"Got somebody who says he's got a line on your girlfriend."

"Girlfriend? What the fuck you talkin' about?"

"La Güera."

"Who's the somebody?"

"Umberto Beltrán. Know him?"

"Yup. Done business with him. What's Umberto got to say?"

"Says she's back in West Texas. With her kid. Says he can take you to where she's at. For a price. Won't say anymore till he meets you and gets paid."

For a few seconds that felt like an hour, Chizik couldn't speak, couldn't think, and could barely breathe. Then his brain unlocked and shifted back in gear.

La Güera. With a kid. Didn't know she had one.

"You still there?"

"What? Yeah. Still here. Need a favor. Actually, three favors. Need more info on Garza, the when and where. Need to know who's chasin' the blonde bitch. And give me Umberto's number."

Benny rattled off the digits. *"I'll get you a line on Garza and the bitch. We'll reach out to some lawdogs we own."*

That rankled. Back when he was running crews, he did the owning and the reaching out. No more. Strictly a contractor, now. A bit player. But one who still had teeth.

"Make sure you reach out to your *narco* contacts and not just the lawdogs, *pendejo. La Güera* will draw *sicarios* like a bitch in heat. About to wrap things up here. I'll be in touch."

"Keep it low, brother. Lotta people lookin' for you. Not all of them wearin' badges. Just like her."

"How 'bout I wear a blonde wig and a hat?"

"I said 'keep it low, brother,' not 'keep it loud'."

Seventeen

Rhonda Mae liked rocking on the front porch of her two-room hideaway at sundown, smoking unfiltered Delicados, cradling a CAR-15 in her lap, and watching the darkness creep across the land, slowly stealing the details of the brush, rocks, and sand that surrounded her sanctuary.

It felt strangely familiar, sitting there in the advancing gloom with a full-auto carbine and a strong Mexican cigarette, reviving the reflexes of life on the lam after almost four years of the small-town routine that dulled the watchful habits she swore she'd keep sharp.

Back in Cortez, she thought she was building a safe and quiet life for herself and Charlie. But six booming rounds from her Colt Python shattered that illusion. In the time it took for a slug to leave the barrel and smack flesh, she became a born-again killer, snuffing out the muscle-bound thug who threatened mother and son. No hesitation. Quick and violent. From guardedly passive to lethally active. In the twitch of an eyelid. Then out the door and on the road, burning the deep night miles between Cortez and Faver.

She surprised herself with the sudden shift into high fugitive gear. Carlos the cook told her to go it alone, Charlie would slow her down. Not really. He was an easy keeper who took long naps and, when awake, showed great delight in the changing scenery of new places and people.

But life on the lam, running from lawdogs and gunsels, was no place for a four-year-old kid. Charlie's favorite blanket, a torn blue cotton-poly blend with a Star Wars logo, wasn't bulletproof. And his Stretch Armstrong figure could still live up to its name but couldn't shoot the bad guys.

Better to leave him with people who could shoot straight and keep him safe.

The other lies she told herself:

She wasn't abandoning her son; she was shielding him. She was just like a mama deer or fox leaving her offspring in a hiding place while she led the predators elsewhere, down a trail where she was the only prey.

Another whopper, cutting closer to the truth:

To keep them both alive and free, she needed a singular and ruthlessly selfish focus, not one stretched thin between a mother's worried duty and the wily brainpower it took to stay two steps ahead of the hunters on her trail.

The guilty truth was she felt unfettered and more fully alive with Charlie safely tucked away at Nancy Jo's house, protected by his father's family and their fearsome talents.

Perched in an adobe shack with a tin roof and a hand pump out front for well water, hidden by brush, rocks, and high ground rising around her, she felt the welcome rush of some of her old bravado, shot through with that vengeful streak that made her just as dangerous as any clawed and toothy wild thing backed into a corner.

Let them come. I'll kill them all.

She still missed her son. Terribly. But she told herself keeping him close would get them both killed. She also missed Charlie's father, Armando Ruiz. His quiet strength and loyalty propping her up after Tommy Juan's death. His constant presence protecting her while she ran the *La Güera* game, hustling guns to the *narcos* and plotting her revenge.

They were close, bonded by the dangerous thrill of being on the run and hunted. Sharing the same danger, the same food and drink, the same hideouts. Sharing the same bed was a natural progression, an unconscious act based on need and nearness instead of the age-old carnal calculus or that thing called love.

One night, she just stepped out of her panties, lifted a thin sheet, and climbed into his cot. Pale moonlight lit the room of the adobe shack that sheltered them. No words. Just the hunger and the slow then urgent moves that fed their desire. She mounted him, and their fevered thrusts caused the cot to skid across the tile floor, springs squawking a rhythm to their cries and grunts. They shared a Delicados in the afterglow as a night breeze cooled their sweaty bodies. She left him with a kiss and returned to her own cot across the room.

That became their routine. She would come to him. They'd fuck. Maybe once. Maybe two or three times. Then share a smoke. Not every night. But often enough. When the sun rose, they didn't hold hands, kiss, flirt or talk about the night. Both slipped into their workaday roles—leader and top lieutenant.

Charlie was the inevitable result, but Armando was killed in that desert shootout before his son was born, before she even knew she was pregnant. She could have ended it, but that felt like a betrayal of Armando and the other members of the Ruiz family who followed her and died. She felt a guilty obligation to let Charlie be born.

She lit another Delicados from the ember of the last one and scanned the darkness, thinking about her next move. She relaxed and let her peripheral vision pick up the darker outline of a tarp-covered CJ-5 with rust streaks and a ripped canvas top. Borrowed this old, off-road warrior from one of Nancy Jo's cousins, Hector Ruiz, one of the few who didn't hate her and would keep his yap shut. Parked Big Russett in his barn, covered with a patched-up canvas tarp, cash still hidden behind the springs of the back seat.

Hector also owned the adobe shack and the surrounding desert nowhere that made it a sanctuary. He brought her food and cigarettes. He also got rid of her Colt Python, the one she used to kill that thug in Cortez, bringing back a Smith & Wesson Model 19, a four-inch .357 wheelgun with the same silky blue-black finish.

She was grateful to him, but he was almost as old as Nancy Jo and could no longer practice the deadly arts of his kin. She needed more powerful help. From someone she could trust. Needed to know who was on her trail. That meant someone with some pull, someone younger and more mobile. Handy with a gun. Solid in a firefight.

Only guy in these parts who ticked all her requirements was that old P.I. and rescue artist, Ed Earl Burch.

Heard he had a badge again. That surprised her, even though he once told her that, deep down, he'd always be a cop. He might say that, but when the bullets started to fly and bodies started to drop, he acted more like an outlaw than a cop. She knew. She'd seen him in action. He was a killer with a code, a ruthless gun hand who didn't hesitate.

Tomorrow, she'd drive the twenty-five miles to the nearest phone in that rust-streaked CJ-5. Just to find out which Ed Earl Burch was walking the earth these days. She'd also ask him for a mighty big favor. Help her save herself and her son. And let her get away.

The vibration and echo from Cucinotta slamming his office door with a 'FUCK YOU!' bellow were still quivering when Burch's phone started ringing again. Not good. Not at this hour. Doggett. And he was in a mood.

"I don't want that New York greaseball flat-hatting all over my county, rousting folks to help him find your girlfriend. I want YOU to do the rousting to get a line on whether she's even in the same area code—you and Bobby—and ride herd on him and his crew."

"That'll go over like a lead balloon. Deputy Cucinotta has my two favorite character traits—he's too dumb to live, and he's arrogant for no damn reason."

"Charm the fuck out of this guy and persuade him, Burch. Better yet, get Bobby to do the sweet talkin' while you keep your yap shut and give these guys the evil eye. You're good at that."

"Thanks, I guess. Figured you'd want to play it this way, but there ain't that many of her old outfit left to track down. Not sure it'll be enough of a show, but we can lead those marshals on a grand tour of rough country to talk to the ones still above ground."

"You've also got Nancy Jo Quartermain."

"Yeah, but I'm not letting those guys get within ten miles of her. She'll throw down with that ten-gauge she's got. Best if I go over there alone and see if I can have a quiet word without getting a skinful of buckshot."

"To what purpose? Let me remind you about that badge you carry. You best be aimin' to bring in girlfriend and her kid nice and quiet so we don't wind up with another Fed fuckup. You hear me?"

"Loud and clear. What about Chizik? While we're babysittin' these fuckin' Feds, the trail on him will get cold again."

"That's a question that answers itself, Burch. Quickest way to find Chizik is to put the arm on your girlfriend. He'll home in on her like a heat seeker."

"Shit. You want me to dangle her like bait? Chizik ain't the only one after her."

"I understand a lot of hombres malos want La Güera dead, but I don't give a shit. We've got a serial killer to catch. ¿Sabes?"

"Si, jefe."

"Well, awright, then. Best go home and get your beauty rest. You and Bobby got a busy day tomorrow. Keep me posted."

Burch cut the connection then dialed the number Cucinotta left him. Left a time and place to meet in the morning on his voicemail. Dialed up Bobby and left the same message on his answering machine. With an add-on: tagging Bobby with leading the charm offensive on the fat-assed Fed. Per Doggett's order.

Blew out a long breath, hung up the phone and checked his watch. Quarter till eleven. Too late to call early risers like Alma or Carmen for the Fat Man's Perfecta. Pickin's were even slimmer back at the house. Spam, tomato soup, and baked beans. Canned delights with a side of Premium Saltines. Too far to drive to Alpine for a Whataburger triple. Guess some fine cuisine from the steam table at Billy Mac's truck stop will have to do.

Oh, yew bet. Open 'round the clock, by God. Just tool yourself on out to U.S. 67 for some terminally irradiated fried chicken. Chow down on two breasts mummified from hours under those red warming lamps. Rock-hard crust. Desiccated meat. Congealed chicken fat. Dee-lightful. Go for the Frito pie, instead. And a cold Big Red. Greasy, gristly, and salty. Washed down with liquid bubble gum.

Fuck all that. Piss-poor substitutes for that chicken-fried steak fantasy with the horizontal chaser.

Burch reached for the bottle of Maker's in the bottom desk drawer. He needed another pull to make it home for a nightcap of Spam and Saltines. Twenty miles never seemed so far away.

Eighteen

Chizik watched the lumbering lawman stomp out the double doors of the Cuervo County Sheriff's Office then pause on the sidewalk to turn around and flip both middle fingers at a dimly lit, second-floor corner window.

He could hear the man shout something to reinforce the double bird. Choice profanity, no doubt, lost to the prevailing wind. He chuckled, then steadied the binoculars cupped in his hands to avoid flaring any reflection from a flood light at the near corner of the Main Street building.

That's one pissed-off dude. Not one of the county's finest. Wearing the ballcap and windbreaker so common to oinkers elsewhere. But not in Texas, by gawd. Those boys still ride for the Lone Star brand, proud of their cowboy hats and boots.

This dude didn't and wasn't. Stuck out like a church lady at a stripper's convention. You ain't from around here, are you, son? Bet you're a Fed. Maybe Fart, Barf, and Itch.

Maybe a U.S. Marshal. Maybe tracking the blonde bitch. Wouldn't that be convenient?

Whatever this dude was, he was backlit, so Chizik couldn't figure out the lettering on the cap or windbreaker. When the man reached the far side of a dark, unmarked Chevy Suburban, he opened the passenger door and ducked inside. Popped into sight again then quick-walked to a dust-covered, pea-green Blazer with a county sheriff's decal on the driver's door. Flicked his head right and left then did a full three-sixty looksee that was freight-train stealthy before squatting behind the back bumper and reaching underneath its bottom lip.

Well, fuck me runnin'. Lawdog planting a transmitter on the ride of a fellow lawdog. That ain't very friendly. Then again, locals hate a Fed, and the Feds hate 'em right back. Ain't it great? Sure made life easier for a sinner like me.

Under Chizik's magnified gaze, the lawman climbed into his Suburban, reached into the glove box, and pulled out a small, black box he powered up, waking a backlit dial and a tiny red indicator light. Making sure that transmitter was sending a signal. Test over, the big man slipped the powered-down receiver into the glove box, fired up his rig, and pulled away from the curb.

From his perch on the flat, rolled asphalt roof of a shuttered garage just off Main, Chizik shifted his binoculars from the fading taillights of the Suburban to the lit corner window. He didn't know who was in that second-story office.

Might be anybody. Could be Burch. Or maybe the High Sheriff himself, the almighty Sudden Doggett, rodeo hero and the first mixed-race candidate ever elected to anything in Cuervo County.

Fuckin' Spigger. Goddam Mexicoon. Should have whacked him when he raided the first ranch my crew was runnin' guns from. Would have been a righteous kill, then, just desserts for a lawdog who fucked with The Brand. Now, he's a luxury I can't afford.

Besides, Doggett ain't a rung on my Judas Ladder. But that cocksucker Burch sure is. Damn tempting to pull a Sweeny Todd on his sorry ass right now if he's the one up in that office. Doors're wide open. Sneak up there and slice him ear-to-ear right now.

Cool your jets, pendejo. *Stay frosty. You kill Burch now and you lose your best chance of catching the blonde bitch. If you play it right, the old bastard will serve her up on a silver platter. Just be patient. Shee-hit, fuck that. I'm on the run and on the clock. Gotta force the action with a little sumpin' sumpin'. Straight from the darkest chamber of my black heart.*

Yeah, what I got in mind'll paint the walls red and cause that blonde bitch to bolt out of her hidy hole and run screamin' and hollerin' to Burch. Gee, wonder what would cause a mother to do that?

Chizik savored the moves he was about to make. Required just the right mix of finesse, manipulation, timing, and seduction. And spilled blood.

The second-floor office window went dark. Chizik counted to thirty, then raised his binoculars to focus on the double-door entrance. Another big man walked out. Barrel-chested with big shoulders, this one had a familiar limp, a slight drag of the left leg. He focused on the face, but all he could see under the broad brim of a cowboy hat was a white beard. Watched him fire up a cigarette, snap the lighter closed, and put it back in his shirt pocket.

Bet that's a Zippo. Bet he's smokin' a Lucky. Didn't need anything else to know it was Burch. He licked his lips and locked on his prey like a mountain lion lining up a deer for dinner. *Easy,* cabron. *Not now. But soon. Soon enough.*

Took the rest of the old bastard's inventory. Along with the big hat, Burch was wearing a dark shirt with snaps, tan slacks, and brown boots. Gun belt held a badge and that .45 that blasted Chizik in the desert, taking out an eye and a knee. Odds were six-to-five and pick 'em on who had the worse limp, with Chizik the slight underdog.

Had to admit the old bastard looked sharp, like a true Texas lawdog. He'd make a good looking corpse, long as they kept the shirt snapped over the second smile he planned to carve deep across the man's throat.

Temptation kept knocking. Chizik could tail Burch. Maybe get lucky and get led to *La Güera.* Could rush in and kill him right here, right now. Or trip up and give Burch the chance to paint a terminal finish on his hollow-point wrecking job.

Won't make that mistake again. My best bet is keepin' the door slammed shut on temptation, slippin' outta here, and slidin' on over to Cindy's. And slippin' and slidin' my dick into every hole she's got. Gettin' hard just thinkin' about it.

Cool it, macho. *Burch ain't even gone yet.*

Chizik kept his binoculars focused on the old bastard, watching him climb into that dented Blazer with the transmitter riding on the bumper lip, grind the starter four or five times before the engine fired, then pull away from the curb, trailing a thick cloud of bluish-white smoke that rose into the Sheriff's Office floodlight beams—the telltale of an almost-flooded carb.

What a dumbass. Change your fuckin' plugs, old man. Clean the gunk out of that carb. Or get stranded in the goddam outback.

He watched the taillights fade away and felt his pulse lower.

Adios, motherfucker. I'll see you soon. Soon enough.

His mind drifted back to Cindy, Cindy Wiley, she of the long, lean legs that could squeeze the life out of a man, the California bolt-ons that gave her a Double D chest, the wild tangle of dishwater blonde curls, and the green eyes that glittered with anger and deep craziness. Once the main mama of one of his crew at the Bar R L, Butch Malone, now pulling a long stretch for all that coke and heroin pulled out of the secret chamber underneath the barn when Doggett and the Feds came calling.

Saw Chizik on the side before the ranch got raided. Every Thursday afternoon at the Cactus Blossom Motel on the outskirts of Faver.

"I don't know why I waited so long to fuck you. You got a buzz saw for a tongue and a diamond drill bit for a cock."

"You were in training, working your way up the progression of reps and weights until you were ready to max out with me."

"Jesus, didn't know I was jumping Arnold Schwarzenegger's bones."

"Thas' right, baby. I'm the Terminator."

She straddled his face.

"Terminate this, lover boy."

During the sprawling gun battles of the ranch raid, Chizik escaped arrest by killing Doggett's chief deputy and sneaking down a game trail and out the back fence gate. Hid out at Cindy's for a couple of days, then commandeered her dead husband's old Jeep Wrangler, bouncing between back-country hideouts and hunt camps, working his way to Las Cruces and a rundown RV park called Jerry's Retreat. Owned by an ex-con and biker named Jerry Deukmejian, once a West Coast wheel with the Armenian mob, who coordinated drug-smuggling runs with the Outlaws, Mayans, and Hell's Angels. The park catered to thugs on the run.

Jerry, now content to sit on his fat ass and even fatter bank account and tinker with his Harleys and vintage Airstreams, took the long, ecumenical view on who could stay at his park. Lions and lambs, he told his prospective tenants. Leave your beefs at the gate, park your rigs, mind your own fuckin' business. Or his young cousins, two scowling, hulking, and long-bearded enforcers named Aleksandr and Aram, would shoot you.

Lots of holes in the fuckin' desert, Jerry said. Don't be one of them.

Jerry owned the local cops. Cartels and biker gangs also left Jerry alone because nobody wanted to fuck with an Armenian mobster, even one who had parked himself on the sidelines. Might still have strong ties to the Russian *Bratva*.

The Brand did business with Jerry but also kept a respectful distance, using Chizik as the sole point man to buy crates of Warsaw Pact weapons, including the occasional batch of Zastava M70s, Marshal Tito's unauthorized clones of the Russian AKs. Jerry liked him and stuffed his belly with *khorovats, kyufta,* and *manti,* and got him drunk on mulberry *oghi* and Ararat, the high-grade Armenian brandy.

Fear and loathing made Jerry's Retreat the perfect safe haven for the fugitive Chizik, plotting his next move against *La Güera* from a restored '68 Airstream Excella, reaching out to friends in the drug gangs up and down the river for a line on her whereabouts, sussing out the deal she made with *El Duque,* the Ojinaga drug king, to sell him her last cache of military-grade bang bangs.

Once he knew the time and place, he pulled together a pick-up crew of ex-mercs, bushwhackers, and manhunters, tapping his own network as well as Jerry's for rent-a-guns willing to kill or be killed for a fat stack of cash.

Gonna wreck that deal and kill that blonde bitch. Grab the weapons and sell 'em to Jerry. That was the plan. Didn't count on me getting wrecked, too. Or the bitch getting away. Thanks to Burch, the old bastard.

Something about Cindy still spoke to him, something beyond the physical. It was her wildness and anger, a woman skating on the edge of madness. He knew that dangerous boundary all too well. She lived in a rock-and-timber ranch house she inherited from an elderly husband with a bad ticker, built on an isolated flat-top mesa northeast of The Devil's Backbone, *El Espinoza del Diablo*, a sharp-spined, two-thousand-foot-tall ridgeline splitting the old Hulett ranch in half.

When the gunrunning schedule was slack, Chizik would jump into one of the ranch's old Jeeps and rattle his teeth up the rutted trail to her hideaway for a horizontal breather, sat phone in his go bag to stay connected with the crew. He also tapped Cindy to mule the occasional brick of coke or Mexican brown to special clients with drug-addled friends. Mostly rich and politically powerful guys in Alpine, Fort Davis, or Midland that The Brand wanted to keep extra sweet with powder at a brother-in-law price and a dose of Cindy's carnal talents.

Pay to play for both types of party favors. Greenbacks squirreled away in a lockbox hidden under tip-up rear seats in the cab of Cindy's four-by F-250 HD XLT Super Cab in medium gray and wild strawberry metallic, another bequeathed bauble from dead hubby. Dead-solid perfect rig for a hard hitter like her.

"Cash and cock, baby—two of my favorite things."

"Cash first, then the cock. Keep 'em droolin' until you get the money in the lockbox."

Cindy pouted.

"I wasn't born yesterday, baby. I know how to keep a man pawin' at the ground until the deal is done."

"Thas' my girl. See you in two days."

He tucked a Browning Hi-Power under the belt above her right hip, then cupped her ass with his hands and drew her close. Her goodbye kiss was all tongue and suction.

Clients didn't stand a chance.

Chizik stayed away from Cindy during the long months of healing after Burch nearly killed him, hardening his body and feeding his murderous obsession with irradiated hate. Figured she was listed as a known associate, a KA in lawdog parlance. Wouldn't do for a dead man to be seen frolicking naked in a hot tub with a hard-bodied widow who loved to fuck anybody wearing The Brand.

Better to stay mobile and avoid all of his old haunts, buddies, and lovers. Be a stranger, a one-time John or an anonymous pickup at any random roadside bar in Fort Stockton, Las Cruces, Rankin, Iraan, Ozona. Or Van Horn.

What's your name again, honey? Sharon? Call me Burt. Let's find the nearest no-tell and do the Horizontal Bop. Or, say 'yes' if she decided to drag him home and share her bed for a day or two.

Chizik worked hard to stay below the radar. That's why his only points of contact were Bruno and Chugger, men he did time with at Chino and Pelican Bay. And only to get a line on the next piece of wet work. He did keep tabs on the few survivors of his gunrunning crews. Never knew when an extra gun hand might be needed. Needed reliable types who knew West Texas and kept their mouths shut. Like Lonny Dalrymple. Until he got blown away. Another reason to slice Burch wide open. Payback for Lonny.

But once he started climbing his Judas Ladder, he cut off Bruno and Chugger and quit reaching out to his old crew.

Signed up Bunny Ranch Benny as his eyes, ears, and answering service. Cost him the stack of green sitting in Benny's safe—Mueller's payment for whacking Jingles McCoy and his kid. With Benny, Chizik was playing a hunch. Going with his gut. Betting on vibes from their brief phone conversations. He was also banking on the power of the mighty American greenback.

Greed and good vibes would have to do. Beats shit out of ever talking to Whitey Mueller again. Shithead. Loose-lipped creepy-crawler killer with the soul of an accountant.

Chizik knew Umberto Beltrán from his gunrunning days, a lean, hatchet-faced hitter for Adolfo Medina's crew, a killer you didn't cross but a standup guy. Met him to trade cash for information at Cruce de Cabra Muerta—Dead Goat Crossing in Anglo—a desert crossroad halfway between Faver and Marfa.

"This is solid. A tip from my nephew that I checked out myself."

"You saw *La Güera?*"

"Sí."

"Where?"

"At Nancy Jo Quartermain's house. Outside Faver."

"When?"

"Hace dos dias. I've had men watching the house. She's not there now. But her kid still is."

Sweet Jesus, La Güera. So close he could smell her. Made his mouth water and his dick get hard. And Nancy Jo Quartermain. I remember that old bitch. Used to run a brothel way back in the day. Used to run weed, too. Kept the ranch kitchen running smooth for that blowhard bastard, Thomas 'T For Texas' Bondurant.

That gave him his big, black-hearted idea. Forget about killing Valentina Garza in El Paso. Pay a visit to Nancy Jo Quartermain. Snatch *La Güera's* kid. That'll force her out into the open.

But he needed to take an important side trip before visiting the old whore, madam, and weed smuggler. A few hours after meeting Beltrán, he parked the Blazer behind the roadside brush at the base of the mesa where Cindy lived and waited until well after sunset.

As the light faded, it turned into a clear, cool night with a full moon overhead, so he didn't need his headlights or the flood lamps on the bar above the Blazer's cab to slowly climb the gravel switchbacks that led to her house. When he got to the top, he saw the deep black outline of the house, lit only by the endless spread of stars in the desert sky and the fickle glow of a shape-shifting moon. He slowed his roll to a crawl, aiming the nose of his rig at what looked to be the front door while easing his Smith & Wesson Model 59 from behind his back.

He was still twenty yards out when floodlights at each corner of the house and across the roof ridgeline popped on, blinding him. He slammed on the brakes, his boot slipping from the clutch pedal and stalling the engine out with a mighty lurch of mis-meshed gears. He dove across the front bench seat, tucking his body below the dash while catching his ribs on the shift levers, wincing the pain away while waiting for the first storm of bullets to smash glass, sheet metal and body parts. His body parts.

He waited.

He waited some more.

Seconds dragged out longer than black bean soup farts. His ribs were pulsing in pain. He needed to take a piss.

He heard the creak of a door opening and the low growl of a dog. *When the fuck did she get a dog? How big and how mean?*

Cindy's voice: "Who the fuck is in that truck? Step on out with your hands up before I start shootin'."

Chizik grinned and rose up slowly. He eased the driver's door open, keeping his right hand in the air, squinting from the bright floodlight beams.

"Nice and slow, mister, or I'll sic Roscoe on you."

There she was, standing a yard or two outside of the open front door, a pistol in her right hand, a long-tubed flashlight in her left. Looked like a Kel-Lite, the heavy, six-battery flash cops once carried and used as an alternative night stick to crack skulls.

"It's me, Cindy. Mister Diamond Dick."

She yowled like a bobcat, closing the distance between them and hurling herself against his chest, wrapping arms and legs around him, banging pistol and flashlight across his back and shoulders.

"Sweet Jesus, Chizik. Everybody said you was dead."

"Not hardly."

They never made it to the bedroom. Jeans, boots, boxers, and a bra marked their staggering path from the front door to a cowhide couch facing a massive rock fireplace with a gas log insert throwing flickering heat across their sweaty bodies. Cindy was busy with her head in his crotch, trying to coax Round Three out of his dick with mouth and hand.

"Give it a rest, baby."

"No, I want you in my ass this time."

Chizik grabbed a handful of curls and yanked her head toward his chest.

"That hurts, goddamit!"

"Need you to pay attention. Need to tell you sumpin'. It's important."

"Oh-fuckin'-kay, baby. I was just tryin' to get you hard again. No need to jerk my hair out by the roots."

"You told me one time you always wanted a kid but sumpin' happened, and you couldn't have one. What if I told you I found one that can be yours to keep?"

"What the hell are you talkin' about?"

"I need you to babysit a kid for me. For four days. Maybe five. There's thirty-K in it for you on the front end. Once the job's done, another thirty-K. You can either keep the kid or drop him off someplace and let the cops know where he is. Your call."

"Damn, that's kidnappin'. We get caught, we do a lot of time."

"I'll make it worth the stretch. A hundred-K, all up front. Just for sittin' on a four-year-old, keepin' him fed, keepin' him quiet with some Valium in his orange juice."

"Where will you be?"

"Busy takin' care of some old business with the kid's mother and a cop."

"So, the kid's bait, right?"

Chizik chuckled and stroked the side of her face.

"No, baby. He's my gift to you."

"Nobody ever done nothin' like this for me before."

Her green eyes glittered. Not with anger or craziness. Tears.

Squealing brakes, skidding rubber, and the blast of a car horn snapped Chizik back to the present. Below him on Main, a white Ford F-250 with a stake bed was stalled halfway out of a side street, the driver flipping the bird and yelling at whoever was behind the wheel of a dark blue, four-door Impala halted just short of a T-bone crash.

Chizik waited until the Impala backed up and let the truck pass, the car's driver seizing the moment to give his own single-finger salute and bellow a gravelly "Fuuuuccckkk yew, asshole!" that echoed down the empty street.

He duck-walked across the roof and climbed down the same drainpipe he used for access, then headed for his Blazer parked behind a vacant house an uphill block away, sticking to brushy shadows.

Higher up the hill, a man named Jake Sartain sat behind the wheel of a nocturne blue '68 Olds Delta 88 coupe, partly hidden by a chest-high wooden fence. He had been watching Chizik and the Sheriff's Office Building for more than two hours, and his belly was rumbling for a fresh jolt of food. Anything greasy, salty, and peppery would do.

Sartain tapped the shoulder of his sleeping partner, Terry Balaban, now the leader of the six-man crew hired by Danny Ray Mutscher to find his daughter since Mike Perry got dead. Used to be eight before Mike got clipped and they had to permanently park Arnie Klein in a Colorado garbage dump for being a terminal dumbass.

"Got action?" asked Balaban, blinking his eyes then rubbing the sleep out of them.

"Yeah, Burch just left and asshole here is takin' off."

"We know who asshole is yet?"

"Pretty sure he's a guy who's s'posed to be dead."

"Chizik?"

"Yup."

"What else?"

"That Fed left a tracker on Burch's rig."

"No shit? He find ours?"

"Nope."

"Good deal. Burch is drawin' a crowd."

"Like shit drawin' flies."

"You got it. Might be nice to find out what the others are up to. Max got all hot and bothered about what some asswipe dealer told them. Got 'em chasin' a rabbit, most likely."

"You don't care much for Max, do you?"

Terry shrugged. "Not much there to like, is there? He's an asshole, but he gets the job done. Long as he don't get too big for his britches, we're fine."

"And if he does?"

Terry looked at Jake. "You remember Arnie, doncha?"

"Who? Don't see much of that guy no more."

"Exactly. Fire her up and let's roll."

"I love drivin' your car. Like ridin' a magic carpet. Sleek, smooth, and mighty. Got one question—why risk this jewel on a job like this?"

"Because life's too short to ever drive a boring car."

"Figured you'd say that. Whaddya wanna do now?"

"Let's tail Pally here a bit. See if it is Chizik. See where that leads us. If it looks promising, we'll yank the fellas out of their rabbit hole. If not, head for the barn, wait on the happy wanderers, and check in with the boss."

"Watchers watching the watcher. Sounds like a plan."

Nineteen

Good news is rarely on the line when that phone rings long after midnight.

Parents with bad-seed kids dread this call, praying it only means a trip to the bail bondsman and the local jail. Not the morgue. So do plant managers who preside over the production of flammable fuels, toxic chemicals, or an atomic engine that cranks out electricity for a million people but can turn a hundred-mile radius of farmland into a contaminated evacuation zone.

Murder cops skip the prayers and already know the news is bad. Always is. They accept the inevitable. Stoically. Like a Jesuit yielding to the lash. Comes with the territory. A body soaking in its own blood somewhere, dead from a bullet, knife, axe, garrote, bare hands, or the thousand other ways humans kill each other.

Duty calls. Get here now. Coroner's on the way.

They can sleep like a dead man until that bell goes off but are never surprised when it does. Some nights they dream of a ringing phone, reaching for it in their sleep seconds before the clamor starts in real life, and they wake up to find their hand already on the receiver.

Burch used to be that way. Back when he was a Dallas homicide detective. When he got those dead-of-night calls, his brain flipped a switch and he was Mister Cool, Calm, and Collected. Even though his heart started revving, and he had to suppress a nanosecond of dread about the horrors waiting for him dead ahead.

Strictly routine. Nothing you haven't seen before, buddyrow. Nothing you can't handle. Get up. Get dressed. Get your ass out the door. Get two fresh packs of Luckies and two large black coffees to go, one for you, one for your partner.

Fast forward two decades. He carried the gold badge of a Cuervo County District Attorney's investigator. A murder cop again. Had been for almost four years. The gold leaf on his badge was barely scuffed. But those reflexes he used to take for granted were badly frayed or fried. When his phone rang in the wee hours these days, his brain hit the panic button, his eyes popped wide open, and he ripped open the night table drawer to fill his left hand with that five-shot nickel-plated belly gun he took off a Dallas pimp and drug dealer.

Then he'd answer the call.

Used to be a whole lot worse. Used to wake up screaming, with visions of winged serpents, jaguar knights, and Aztec heart sacrifice rushing toward him. Used to reach for his Colt, then grab a bedside bottle of Maker's and a plastic vial of yellow Percocet tablets to chase those demons back down in their holes. The heavy hitters, with ten milligrams of oxycodone, courtesy of an open-ended script from a bent doc in Dallas.

Fuck answering the phone. He had to take his medicine. Motherfuckers would call him back. They always did.

He'd answer if his heart had quit doing the Jackhammer Bop and was slowing down to a lively Texas Two-Step. Tell 'em he was taking a shit or throwing up a quart of bourbon during their first string of ringy-dingies. They'd buy that.

The worst of those really bad days of round-the-clock nightmares and paralytic panic took place well after he lost his gold detective's shield in Dallas. His deep dark-thirty calls those days were from clients, ex-lovers, and thugs who wanted to kick his ass on behalf of somebody he tracked down who didn't want to be found.

Usually, the muscle was working for a chiseler, a deadbeat partner who didn't have enough money to pay off a savings-and-loan note but could scrape together enough green to hire a cheap knuckle-dragger too stupid to avoid calling to tell him they were coming after him.

"Best make out your will, Burch. You fucked over a friend of mine and I'll be visiting you real soon."

"Looking forward to it. So's Black Betty. She'll be very glad to meet a brain-dead, pop-dick cocksucker like you and slap you into dreamland."

"Listen to me, you pill-poppin' lard-ass. When I get through with you, you'll wish we never met, asshole."

"Shit, bubba. I already wish that. But I'll be waiting for you anyway now that you tipped me off. Much obliged."

Life got much better once the demons left him alone and he weaned himself from those numbing yellow pills. A sweaty, white-knuckle ride he wouldn't wish on his worst enemy or ex-wife. He didn't ditch the Maker's, though. Had to keep at least one crutch to prop up his fractured sanity. And keep his liver company.

The phone stopped ringing. He took a pull from the bedside bottle and put the pimp gun back in the drawer. He waited thirty more seconds, then reached for the phone. It rang again as soon as he touched it. Spooky.

"This better be good, Bobby. I was having a nice wet dream when you called."

A woman's laughter rang down the line like the dinner bell at a Mississippi boarding house. Burch froze. Didn't sound a bit like Bobby. But it did sound familiar.

"Is that you, Carmen?"

"Carmen? She the latest squeeze? What the fuck happened to that little blonde hellraiser? Take another guess, Gramps."

"Well, shit. How'd you get my number?"

"You gave it to me, remember?"

"Apparently not. I know you're in bad trouble with the wolves chasin' you. Had a deputy U.S. Marshal pounding on my office door this evening, matter of fact."

Burch heard background noise on the line—a semi rolling down the road, a car door slamming shut, an engine starting.

"Where the hell are you? Sounds like you're using a pay phone out on U.S. 90 somewheres. Are you nuts?"

"You know the answer to that better than anybody. And I'm closer than you think."

"Meanin' you ain't up on 90. Better not be pullin' into my driveway anytime soon. Got eyes on me betting I'll lead them to you."

"Not gonna get that close, but I need your help."

"You know I'm wearin' a badge these days, right Slick?"

"So they tell me. But I'm hopin' to make a pitch to that outlaw heart of yours we talked about over cheap whiskey. The one who loved my grandmother and did his damnedest to make her last wish come true."

"I did love your granny but you've got the heart part wrong, darlin'. I said I'd always be a cop deep in my heart no matter how much of an outlaw I appeared to be."

"Well, shit. I was hopin' to get your help blowin' down some of these bad hombres who're chasin' me."

"Where's Charlie?"

"Not with me but somewheres safe. I'm kinda like the mama muley leadin' the wolves and coyotes away from her baby."

"Makes sense. Wherever somewheres is, I hope it's got better firepower than a double-barreled ten-gauge."

"What's a ten-gauge?"

Burch chuckled.

"Now you're tryin' to kid a kidder. Look, darlin', the best I can do is protect you for a handoff to the U.S. Marshals. Be happy to blow away any bad hombres that cross our path until that deal gets done."

"Just like old times, right, Gramps?"

"Not hardly. But it's the best I can do while wearin' this badge."

"What would happen if you weren't?"

"Weren't what? Wearin' a badge?"

"Bingo."

"I'd be tellin' you a whole different story."

"Why don't you study on doin' what you need to do to tell THAT story, Gramps?"

"Quit hustlin' me, Slick. I ain't some cartel douchebag droolin' over your *La Güera* act. I'm bound by that badge and the oath I took to carry it. Don't matter how much I loved your granny and her favorite granddaughter."

"What did you say about my granny and her favorite granddaughter?"

"You heard me. Now, study on the story I'm able to tell you right now. And take the deal I'm offerin'."

"I'll think about it."

"Think hard and think fast. The wolves are circlin' and the clock's tickin'."

"Damn, but ain't you a walkin', talkin' cliche machine."

"I mix metaphors, too."

"I'll call you tomorrow night. G'night, Gramps."

Click.

Burch hung up the phone and flopped back down on his bed, sliding two pillows under his head to make it more comfortable to stare at the ceiling and catch the random thoughts flying around up there.

He grabbed four.

Dump that fuckin' Fed in Bobby's lap.

Go visit Nancy Jo Quartermain.

Take another pull of Maker's, set the goddam alarm for 0430 and get some sleep.

Ignore the bright red numbers of the digital clock that reads 0200 right now.

Rhonda Mae stared at the pay phone and shook her head. She had just lied to Gramps. It was only a little white lie. And she told it only because he guessed right, and it annoyed her. She *was* up on U.S. 90, at a twenty-four/seven stop n' go called Pancho's on the outskirts of Marfa.

She was hungry and sauntered into the store like somebody without a care in the world, her tattered maroon Lonestar Stockyards ballcap pulled low across her brow, her barn coat open, her jeans and Justins spattered with mud. Just another horse-crazed woman, headed to the barn at oh-dark-thirty, fueling up to chase her West Texas cowgirl dreams. With a Smith & Wesson .357 in her purse and a CAR-15 in a toolbox welded to the floor of a borrowed Jeep.

She browsed a refrigerated display case of nuke-able food wrapped in white waxed paper while clocking every person in the joint. Clerks and patrons. No threats. A couple of dumbasses jawing about the Cowboys. And one drunk cowboy mainlining black coffee at a window table. She clocked him twice. Three times. Maybe she'd keep a covert eye on him.

Nuke a *carne asada* burrito in the microwave. Grab a Big Red, a bag of Fritos, and a Powerball ticket. Head out the door. The cowboy was at the coffee pot on the back counter, pouring himself more black jolt juice.

Fire up the Jeep and crank up the mental grinder on that little white lie. Why an on-target guess by Gramps annoyed her had something to do with their tangled ties of shared danger, saving each other's ass a time or two, and a mutual love for her dead grandmother, Juanita Mutscher.

Also had something to do with mutual respect and love for each other, truth be told. Something he flat out admitted over the phone. That's what truly annoyed her, having to own up to giving more of a damn about Gramps than she wanted to. That's why she told him that little white lie. Just to knock him back on his heels a bit. Gave him a little verbal misdirection to make him think she was much closer to Faver. Closer to that adobe and tin-roofed house he lived in, set a half mile up a box canyon just off a ranch road thirty miles from town. But not sitting in his driveway.

Yeah, she knew about the place from Hector, who did a little surveillance of the Burch *ranchito* a week ago, describing it as a spare and lonely patch with a big barn, twenty acres of fenced-in rocks and sand but no horses. Not even a dog. *Triste y solitario*. Earlier in the day, Hector resumed his rounds, prowling past the watering holes where killers might lurk, the safe houses the Garzas kept on this side of the river, the homes of whores and girlfriends, looking for flashy new rides with Chihuahua or Coahuila plates.

Trolling for hard men with stone faces and cold-eyed stares. Eyes that never blinked, the look of a predator.

Rolling slow in his primer red '59 Apache pickup with old oil barrels, warped and weathered lumber, rusty chains and other junk piled in the bed, Hector looked like the day laborer and trash picker he pretended to be. With these accessories: a steno pad and Polaroid camera on the bench seat and a Stevens 520 twelve-gauge pump on the floorboard tucked behind his boots.

When he returned, he showed Rhonda Mae a small stack of photos—license plates and men, some she recognized from her days dancing the *La Güera* hustle. Garza *sicarios*. Others were killers she didn't know.

"They are close, *mi hija. Muy cerca.* Too close for you to stay here."

"Do these *hombres* know you? From the old days?"

"I sincerely doubt it, *guapa*. It's been a long time since I made people disappear for Malo Garza. Or anybody else. The men in those photos looked at me like I was a *peon*. Had no idea I used to slit the throats of men just like them for a living."

"Bet you wanted to slit a few throats today."

Hector smiled and ducked his head.

"Maybe take a scalp or two, *hija*. Maybe three."

She laughed and slapped him on the arm.

"I knew it! Such a polite killer. *Un asesino modesto*. I think I'm still safe right here as long as you're here to protect me."

Hector laughed, his dark and wrinkled face brightening with a warm smile. But only for a second. Like a snuffed match, the smile disappeared, the lines on his face deepened, and his eyes looked tired and sad.

"They're coming for you, *mi hija*. And I am no longer man enough to stop them. You must go. I know a place. I'll take you there."

"Not tonight, Hector. I have something I've got to do. You can take me to the new safe house tomorrow. *¿Mañana por la mañana, ok?*"

"As you wish, *guapa*. It will still be there *mañana*. Will we?"

Their safe signal was simple—a light above the door of Hector's barn. Lit and all was well. Dark and run like hell.

Day or night, it was easy to spot from her hideaway or through a gap in the brush on the last uphill switchback of the rough trail leading there. A single-bulb beacon just below the dark line of a ridge top more than a mile away.

A fatherly note from Hector. *You're still safe, mi hija.*

Muscling the Jeep through a brushy tunnel of rocks and ruts, she saw the stars sweep into view and knew she had hit the gap. She looked to her left, searching the dark mass below the horizon for Hector's signal, downshifting for the trail's final ascent.

Nada. No welcome home from Hector. Nothing but desert darkness.

She stopped the Jeep, set the emergency brake, and switched off the engine. She was fucked, and she knew it. Killers were waiting up top. Heard the Jeep, knew she was coming. Might be one or two on the trail below. She couldn't turn around. And backing down this twisty, hilly goat track under fire wasn't an option.

No choice but to kill or get killed trying. Take it to them. Don't wait on death.

She eased out of the Jeep, pulling the Smith & Wesson and two speedloaders from her purse, tucking the pistol behind her back and pocketing the extra rounds in her barn coat. Leaning over the back seat, she unlocked the toolbox and pulled out the CAR-15 and two spare thirty-round clips.

The high side of the switchback was thick with creosote, mesquite, and ocotillo. She spotted a game trail and ducked into its narrow opening, moving slowly uphill toward the hideaway where killers were waiting. One gunman would be inside. Another, maybe two, would be hiding in the brush. Ready to outflank her. Anyone posted below the Jeep would move up and close the trap.

If killing her was the only name of the game, they could have sprung the whack anywhere on the trail. Anywhere else at all, really, if they had been glued to her ass while she drove to Pancho's. She'd been damn careful, though, jinking down a ranch road or two, doubling back a couple of times on U.S. 67, and eyeing the mirror for headlights taking a sudden U-turn, ducking into the parking lot of a shuttered auto parts store then the shadows of an abandoned Shamrock station further up the road on U.S. 90 and watching her back trail.

Skills Tommy Juan and Armando taught her. One more look. Then another. Nada.

That told her two things. Somebody close to Nancy Jo or Hector ratted her out to these *pinche pendejos*. Maybe a bitter Ruiz widow or mother. Maybe the truth was burned out of Hector or Nancy Jo. The tea leaves also told her they were here to grab her up and take her somewhere, not kill her on the spot.

Dear ol' daddy? Or somebody who hates me a lot, wants to tie me up and kill me real, real slow?

Gave her an edge on these motherfuckers. They might hesitate before pulling the trigger. She wouldn't.

She eased her way past stabbing branches and slashing thorns, moving slow up the steep slope, always to the right, always angling toward the backside of the shack. Pausing to listen and catch her breath, freezing in place when she heard a twig snap or a scurry in the sand, dreading the warning *buuurrrrrrr* of a diamondback. Once she made the top, she spotted the two thick clumps of creosote and mesquite flanking either side of the pathway leading from the trail's end to the hideaway—perfect blinds for outriders looking to herd her into the house at gunpoint.

She dodged both, looping through the brush to the far side of the shack, edging up to an open window that funneled the cold night air, causing a big man sitting in the dark to curse softly and hunker down in a black leather jacket that was too thin for the falling temperatures.

In solitary shadow, he oozed the air of an alpha dog, a self-appointed honcho, waiting for others to drive her to him. Facing the open front door, puffing a cigar, cradling an AK of some persuasion. His head was large, shaved clean and in profile, sitting like a melon on broad, hunched shoulders.

Her CAR-15 had a mind of its own, muzzle up and locked on the melon, stock already extended and welded to her cheek like a lover waltzing with her in the dark. *Like Tommy Juan. Like Armando.*

She smiled and squeezed the trigger.

Muzzle flash from a full-auto rip of rounds lit the room like a strobe light, wrecking her night vision. Stuttering images of skull fragments, brain pulp, and blood mist danced in the iron sights. Staccato blasts deadened her ears.

She dropped away from the window, tucked her shoulder, and rolled to her right. Rounds chewed up the window frame, shattered the top glass and smacked into adobe on either side. Even a blind man could have spotted the flash of an AK from the nearest brushy clump. Still on autopilot, the CAR-15 swept up and emptied the rest of the thirty-round mag without a single commanding thought from her.

Slip the brain back into conscious gear. Drop the spent mag. Pull out a fresh mag. Slap it home, trip the bolt, punch the forward assist button.

Ready for more rock n' roll. Tuck the shoulder and roll right again. Scrabble through the rocks and sand. Find cover to watch both clumps for further rude behavior. She took three deep breaths and felt her hammering pulse start to slow. The tunnel vision of sudden violence widened in scope. Her hearing and night sight slowly returned. She watched and waited, her eyes sweeping the clumps and the pathway from the trail.

Movement in the far clump, sensed rather than seen. Up with the CAR-15 but she held her fire, waiting for a target she could truly see. She heard a thump, a cry, and then a muffled scream. She waited. One minute became three, then five.

"Don't shoot, *guapa*. It's only me."

"Step out where I can see you, Hector."

"I'm afraid I can't, *mi hija*. This *pinche cabron* had his own knife to stab me with."

She rose and moved slowly to the nearest clump, the one she hosed with the last of her first magazine, CAR-15 leading the way. Another dead killer in a black leather coat too thin for the cold night air. This one had straight, black hair but only half a dark-skinned face, the left side of his jaw blown away by 5.56 mike-mike rounds. He was on his back, his right arm flung away from his body, still clutching the pistol grip of his AK.

She rushed to the second clump and found Hector leaning against a rock, clutching his belly with both hands, dark blood oozing through his fingers. A dead man was lying on his back at Hector's feet, a knife jammed hilt deep into his chest.

"I'm afraid I'm not the man I used to be. Had this *chupaverga* right where I wanted him. Ready to slit his throat. Just like the old days. Then I slipped."

"Shhhh, Hector. Save your strength. Rest for a bit and I'll get you out of here."

"No, *mi hija*. You must go. There's a map and a set of keys for the new place in my jacket pocket. Take them, go get your money, go get Charlie and get away."

"Not yet. I'll stay with you a while."

She sat next to him and cradled his head on her shoulder. He told her when the killers came, how he saw them on the road below, how he hid in the brush while they searched the house and barn. They turned on the safety light then made a beeline to the hideaway. He flipped it off before following them on foot, too slow and too late to flag her down before she headed up the trail. His words tumbled out in a raspy rush halted by a long, ragged coughing fit.

"Easy, Hector. Save your breath."

Hector ignored her command. His story had a point and he was running out of time to make it.

"They knew just where to go, *guapa*."

"Someone told them."

"Somebody *showed* them. On a map. Gave them directions. They knew just where to go. They didn't wander or hunt. They flew right here. Someone betrayed you."

"I know. Were they Garza's men?"

"No."

"You're sure?"

"*Sí.*"

He leaned his head back and grinned.

"I must tell you something, *guapa.*"

"What's that, *abuelo?*"

"I slit a man's throat tonight. Just like the old days when I was really a man. You'll find him down on the trail, just below where you parked the Jeep."

"You see? I was right. You are *un asesino modesto.*"

"*Sí.* A clean kill. One last time. But listen, he was a *gringo* and the Garzas don't hire *gringos.* As a rule. I also heard them talk. They didn't sound like Texans or Mexicans. They sounded like they came from up north. Chicago, maybe. Did you know I used to live there? Many years ago."

"I did not know that, Hector. Thank you for telling me this."

"*Por nada, mi hija.* Now you must leave me and this one to the coyotes. We killed each other. A life for a life."

She held him as the light faded from his eyes. He was still smiling.

No pain or worry. No regrets. Like a sleeping child, grinning through a sweet dream.

Like Charlie.

Twenty

In a restless dream, Burch was back in the dark blue of a Dallas street cop, rousting a scumbag, pounding on the standard-issue steel door of an apartment in a no-name complex off Live Oak, bellowing the routine command to open up that really meant the *poh-leece is here,* ready to kick the ass of anybody who didn't cooperate.

Or shoot 'em.

The rolling boom from the door grew louder. He kept pounding the dream door because he kept hearing the sound. He kept hearing the sound because he couldn't stop hammering the door with his fist. He also couldn't breathe and started to panic, willing himself to wake up and make the pounding stop. His eyes popped open. He gasped and gulped air through his mouth like a dying trout, sprawling across the bed to reach for the pimp gun in the night table drawer.

He was wide awake now, heart tripping fast, breathing hard. The pounding continued. From the dream to real life. That pissed him off. Felt like a cheap conjurer's trick.

"Knock it the fuck off, I'm coming."

"Open up, Gramps. Don't want to get my ass shot on your front porch."

He yanked on his jeans, buckled up, and walked barefooted and bare chested, bare belly flopping over his belt, across a living room lit only by night lights in wall sockets. Angling toward the solid oak front door, ignoring the cartilage pops from his knees.

Flipping on a goose-necked brass reading lamp, he traded the pimp gun for the Colt sitting on the end table next to his recliner, easing the slide back to make sure there was a round in the pipe, then killing the light.

Tripped the two deadbolts and the mortice lock then pulled the steel door bar from cradles bolted to six-by-six oak posts sunk into concrete piers under the house. He swung the door open with his right hand, stepping back and to the side, his left raising the gun muzzle head high.

"Jesus, Gramps. It's just me. You can put the gun down."

"Better get your ass inside, Rhonda Mae. Welcome to my humble *casa*."

"We need to talk."

"We will, but I need to watch your back trail a bit. Go make us some coffee or pour us some whiskey. You'll find both in that skinny-ass excuse of a kitchen I've got."

"They call it a galley, Gramps."

"Yeah, but we're in the desert, and this ain't no boat. Make yourself at home."

He grabbed a red and black Navajo-patterned blanket from his recliner, draped it over his shoulders, and stepped into the star-splashed cold, pulling the door shut and easing into a rocking chair on the northeast end of the porch to wait for the night to reveal itself.

Fingers snagged the strap of a pair of M17 7x50 binoculars hanging from the top rail of the rocker in a scuffed, brown leather case. They were World War II vintage lenses with Bausch & Lomb glass he bought off a retired artillery officer while stationed in Germany with a tank battalion back in 1967. Damn fine gear with a wide field of view and big lens barrels that let in plenty of light. None too heavy, either. Easy to swing slowly through an arc of interest, relaxing to let his peripheral vision take the lead.

The artillery officer used them to spot Tigers, Panthers, Panzer IVs, Stug IIIs, Wehrmacht panzer grenadiers, and Waffen SS troops pouring through the Ardennes, calling in hellfire from 105s and 155s during the Battle of the Bulge. Almost fifty years later, Burch felt a sliver of shame for using these historic lenses just to sweep over a sorry-ass stretch of West Texas desert, spotting a coyote, a trio of javelinas, and two jack rabbits. Critters too scrawny for a fire mission.

From his perch, he could also study the magnified outline of his barn, the north wall of the box canyon that loomed above his home, and the fenced-in rocks, sand, and brush that gave "pasture" a bad name, split by the caliche trail that started deep in the canyon, looped by his front door, and ran the half mile to Dry Branch Road. His view of the road was limited by the canyon wall and a low rise that rolled across the north side of his cactus paradise, giving the trail a short summit before it dipped down to the pipe-gated entrance with cattle guard and the rough barbed-wire fence that bordered the only route to Faver.

Watchers could post up on the rocky shelf that rose above the far side of the road. If they were bold or stupid, they could hop the gate and grab some brush at the top of the rise. But that would have spooked the critters he could still see rooting around the near side of the rise. *Hombres malo* could also keep tabs on him at a distance. When he got home an hour or two ago, he grabbed a flashlight and slid his fat ass under the Blazer, checking the frame rails, cross members, and bumpers for transmitters. He found two. Left them there.

Let the bastards think I'm clueless. Let 'em think I'm home for the night. When I need to, I'll dump these trackers. Put 'em on a bus leaving town. Be long gone and elsewhere before they figure it out.

Don't think, dumbass. It hurts the ballclub. Keep looking. He slowly scanned both sectors and the barn, then reversed the sweep, humming "Cherokee Boogie," an old Moon Mullican hit.

Well, a Cherokee chief as he dances along/
He does an Indian boogie to a white man's song/
Singin' "Hey-ho-a-lina"/
"Hey-ho-a-lina"/
Well a "Hey-ho-a-lina wup-wup a-wittena-yea ..."

Rhonda Mae stepped onto the porch, balancing two stoneware mugs that cast the scent of strong coffee into the cold night breeze, causing his nose to twitch. She handed him one then dragged another rocker over to sit close.

"Found a bottle of ninety-proof sweet'ner for that."

"Knew you would."

He took a deep gulp and smacked his lips.

"Nectar."

"Anything out there?"

"Night critters. Javelina, a coyote, couple of jackrabbits. No bad guys. Yet."

"We need to talk."

"Talk while I keep watchin'. I can also walk and chew bubble gum at the same time."

"Smartass."

"Keeps me young."

She told him about Hector's hideaway and the four killers waiting for her return from Pancho's. In taut, flat tones, she gave him the details of the two she killed. Her voice broke when she spoke about Hector, how he killed the other two before he died and the father's love she showed him.

Burch, still scanning the night, murmured, "I'm sorry."

"Hector got a good look at those assholes. He said he didn't think they were Garza *sicarios* because one of them was a *gringo*."

"That doesn't mean that Valentina Garza didn't send them. Her daddy was known to bring in some freelancers on occasion. And she's her daddy's little daughter and follows his ways."

"Hector also said they didn't sound like they were from here. He thought they were from up north, Chicago, maybe."

"The Garzas wouldn't hire anybody from up there. Too many killers to choose from right in their backyard. Mex, Tex-Mex, or *gringo*. Take your pick and they ain't that choosy. If the dearly departed were from the Windy City, they were workin' for somebody else."

"Any idea who?"

"Your damn daddy, for one. Danny Ray Mutscher, king-hell asshole supreme."

"Coulda gone all week without hearin' that."

"I know. Got a question. Where's Charlie?"

"I'll answer a question with a question. What's a ten gauge?"

"That's where I thought he was. We need to get him the hell out of there. Let me get dressed and make a couple of calls. Then we'll head to Nancy Jo's. We'll take your ride."

"Why we doin' that?"

"Cause the folks watchin' me know that piece of shit Blazer I got with the sheriff's decal on the door. Also got it wired up with transmitters. They won't be lookin' for a four-door Malibu Classic like the one you're drivin', and we'll make sure it ain't wired."

"You takin' me in?"

"Let's study on makin' sure Charlie's safe. Then we'll worry about petty stuff like the law."

Burch made another back-and-forth pass with the binoculars.

"Aw, fuck it. Ain't nobody out there."

He was dead wrong about that.

Twenty-One

It was quarter past three in the ayem, and Bobby Quintero needed a gallon of hot coffee, a cold shower, and a gnarled divining rod to keep hunting for the most likely places Chizik could hole up, strop his straight-edge razor, and plan his next strike.

What he had was a tin of Bayer aspirin, a fizzed-out bottle of Coke, and a chaw of Red Man as he pushed himself and an unmarked Cuervo County cruiser down the next endless stretch of West Texas blacktop. An added bonus was Deputy Malcolm Collins, youngest sworn officer in the department, snoring like a hog in the back seat.

The killer sure wasn't at that Alice Baker bunny ranch outside Valentine, which felt like a sure thing when a Hoover-nosed snitch named Albert Broomall told him about it—when was that, yesterday? Day before? Time loves an addled-brain hero.

Quintero ignored Burch's command to wait until daylight. He burned rubber from the bloody motel in Sanderson to scout the carnal campground, planting the cruiser in a safe spot so Collins could watch the front gate, then gliding on foot like a wraith past the travel trailers and adobe cottages, listening to the grunts, giggles, and cries of the whores and their johns.

When he paused his ghostly stroll by an open window of the squat cinderblock building that housed the office and mirrored lounge where the ladies paraded their assets, he heard a guy named Benny bitch on the phone about Chizik being a no-show who owed him money. Sounded like a man getting his ass chewed by the other party on the line.

Replay:

"Hell no, I don't know where that motherfucker's at. He told me he was on his way here three days ago."

Screeching and screaming from the other end of the line.

"If I knew where, I'd tell ya. Yessir, when he calls, I'll tell him to call you. You bet. And I'll give you a heads up. Nosiree, I won't let you down."

Another dead end. A duster. A dry hole. Made him feel lower than an Odessa wildcatter down to his last dime as he crept back to the cruiser. Until another snitch came to mind who might point him to paydirt, a hometown boy named Zeke Quarles, a turncoat member of the Aryan Brotherhood of Texas, the scorned white-trash cousins of the Aryan Brotherhood founded in California prisons.

"C'mon, kid, the motherfucker ain't here. We're headed for home."

"What's the plan?"

"No plan for you except sixty minutes of sleep in back and a return to your regular duties. Thanks for ridin' shotgun, but Burch and me will be back in harness later today."

"What's it like workin' with Burch? I hear he likes to shoot people."

"Only the ones what need killin'. Let's just say he ain't housebroke."

Which was a severe understatement. Truth be told, Quintero was torn. He liked Burch, found him fearless and unwilling to take shit from anybody. But he was unpredictable and reckless, likely to barrel straight into something that could get them both killed.

Burch was also brutal as hell, willing to beat the shit out of a scumbag. With a blackjack, a phone book, his fists, or his boots. White, black, brown, or yellow. Didn't matter. Make 'em a true believer, ready to rat out their mother. On the plus side, the old cuss was never boring.

Took him less than an hour to get back to Faver and whip the cruiser into the deep shadows of a dark patch of oil-stained cinder behind Tio's, an all-night gas n' go on the corner of Contreras and Main, right where the town's central artery widened into a smooth, blacktop spur with a suicide lane running northwest to U.S. 67. He knew he'd find Quarles at his customary post, perched on a high swivel stool behind the store's cash register, cigarette smoke curling from a black plastic ashtray, a twenty-ounce Dr. Pepper within easy reach.

Once a skinhead, the ex-con was hiding in plain sight, his iron gray hair now shoulder length and masking the swastika tattooed on the back of his skull. His beard was long enough to rival Billy Gibbons, and his Texas driver's license, an artful forgery, listed his name as William Frank Martin.

Billy Frank to his friends. Not that he had many. Most of them were dead or in prison.

Quarles did a dime of a fifteen spot for armed robbery in Huntsville, where he earned his ABT stripes with a little wet work, much rumored but never proven. Joined Chizik's first gunrunning crew, working out of a ranch north of Faver that got raided by the Feds and Doggett back when he was Blue Willingham's chief deputy. He rolled over on Chizik and the rest of the crew. Got out in two years instead of ten. A walking dead man under normal circumstances, a rat ripe for extermination by any righteous AB brother.

Quarles caught a break, though. Another member of the crew, Tommy Juan Jaeckel, was an even bigger rat, a trusted Chizik lieutenant who also had balls that clanked so loud he set up his own gunrunning gig and poached his boss's clients. It also helped that Chizik's fury was volcanic and narrowly focused on Tommy Juan and his girlfriend, the infamous *La Güera*. Quarles and his betrayal slipped into the shadows, out of sight and nearly forgotten.

Count your lucky stars and run, son. Get the hell out of Dodge and don't look back.

But Quarles was born and raised in Sanderson and couldn't bear to leave his mother or West Texas. Not necessarily in that order. But never again. Which was the sentimental reflex of a terminal mama's boy with a twangy death wish. Thought if he changed his name, grew long hair and a beard, and moved to Faver, he'd be okay. After five years, his luck was still holding, and he could go see mama twice a week at the Alpine Valley Care Center.

He bought a concrete-and-stone house with a tin roof on the west side of town and kept his nose clean, avoiding old haunts and friends and working the graveyard shift at Tio's even though he was part owner.

Kept his Harley, though, and still sold weed and pills. Nothing heavy. Just enough to put some extra jingle in his pocket, dealing to a small group of herbally-minded retirees and some long-haul truckers who needed a chemical jolt to keep their rigs running between the ditches.

Placed him where he could hear things, see things, and sell that info to Bobby Quintero, who kept the heat off him. His latest score—spotting Lonny Dalrymple at that hunter's shack while scouting for muley tracks and dialing up Bobby. That earned him a hundred bucks.

There was only one customer in the store when Quintero strolled through the door—a wiry, bald-headed guy with a pigtail of gray hair hanging down his back and bulging eyes behind thick bifocals with a black plastic frame. He was sweating, and those eyes looked ready to pop out of his skull as they shifted back and forth between Quintero and Quarles.

Quintero held the door open as the man scurried into the night, angling toward a rust-streaked '65 Ford F-100 step-side that was once shiny and green.

"You have you a good night, sir."

The man looked back and almost tripped over his boots. Quintero shook his head and turned his attention to Quarles, ready to keep up the fiction of the snitch's assumed name.

"Who's that nervous joker, Billy Frank?"

"A fella by the name of Jake Babcock. Welder at Donny Moore's shop over on Pershing. Not a bad sort. He's the high nervous type and got the glaucoma real bad. I help him out some."

"Weed and 'ludes?"

"Sumpin' like that. What can I do you for, Bobby?"

"I need a line on a man who's supposed to be dead. You know him right well, but he ain't no friend. Probably the last guy you'd want to see walkin' through that door."

"Cleve Chizik. Thought your partner iced that sumbitch during that shoot 'em up a few years back."

"So did everybody else, including my partner, who's right pissed about Chizik walkin' around killin' folks. Seems like he's settlin' old scores, Billy Frank."

"Like who?"

"Brad Settles, for one."

"That popdick motherfucker needed to get dead. Good riddance."

"Couldn't agree more. Seems like Chizik's still hangin' around here, though. Like to get him dead for certain this time before he slices anybody else's throat. Like yours, maybe."

"Naw, he ain't after me. I'm way off his radar screen and plan to keep it that way."

"What have you heard about the bastard, Billy Frank?"

"You know I stay as far away as possible from those dudes, Bobby."

"And well you should. But I know you keep your ear tuned to the coconut telegraph."

"That I do. Got to find out the latest and greatest to keep getting double sawbucks from you."

Quintero slid two twenties across the counter.

"Speakin' of which."

Quarles palmed both bills and slipped them into the front pocket of his jeans. He glanced right and left then scanned the parking lot before speaking.

"One of my regulars is tight with two guys who worked those Chizik crews. Both of 'em are Alice Baker, and I know 'em both as solid brothers who'd slit my throat in a heartbeat."

"So you don't wanna see either one of 'em comin' through that door but think they ain't full of shit."

"Right you are, Bobby. One of 'em don't believe the talk about Chizik bein' alive. Not that there's a helluva lot of that kind of talk on the wire—not after a brother got his throat slashed for blabbin' about Cleve Chizik bein' rose up from the dead like Jesus H. Christ."

"What about the other brother?"

"He's a believer. And I don't mean the church-goin' kind. He says he seen the bastard couple of years ago in a bar in Las Cruces and more recent at a gym in Van Horn run by an ex-Delta Force operator. Don't got a name."

"If he is hangin' 'round here, where's he hidin' out?"

"My money would be on Cindy Wiley's place, just above the north end of the Devil's Backbone on the old Hulett ranch. Fancy house built on a mesa by her dead husband.

She's a crazy bitch who fucked anybody in pants on Chizik's crews before zeroing in on him."

"Including you?"

"Including me. Pretty near fucked my dick off, that one."

Bobby snorted a laugh then asked: "Anyplace else?"

"Not too many other places he'd be welcome. Needs to steer clear of the Ruiz family. They blame him for Armando's death. And I hear Valentina Garza's got her hitters lookin' for him. That's why I say Cindy's place is your best bet."

"Second best place?"

"Okay, if you've gotta have another choice, I'd say the old Kincannon place, the Bar Triple T. Where we were runnin' guns from before Sudden Doggett busted us. Nobody but distant relatives have had a thing to do with that place since then. Nobody lives there. Be a good spot to hole up once you chased out the rattlesnakes and tumbleweeds."

"Much obliged, Billy Frank. Might be a good idea for you to hop on that Harley and hit the road for a few weeks. Until we get the bastard."

"Cain't do it, Bobby. Gotta watch the store and keep an eye on mama. Besides, seems like the more I stay in place, the more invisible I get. Kinda like Alice and that Cheshire Cat. Pretty soon, all you'll see of me is a shit eatin' grin."

"Not if you keep that beard. Keep your head on a swivel, *hombre*."

"Same to you, Bobby. Same to you."

Twenty-Two

"We got company."

Rhonda Mae jerked her head around to stare out the back window of Big Russett.

"Where?"

"Pretty far back. Maybe half a mile. No lights. Ever' so often, he picks up some starlight. Must be a shiny ride."

"Go dark and lose him, Gramps."

"In this thing?"

"It'll scoot. Punch it."

Burch dumped the lights and dropped the hammer. Big Russett leaped ahead, pressing him back in his seat with the sudden acceleration.

"Damn. What the hell's under the hood of this sled?"

"Dunno. You'd have to ask a guy up in Colorado named Carlos. He overhauled the engine when I bought it. Said something about a Q-Jet, a street and strip cam, cylinders bored out for bigger pistons, and a dual-plane intake. Oh, and a dual exhaust with DynoMax mufflers."

"That'll do it."

They were booming down a long straightaway on Arrowhead Road, hurtling toward a bobby-pin curve about a mile ahead that skirted the rocky face of a mesa. Miss the curve. Kiss the mesa.

The huge secondaries on the QuadraJet carb were wide open, adding a bass note to the roar of Big Russett's tweaked 400 cubic-inch engine. The hombres tailing them realized they'd been made, rocketing to close the gap and flipping on their headlights, twin side-by-sides on each end of the grill, old-school high beams glaring in the rearview mirror.

You boys are hunters, now. Not just babysitters. Different game, different rules. Higher stakes. Kill or get killed.

Burch braked hard before he hit the bend, bleeding speed and slapping the automatic transmission into low. The big Chevy dropped its nose, engine and tranny screaming, as he muscled into the sharp curve, the rocky face of the mesa filling the windshield.

Rhonda Mae started chanting: *Jesus, Jesus, Jesus ...*

The rear fishtailed then held, the outside tires crunched shoulder gravel, and Burch fought a suicidal urge to stomp on the brakes. He held his breath as he felt the car lose its grip again before the rubber bit blacktop and didn't let go.

... Jesus, Jesus, Jesus ...

Big Russett spat out of the back end of the curve like a gristly piece of meat hawked up by a big-bellied banker. Burch spotted the ghostly trace of a ranch road dead ahead and cranked a hard right, trading smooth asphalt for rough, brush-choked caliche and ruts that punished the shocks and chassis.

The trace climbed the shoulder of a rocky hill, topping the lip of a clearing where the mesquite, creosote, and salt cedar had been knocked back far enough for a pickup and horse trailer to park and turn around. No exit. A dead end. No way out but the way they just came in.

Burch jammed it into low-low and coaxed Big Russett into an about-face, branches screeching down the flanks, scraping off paint and primer. Kept his boot off the brakes and the taillights they'd trigger, then slipped into neutral and let the car creep to a stop on its own, more or less facing the road they just left.

"You still can't drive worth a shit, Gramps."

"Shut up and rip out that dome light, willya? Don't want to send a signal to the bad guys when we step out of this rig."

"Don't have to rip it out. Just pop off the lens and take out the bulb. Like this."

Burch heard a plastic pop and a metallic click. He could see her smile as she held up the dome light lens with her left hand and the bulb in her right. She opened the glove box and dropped both inside.

"Remind me to buy you a subscription to *Popular Mechanics*."

"Make it *Hot Rod*. I want to figure out how Carlos souped up this car."

"If you live that long."

From where they sat, they could see the long grade of Arrowhead Road climbing northeast toward a saddle in the Cuesta del Burro, a range of rugged hills named for the wild donkeys that roamed the slopes. Rhonda Mae pointed toward the headlights of a car about two miles up the grade, well beyond the ranch road cutoff.

"Looks like they blew on by without a clue."

"Not so fast. They'll figure it out in a second or two."

Taillights flared. Headlights swept the bumpy arc of a car that had to use both gravel shoulders of the road to reverse course and head their way.

"I hate it when you're right."

"Should be used to that by now."

Burch eyed the bandit car as it slowed so the hombres could hunt for the spot where Big Russett left the road. It was a sinister ride in a deep, dark color. Black or nocturne blue, just like his Four-Four-Two. With a satin shine. Two guys in the front, none in the back.

Looked like an Olds or Buick. Late 60s or early 70s two-door. Not the ubiquitous black SUVs of arrogant Feds and hired corporate killers. Sleek and flashy, but not chopped, jacked, and tricked out like a *vato* banger ride. Damn sure wasn't a hooptee.

These boys ain't from 'round here, Sport Model.

No Wynn, they ain't. But they surely do love a classic piece of American Iron.

Love to drive it, too. Long distance. Not just leave it in the garage to look at. You like to see that.

Beg to differ, old friend. I think it's a tad arrogant for hired goons to drag a sweet ride to a gun fight. Must think they're so good there ain't nobody who can shoot the shit out of them and that car.

You and your girlfriend here are about to disabuse them of that notion, ain'tcha?

If they drag that ride up here, we will.

You know them boys ain't got no good intentions, right, Sport Model?

Right.

So fly the Black Flag. Smoke 'em.

"You bet."

"You bet what? You talkin' to yourself again?"

"No. My dead partner."

"Jesus, Gramps."

"Don't start. Assholes have found the trail. How many mags you got?"

"Three. Thirty rounds each. Got a Smith & Wesson with two speedloaders. You?"

"Got plenty. More than enough to keep these shitbirds entertained."

The bandit car left the blacktop and headed toward them, lights off. Burch and Rhonda Mae stepped out of Big Russett. He reached back in over the front seat and pulled his M1 Garand from its canvas case. Also grabbed the six-clip cloth bandolier to drape around his neck.

Rhonda Mae was already staring across the car roof at him, cradling her CAR-15, when he straightened up, racked a round in the chamber of the Garand, and looked her way.

"Remember the last time we did this?"

"How could I forget?"

"Awrighty, then. Pull that bandana over your face. You go right with that bush burp gun. Stay low. I'll go left and stay high. Catch 'em in a crossfire without shootin' each other."

"That'd ruin our day."

"We don't want that. Now, go, baby girl. Keep it low, shoot straight, and don't get dead."

"You too, Gramps."

Balaban held up his hand: "This is far enough, Jake. We'll walk from here."

Sartain took his foot off the accelerator and let the upward slope of the trail stall the 455 Rocket engine before setting the emergency brake and slipping the tranny into park. About thirty yards ahead, the trail topped the lip of a rise and disappeared from view.

"You sure about this, boss? Might be better to pull back and go get the others."

"Where are your balls, brother? Let 'em drop. The target's right here, right now. So's that fat bastard who needs to get whacked. We grab her, we clip him, and we all get a big payday. C'mon, let's gear up."

Sartain pulled his Browning Hi-Power from a shoulder holster as he stepped out of the Olds and eyed the ghostly, dirty-white trail ahead, covering Balaban as he popped the trunk to slip on a Kevlar vest and grab an H&K MP-5 and a couple of spare mags.

When he felt Balaban tap him on the shoulder, he stepped back to the trunk to strap on his own vest and grab a Mossberg 500 twelve-gauge riot pump, stuffing extra shells in the cargo pocket of his dark gray utility pants before racking a round of buckshot into the chamber.

The loud *shiiiiing-shiiiiing* broke the night's stillness and drew a hissing rebuke from Balaban, delivered in an angry whisper as Sartain stepped onto the trail and rejoined him in front of the car.

"If they didn't know we were here before, they sure as shit do now, fuckhead."

"They already knew. Might as well put the fear of God into them."

"Shut the fuck up and work the left side of the trail. I'll take the right."

They turned away from each other, each taking two or three steps before a voice in the dark above shouted: "Hey, assholes!"

They looked up, frozen in mid step, silhouetted against the caliche dust of the trace. The perfect pose to get chopped down by a high-velocity storm of jacketed rounds, their jerking bodies lit up by muzzle flashes. A death dance paced by the loud staccato chatter of Rhonda Mae's CAR-15 and the slower, deeper boom of Burch's M1 Garand. Their Kevlar didn't save them. Head shots from a battle rifle made in 1942 made sure of that.

Their sleek ride fared a little bit better. Stray rounds blew out the paired headlights on the driver's side, stitched a line of frosted holes in the windshield, and ripped up the dark gray imitation leather of the headrests and seatback of the split front bench.

Good news for classic car aficionados, though. Bullets didn't leave a mark on the satin sheen of that dreamy midnight blue paint job. No holes in the sheet metal at all—hood, fenders, doors, or roof. And the 455 Rocket would still fire up, which Burch found out after he and Rhonda Mae collected their guns and wallets and dragged the bodies into the brush. Dinner for the coyotes and buzzards.

They drove the Olds over the lip of the rise, parking it in the clearing next to Big Russett, dumping the dead men's guns in the Chevy's trunk and their own weapons in the back seat, covering them with a quilt. Burch fished a small Maglight out of his jacket pocket and flipped through the wallets of the men they'd just killed.

Terry Balaban's had a Wisconsin driver's license with a Milwaukee address, a private investigator's license, and a pistol permit. Jake Sartain's had a Louisiana driver's license with a Baton Rouge address, a concealed carry permit, and ivory-colored business cards that listed his name, phone number, and simple title: Problem Solver.

He handed the Maglight and driver's licenses to Rhonda Mae. She studied them both, shuffling from one to the other three or four times.

"Know either of these fuckheads?"

"No on Balaban. Maybe on Sartain. My dearest daddy did a lot of business in Baton Rouge with a guy named Bertrand Sartain. Still does, probably. Meth, smack, coke, pills, weed, and guns. Sartain offered a smorgasbord of criminal delights."

"That's close enough to say these guys were working for Danny Ray. We'll nail it down later. And those four you and Hector smoked. Right now, we need to beat feet and go get your boy."

"Crank it up and get us the hell out of here, Gramps."

Twenty-Three

Burch could smell the blood and burnt gun powder before he crossed the threshold of Nancy Jo Quartermain's shattered front door at dawn. His boots automatically slid into a slow combat shuffle as he scanned the living room, both hands gripping his Colt 1911, arms outstretched, letting the pistol lead the way, his eyes taking in details framed by the gun's iron sights.

To his right, Nancy Jo was sprawled face up between the couch and what he remembered as her favorite easy chair, her thick gray hair cushioning her head, blood soaking the lap of her dress and pooling on the tile floor beneath her, her eyes tracking him and her lips moving to form words only she could hear.

Her right hand was still wrapped around the straight grip of her L.C. Smith ten gauge, the pitted, bare steel of its double barrels pointed toward the far corner of the room. Both hammers were down. She had emptied the gun before falling gut-shot to the floor.

Her target was crumpled in the corner like a burlap sack of potatoes the hogs had torn up—the ragged body of a woman with wild blonde curls. The left side of her face was blown away, blood and brain matter dripping into the hole where her eye socket used to be. Double-ought buckshot had ripped open the Double D chest, turning flesh into a pulp of blood, meat and silicone gel.

A hoarse, anguished cry from Rhonda Mae: "Jesus, he's got my boy. He's got Charlie."

Burch turned and looked her dead in the eye: "I'm gonna get him back, ya hear me?"

Quick as a snake, her face turned hard and her voice snapped the air like a bullwhip.

"You ain't good enough to do this on your own nickel, Gramps. The two of us might be."

"Make it three once Bobby gets here. Guess we'll find out then."

Burch quickly cleared the rest of the house and checked the utility shed out back. When he stepped back into the living room, he spotted a folded piece of paper sitting on the seat of Nancy Jo's easy chair. Missed it on the first pass.

Inside, in a spidery pencil scrawl, was a three-line note, all-caps:

TRIPLE T

TRADE—YOU FOR HIM

LIFE FOR LIFE

Knew it wasn't meant for him. Knew it was penned for a hard-ass woman with a kidnapped child. He pocketed the note then looked at Rhonda Mae cradling Nancy Jo's head in her lap, stroking her hair. He kneeled close to the tough old woman to hear what she had to say. Her black eyes were fierce and defiant, locked on his, hot and angry about her life ending. She grabbed the front of his shirt and pulled him closer.

"Chizik," she hissed. "Chizik got Charlie. You go get him back from that bastard. Kill him for sure this time, *pendejo*."

He almost laughed. Calling him an asshole with death knocking on her door. Once a whore, a madam, a weed smuggler, and a wife, she was a revered elder of the Ruiz family of outlaws and killers, a short, stout human cyclone to the very end.

Nancy Jo took a long, ragged breath. Then died.

"Why'd she shoot her instead of him?"

"He was carrying Charlie, would be my guess. And had a gun and shot her, 'cause I don't see one around that body in the corner."

"Who is she? Or was she?"

"Cindy Wiley."

"I remember her from the ranch. Nancy Jo called her a *puta*. Kind of ironic, given Nancy Jo's past. She sure didn't like her. Said she had no honor. Said she would fuck anything with a pecker."

"Was she Chizik's main squeeze?"

"Seemed like she was everybody's punch."

"They were hooked up until tonight. Nancy Jo broke that up. With both barrels. Nasty."

Burch heard a footfall outside. Still on his knees by Nancy Jo, he turned his head and upper body toward the door, left arm extended with the Colt in his hand.

"Easy, partner. It's me."

"Show yourself, Bobby. Hands where I can see 'em."

Bobby Quintero stepped through the door, smiling, hat pushed back on his head, both hands empty and held in front of his chest.

"Jesus, Burch. I barely got you broke in. Sure as hell ain't gonna shoot you."

"*Nunca se sabe, Bobby.* You might got a better offer."

"Best they could do was five dollars. I'll dance with who brung me."

Burch stood slowly, knees popping. His smile was tight as he holstered the Colt. Hard to see under his beard and moustache. Unless you were studying him hard. Bobby was.

"You're still jumpy, partner."

"Got reason to be. Chizik was right here. I can smell him. Gone thirty minutes. Or less. Tops. Grabbed Charlie. Shot Mary Jo. He's gone, but he's still close. For all I know, he's watching us right now."

"Not with that kid, he ain't."

Quintero was scanning the room while listening to Burch, eyeing the blood patterns and bodies, whistling low while looking at the corpse in the corner and the dark red spatter arching above.

"How'd this play out?"

"Looks like he shot Mary Jo then grabbed Charlie. Body in the corner there was Cindy Wiley. She must've froze up when Chizik shot Mary Jo. Old woman was gutshot but strong enough and mad enough to grab that old ten gauge of hers."

"Had to make somebody pay. Couldn't shoot Chizik. Went for Door Number Two."

"Bingo."

"You gonna introduce me to this lady?"

"You mean her? Hell, she ain't no lady. This is *La Güera*. Sometimes called Rhonda Mae Mutscher."

Quintero shook Rhonda Mae's hand.

"So you're the bee in Chizik's bonnet."

"One of them. Call me Rhonda Mae. Or Hey, You. Tryin' to keep *La Güera* dead and buried."

"Will do. Call me Bobby."

"Are you going to turn me in, Bobby?"

"Not unless my partner tells me to. We need to get your boy back first."

"I'd be obliged."

Quintero asked Burch: "You callin' this in?"

"I'll call Doggett and brief him, but we ain't hangin' around. Exigent circumstances. We need to get on Chizik's trail and get her boy. You need to figure whether you're in or out. Could cost you your badge if you're in."

"Half the things we do could cost me my badge, partner. I'm in."

"You need to know that these ain't the only folks who got dead tonight. If we're lucky enough to grab the boy, there'll be a big mess to clean up after."

"They were killers, right?"

Burch nodded.

"I'm shocked more bad guys got dead by you. I also got an idea where Chizik might go to hole up."

"Out with it."

"Snitch of mine named two places. Wiley has a place up on a mesa north of the Devil's Backbone. That was probably where they were going to take the kid."

"Chizik won't go there now. He'll figure we'll identify Wiley and make a beeline for her place."

"Yup. That makes the other place the most likely spot. The Bar Triple T, a small ranch about thirty miles north of here. It's the spread Chizik's first crew was runnin' guns out of before Doggett and the ATF raided the place. My snitch was part of that crew. Says nobody livin' there now except coyotes and rattlesnakes."

Burch held up the scrawled note he found on Nancy Jo's easy chair.

"Does this fit the puzzle?"

A quick scan by Quintero: "Damn. You know it does. And here I thought I was tellin' you something you didn't know."

"That'll be the day. Know how to get there?"

"I do. I was a newbie, but Doggett picked me to be a scout on that raid."

"Because the Army made you such a sneaky, stealthy bastard."

Quintero grinned, knowing that Burch had steadied up. He put a hand on his partner's shoulder.

"*Es verdad, hombre.* I'm still a ghost when I want to be."

"Sack up, Casper. But fuck bein' a friendly ghost."

Twenty-Four

Deputy U.S. Marshal Gabriel F. Cucinotta was in full, red-faced roar, standing at the front edge of Sudden Doggett's desk, stretching his big-bellied, six-foot-five frame to maximum height, thrusting his right index finger toward the sheriff's face as he yelled.

"The United States Marshals Service is not going to tolerate interference and obstruction from a local law enforcement agency in the course of our lawful pursuit of a fugitive we have reason to believe is hiding in your county," he shouted in a precise and formal tone that only made his Bronx accent more obnoxious.

"We expect your full cooperation. And to that end, I've secured an order from U.S. Magistrate Judge Carlton W. Blanchard in Alpine that instructs you to produce the two officers, E.E. Burch and R.L. Quintero, pursuing said fugitive, Rhonda Mae Mutscher, and further instructs them to provide any and all results of their investigation to date, including the names and locations of members of the Ruiz crime organization and the likely places where the fugitive is being harbored. Furthermore ..."

Doggett had listened long enough. He pushed his oak swivel chair with the red leather cushion away from his desk so he could lean back, thunk his boot heels on his green baize desk blotter, and force Cucinotta to bend at the waist to maintain eye contact.

"Let me get a word in right here, Marshal. Go fuck yourself. Go fuck the New York Yankees, for that matter. The two officers you mentioned are, as we speak, in pursuit of a serial killer who has dropped three bodies in my county alone. That trumps your fugitive all to hell and back and is the reason they weren't here to hold your hand on a guided tour of the Ruiz family homes and hangouts."

"I don't need a fuckin' babysitter."

"That's debatable. More to the point, I've taken the liberty of calling the chief judge of the federal judicial district that covers this county. He's faxing you an order that shitcans what that magistrate judge wrote, tells you to quit bothering me and my officers and conduct your own investigation, and orders you to steer clear of Burch and Quintero."

"I know all about Burch. He was a crooked cop who got booted off the force in Dallas and is lucky he didn't get indicted for murder. He's been a bottom-feeder private dick for the past twenty years, working for pimps, drug dealers, smugglers, rustlers, car thieves, and mobsters. Him working for you tells me you're just as crooked as he is."

Doggett smiled and shook his head.

"You're a miserable Yankee cocksucker who wouldn't know a real lawman if they bit you on the ass. Making a lot of noise and puffin' out your chest ain't no substitute for smarts and leadership. That's why you got run out of New York, Philly, Atlanta, and Tampa and wound up in the Colorado boonies. It's also why you can't find Rhonda Mae Mutscher on your own nickel."

"That's because Burch is protecting her, harboring a damn fugitive, keeping her hidden."

"Wrong again, fuckwad. He's using her to find a killer. And I'd gladly take two more of him over a hunnert of you. Now get the fuck out of my office before I have you thrown out."

"I'm not going anywhere until you fulfill the demands of that magistrate's order."

Doggett smiled again.

"Glad to hear you say that, Marshal. Gonna be a pleasure watching some real lawmen take out trash like you. By the way, I've recorded this conversation and will be sending a copy to your boss, the magistrate judge, and the chief judge for this district. He's a friend of mine who comes down here twice a year to hunt dove and muleys."

Cucinotta lunged across the desk but Doggett was too quick for him, jumping out of the path of the marshal's move with the speed that earned him a nickname that outlasted his glory days as a calf roper.

"You sonofabitch!"

Doggett curled his lips over his teeth, using a thumb and index finger to sound a whistle loud enough to startle the perm off his secretary, Myrtle Bodine, and cause three deputies at the far end of a hallway to snap their heads around. A few seconds later, Dub McKee walked in, trailed by two Texas Rangers who formed a Mutt and Jeff combo.

At six-foot-seven and more than 300 pounds, Sergeant Doug Hayes overshadowed Cucinotta. At five-foot-seven and topping 250 pounds, Sergeant Gustavo Cuellar was squat and muscular underneath his fat, like the *luchador* he once was before joining the Rangers. McKee reached into his charcoal gray suit jacket with the Western piping and pulled out a folded set of papers, tapping them on Cucinotta's chest.

"This here's a writ from Chief U.S. District Judge John Paul Moore in San Antonio, the same judge who just shitcanned your pissant magistrate judge's order. Judge Moore orders you to appear before him at four o'clock today to explain your actions to his satisfaction. If you hurry, you might just make it in time. But you best leave right now. Judge Moore has been known to hold the tardy in contempt and throw them in jail."

Cucinotta tucked the writ inside his windbreaker, shook his head, and edged his way past McKee and the Rangers and out of Doggett's office. Without looking back, he shouted over his shoulder: "You're all a bunch of asshole crooks."

Doggett called out: "Pleasure having you visit Cuervo County, Marshal. Come back soon."

McKee waited until Cucinotta's footsteps faded away then scowled at Doggett.

"What's the latest?"

"Burch and Quintero are chasing Chizik, who kidnapped Rhonda Mae Mutscher's boy."

"Jesus. Do they got a line on where he's headed?"

"They think they do. The abandoned ranch Chizik first used for gunrunning. The one I raided with the ATF."

"Let's call out the cavalry and put a cordon around that place tighter than a tick."

"I don't want to do that. Everything'll get ramped up and crazy, and that boy'll get killed. Better to let Burch and Quintero run a two-man game."

"For all we know, that boy's dead already."

"No sir, he's bait. Chizik grabbed him to get Rhonda Mae out in the open. He'll try to trade the boy for Rhonda Mae. This is Chizik's end game. He's obsessed with this woman. He kills her, and he's ready to die. Wants to kill Burch, too, for makin' him a one-eyed cripple."

"Some fuckin' cripple. How many bodies has he dropped?"

"Eight we know about."

"Where's the mother right now?"

"With Burch and Quintero."

"Jesus Christ, Sheriff. We need to get out there."

"Got four of my best headed out there right now. They'll set up at the ranch house and get within shouting distance of Burch and Quintero. I'll be joining them now that we got rid of asshole."

McKee turned to Hayes and Cuellar.

"You two *hombres* are working for Sheriff Doggett. Got a problem with that? That's a rhetorical question."

"We know that, Dub."

McKee looked over his shoulder at Doggett.

"It's your show, Sheriff, but I'm still a pretty good gun hand. Got some Kevlar for an old man?"

"Maybe so. Happy to have you along."

Twenty-Five

Bobby Quintero was sweating like a pig as he slow-crawled through the brush, wishing he was wearing camo fatigues and a boonie rat hat instead of Wranglers, a gray t-shirt, a dark blue Kevlar vest and olive drab skullcap.

He was angling toward a rock outcropping that looked like the blunt bow of a tugboat, flat-topped with a haphazard pile of mismatched boulders that might give him cover and a clear line of sight to the last building he and Burch had to search on the deserted Bar Triple T ranch.

It was a weathered shed row barn, about fifty feet long and thirty deep, with a hay loft up top and a tack room with a door opening on the end closest to him. Used to be a waystation for cowboys working the back end of the ranch, back before the deep drought of the 1950s killed off this and many another West Texas outfit. Now it was just a handy secluded spot well away from the front gate.

Quintero remembered scouting this building before that raid eight years ago. Chizik's crew stored tarp-covered cases of automatic weapons and ammo in the horse stalls and the loft. Had a spring-loaded trap door in the loft floor with an extendable ladder for people to use. But heavy loads had to be hauled up by a rope and pulley attached to a swinging yardarm bolted next to the loft door.

Nothing visible in the stalls now, but he did spot a dusty, dark green Jeep Wagoneer tucked in the brush crowding the far end of the barn. Got the right place, but he saw no sign of Chizik and the kid.

Picking a stone pile that gave him a view of the four horse stalls, the tack room door, and the wide, second-story door to the loft, Quintero stayed low, took a pull of water from a plastic canteen clipped to his belt, then started setting up his lair. He shucked a rucksack, untying a thin, rolled up foam pad from the bottom and spreading it out on the softest-looking rock he could find, a smooth and lovely oval that wouldn't bruise his ribs, elbows, or hip bones too badly. Next came two extra fifteen-round mags and nylon desert-camo netting to drape over his body to break up his silhouette.

He slipped the sling of his FN FAL .308 over his head then eased into a prone position on the mat, pulling the netting over his head and body, unfolding the paratrooper stock and using the four-power scope to slowly sweep the barn and surrounding brush. Nada. He judged himself to be about sixty yards from the barn and adjusted the Trilux 4X scope. Pulling a Motorola HT-90 out of the ruck, he made sure the volume and squelch were turned low and powered it up to talk to Burch, cupping his hand around his mouth so his voice wouldn't carry.

"Think I found it. Auxiliary barn about a mile north of you. Head up the gravel trail. Can't miss it."

"Any sign of Chizik and the kid?"

"No, but there's a Jeep Wagoneer parked beside the barn. They're either inside or out in the brush. Is Chizik enough of a bastard to drag Charlie into a thicket?"

"Oh, hell, yes. Whether he has is a different question."

"When you get up here, we're gonna have to get a lot closer to this barn to get an answer."

Maybe not. Quintero heard a muffled wooden *thunk* and the sound of something heavy being dragged across a floor. No horses. No mules. Not even a buzzard roosted in this barn these days so odds were good the noises came from Chizik rooting around in the loft or the tack room. Couldn't tell which. Couldn't see deep enough into either space.

Then he heard the voice of a young boy cry out: "Mama ... I want mama ...."

"Shut up, kid. Drink that orange juice. Don't make me gag you again."

"I don't wanna."

"Suit yourself."

Quintero felt the anger rise in his chest. He keyed the mic: "They're both here. Just heard Charlie and Chizik. Get your ass up here. The both of us can take him."

"No. Stick to the plan. You're gonna stay put and blast him when you get the chance."

"Shit."

"I need you to stay frosty and stick to the plan."

"Roger, that."

When Burch and Rhonda Mae spotted the barn about forty yards ahead, they ducked to the right side of the trail and took cover behind some thick creosote and mesquite brush. From this prickly vantage point, they could see the loft door was open and hooked in place but couldn't see much of the inside. Same for the open door to the tack room. No movement. No noise.

He keyed the mic on the HT-90 and told Quintero where they were.

"Got it, partner. I'm gonna have to move. Can't see far enough into those open doors to give you good cover."

"Make it fast, Bobby. Think the show's about to start."

"It'll be down and dirty. Will advise."

Like an itch that won't stay scratched, the lousy fit of his Kevlar vest on Rhonda Mae kept bothering Burch. She wore it under a dark blue denim work shirt with the tails untucked and covering the Smith & Wesson gouging a hole in her back. The shirt smoothed out some of the vest's lumpiness. But not enough to suit Burch. For the second time since she donned the vest, Burch had her unbutton the shirt so he could cinch the vest straps tighter. Didn't do much more than annoy her.

"Quit fussin', Gramps. Don't know why you want me to wear this damn thing, anyway. You're the one who needs it."

"Don't argue with me on this. Just say 'thank you'."

"He's just as likely to shoot you for makin' a wreck outta him."

"Sweet Jesus, had to get the last word in, didn't ya?"

The clang and boom of metal striking wood rang out, putting a temporary halt to their bickering. Hard to tell where the noise came from. Chizik's voice was easier to place —from inside the tack room.

"I know you're out there, Burch, you fat old bastard. Took you long enough to get here after that bread crumb I left you. You better have *La Güera* by your side. That's the only chance this kid's got of stayin' alive."

Rhonda Mae answered: "I'm right fuckin' here, *pendejo*. You send my boy to me, and I'll give myself up. Like you said in that note. A life for a life."

"That ain't gonna be the way this works. I'll send Charlie out as soon as you get halfway here."

"That won't work. He'll come runnin' to me as soon as he sees me."

"Then I guess you'll need to get that fat ass boyfriend of yours to step out so you can tell the boy to go to him."

Enough of this goddam noise, Sport Model. Step up and fix this mess.

"Hey, Chizik! How 'bout this fat old bastard stepping out far enough to take Charlie from his mother's arms? Does that fuckin' work for you, *cabron?*"

"Well now, you ain't a totally useless fuck, after all. Imagine my surprise. We'll do it your way, asshole."

Burch checked his Colt to make sure there was a Flying Ashtray in the pipe then looked at Rhonda Mae. There was grim fury in her amber wolf eyes and the hard set of her jaw.

"Let's go get my boy, Gramps. Then kill this sorry bastard."

"Read my mind. Let's go."

They stepped onto the trail side-by-side, Rhonda Mae to the left, Burch to the right, about four feet between them.

Their eyes were locked on the tack room doorway, the inside too dark to see details but light enough to sense movement. Chizik's movement, tracking them with a gun. A certainty you didn't need to see to believe.

"Be ready. This bastard may start shooting early. You break left, and I'll break right."

The words were barely out of Burch's mouth before Chizik stepped out of the tack room, screaming and shooting.

"*La Güerrrrrrraaaaaaa!* I got you now! Gonna kill you and slit your throat! Suck on this, you bitch!"

Burch zig-zagged right, pulling the Colt, pointing it at Chizik, praying Charlie was tucked behind something thick and solid. Like a tank turret. Or a '48 Plymouth De Luxe. He heard slugs smacking something solid and saw Rhonda Mae stumble, then fall forward.

"Goddamit, I'm hit Gramps. Jesus, that hurts."

Chizik, moving toward Rhonda Mae with choppy steps, his semi-automatic aimed at her body.

"This is where the fun begins, *La Güera!*"

Burch, tracking him with the Colt until he was sure of a center mass hit. Then blasting until the Colt was empty and the slide locked back. Chizik staggering then turning toward Burch, firing twice.

A hard punch above his left hip and a searing sensation along the ribcage told Burch he was tagged. He flinched and dropped the fresh mag he was holding in his right hand. He pulled the only full mag he had left, slammed it into the well, and tripped the slide, putting one in the pipe.

Chizik, wobbly but still standing, screeching his hate and anger. He was also reloading.

"I can't *buh-leeeeeeve* you shot me again, you fat bastard! But I got that bitch! I got that bitch! You didn't protect her this time. She's fuckin' dead! I won! I won!"

"Not today, Slick. Not ever."

Eight more Flying Ashtrays rocketing from his Colt. Chizik, jerking and dancing, starting to fall. Then a deeper boom from the brush behind Burch. A dime-sized red hole in Chizik's forehead. A shower of bone, blood, and brain matter bursting from the back of his skull.

Bobby Quintero, making sure Chizik was dead-dead this time with a .308 head shot. Slam that door and nail it shut.

Twenty-Six

T he voice from the tack room was clear, loud and insistent, boosted by all the lung power a four-year-old boy could muster: "I want mama ... Where are you? Mama ...."

"Help me up, Gramps. Need to fetch my boy."

"Fend for yourself, Slick. I'm bleedin' over here."

"You ain't as dead as Elvis. Not yet, you're not. Get your ass up and give a girl a hand."

Burch rolled away from the wounds to his left side. Got on all fours to stand. The pain was instant and exquisite, shooting razor blades and alarm bells up his brain stem and causing him to retch the only thing on his stomach—yellow-green bile.

Bobby Quintero's voice, behind and above him: "You need to stay put. Lie back down and let me check you out."

Quintero kneeled next to Burch, pulling his shirttail up and out, clucking his tongue as he looked at the ragged red line that streaked the ribs and the hole above the left hip, reaching under the back to feel for an exit wound. He showed the bloody fingers of his right hand to Burch.

"It's a through-and-through. You're not bleedin' too bad. Gonna give you this to put some pressure on it. Best I can do for now."

A dark green gym towel. Smelled like sweat, horse liniment, and gun oil. Burch gritted his teeth and pressed the towel over the bloody wound.

"Mama ... I want my mama ...."

"I'll be right there, Charlie."

Quintero hustled over to Rhonda Mae. She was flat on her back, grimacing in pain. He unbuttoned her shirt and peeled it open to check the oversized Kevlar vest underneath.

"Hurts like hell to breathe, Bobby. Feels like I got some busted ribs."

"The vest caught three slugs that I can see. Don't look like you got tagged anyplace else."

"Help me up, Bobby. Got to get my boy."

Quintero helped her to her feet. She draped her right arm over his shoulders, leaning on him.

"Goddam, that hurts like fire. I can feel somethin' grindin' in there."

"Busted ribs, most likely. Need to make sure you ain't got a punctured lung."

"Dandy. Just dandy. Beats bein' this guy, though."

She nodded at Chizik's body as they passed. It was lying face down in the sand, dark-red pulp where the back of the skull used to be, torn forest green T-shirt fabric vented by four exit wounds on his back that looked like somebody had worked him over with an ice cream scoop.

In the tack room, they found Charlie curled up under a wooden saddle stand in the back corner, his arms and legs bound by zip ties, his tear-streaked face red from crying and yelling. Quintero cut the zip ties with a lock-blade knife, then lifted Charlie into Rhonda Mae's arms.

"Mama, I missed you. Where did you go? That bad man hurt Nancy Jo and took me. I was scared."

"I know, Charlie. I know. I love you, son. And I'll never leave you alone again."

It was a promise she knew she couldn't keep. She hugged her son tight and kissed his face and hair. Charlie wrapped his arms around her neck and burrowed his head in the crook of her neck. She looked Quintero in the eye.

"Thank you, Bobby. For saving my son."

"Glad I could help. But you and *Oso Blanco* did the heavy lifting."

"White Bear? Where does that come from?"

"One of his girlfriends."

"How many does he got?"

"Three that I know of."

She snorted a laugh and looked at the man she called Gramps. *Oso Blanco, huh? Three girlfriends. The old man still gets around.*

Burch was seated in the sand, pressing the towel over the entry wound with his right hand, a Lucky on his lip curling smoke, bill of his CCSO ballcap pulled low, watching three county Blazers roll up the trail, lights flashing, with a meat wagon bringing up the rear. The Blazers fanned out when they hit the clearing where the barn stood to let the meat wagon move up. Doggett and McKee climbed out of the rig nearest Burch and walked over. McKee did the talking.

"You finally get that sumbitch?"

"Yup. Face down in the sand behind me. I chopped him up. Bobby sealed the deal with a head shot."

"Dead-dead?"

"Deader than that Yankee in Grant's Tomb."

"Nice work."

Doggett jerked a thumb at the ambulance.

"There's your ride. Get yourself checked out and patched up. We'll get a statement from you later. Need your gun now."

Burch handed his Colt to Doggett. "No attaboy? Dub showed his appreciation. How 'bout you, boss?"

"Shoulda killed that sumbitch the first time you had a chance. Might've saved a few lives. Now get the fuck out of my sight."

Quintero held out a hand. Burch, too mad and stubborn to accept the help, flipped the Lucky to the sand and staggered to his feet. A young paramedic with a buzz cut and biceps the size of grapefruit trotted up to aid Burch but a red-eyed glare stopped him in his tracks. Quintero chuckled.

"Damn but you're a hardcase."

"Part of my endearing charm. Nice shot, Bobby. Saw the bullet hit."

"Sorry I didn't get him before he shot you."

"I'll live. Buy me a Maker's and we're even."

"You bet. Lemme ask you something. Why do you keep pokin' a stick at Doggett? It's gonna get you canned."

"I don't give much of a shit. I'm tired of him gettin' pissed off when I walk through the office door. And you know why I piss him off? Cause I saved his life one night when we were chasin' a bad guy over on the wrong side of the river."

"Why would that piss the man off? I'd be damn thankful."

"That's because you got your shit wired tight, Bobby. Doggett don't. He's one of those folks who just can't stand a dose of saving grace. It eats at them. Reminds them they ain't bulletproof and needed help one time."

They stopped at the open back door of the meat wagon. Burch lit another Lucky, looked at the young paramedic, and nodded his head.

"Okay, young man. Get your ass over here and patch me up."

"You're not allowed to smoke in the ambulance 'cause of the oxygen tanks."

"Then I'll stand right here until I finish. Don't guess I'll bleed out in the time that takes me. Got any medicinal whiskey in this rig? I could use a snort."

Quintero shook his head and walked away.

Twenty-Seven

Burch was sitting on his ass at his *ranchito* watching the javelinas and coyotes slink by instead of chasing the next batch of killers and scumbags. He was on the beach. In drydock. A cop without a badge. Suspended. With pay. Pending an investigation of the killing of those two gunmen he and Rhonda Mae waxed in that dark-thirty shooting on the hillside goat trail.

It wasn't a righteous shoot. The two bad guys never had a chance. Burch and Rhonda Mae never gave them one. It was a cold-blooded ambush, truth be told.

But it was damn sure warranted.

The two hired guns had long rap sheets for violence and mayhem. And murders that were charged but never proven. They were working for Danny Ray Mutscher, Rhonda Mae's father, the incestuous Dixie Mafia drug lord. Killers doing the bidding of a loathsome piece of shit nobody would nominate for Father of the Year.

Given the upper hand, they would have grabbed Rhonda Mae and clipped Burch. Those were their orders. And in a straight-up firefight, they could just as easily have killed Rhonda Mae. By accident. A fatal error in her father's eyes. One that would have earned both gunmen a toe tag in the Cuervo County morgue. Big deal. Wouldn't mean much to Burch and Rhonda Mae. They'd still be dead.

When the lead's about to fly, there's no time for protocol, procedure, or legal niceties. And giving away your edge in a gunfight is a quick way to get dead. Better to shoot first, stay upright and breathing, and deal with the consequences later.

In the statement he gave to the Rangers called in to handle the investigation, he played it straight and framed the shooting as just that type of do-or-die moment. They didn't seem too concerned about the ambush itself. A pair of scumbags taken off the board? Tough shit. They had the same attitude about the gunmen Rhonda Mae and Hector Ruiz killed. Four more scumbags eliminated? Wonderful news. Clearly a case of self-defense. Sorry the old man got dead.

What they were hung up on was the tactical alliance between a former gunrunner and fugitive wanted for murder and a sworn officer of the law. A cop and a criminal in cahoots, killing people. Not a good look. Broke the rules and boundaries of the cop and snitch relationship all to hell and back. You could sleep with a snitch. Happened all the time. You just couldn't team up with them to kill anybody.

Flat pissed off Sheriff Sudden Doggett, too. He had pointedly ordered Burch not to resurrect his Sir Galahad act to save Rhonda Mae and Charlie, reminding him he was a lawman now, not a P.I. free to ignore the book and do anything he could get away with. Burch blew past Doggett's command and jumped right in to help Rhonda Mae. Another rescue mission. Just like the one her grandmother tasked him with four years ago. Staying glued to Rhonda Mae was also the best way to smoke out the serial killer who had her boy.

Not that much different from Doggett's desire to use Rhonda Mae as bait for Cleve Chizik, who had a homicidal obsession about her. But Doggett didn't see it that way. He wanted Burch to be like a fly fisherman casting his feathered bait from the creek bank, maintaining a chaste distance between himself and Rhonda Mae.

Didn't happen that way, so Doggett wanted to grab Burch's badge from his desk drawer, melt it down, and never give it back. Dub McKee, the retired Ranger and Austin *eminence grise* who convinced Doggett to hire Burch in the first place, looked past the bad optics and blood spills and focused on the results. Burch and Quintero took out Lonny Dalrymple and Chizik, two of the last killers running free in the Leigh Burdette murder case.

Burch still felt a lot of guilt about Leigh's murder. He was hunting for Rhonda Mae, but the gunrunners were convinced he was digging up dirt on them. Chizik, Dalrymple, and two other scumbags tortured her, trying to pry loose information on his whereabouts, then sliced her throat wide open and left her to bleed out on the bed where she and Burch had made love.

Nailing Chizik was the final installment of payback for Leigh. Took a serial killer, gunrunner, and hitter for the Aryan Brotherhood off the board, a man tied to at least eight murders in Texas and New Mexico on his personal payback spree and an unknown number of bodies dropped at the behest of Alice Baker honchos. He was also the prime suspect in the murders of six A-B rivals in California prisons such as Pelican Bay and Folsom, each an individual hit with the signature use of a straight-edge razor.

McKee wanted Burch to keep his badge because he got results like this. He'd lean on Doggett the same way he did to get the reluctant sheriff to initially hire Burch. And he'd keep a lid on the shooting investigation.

"You did exactly what needed to be done. Now, hang tight, keep your nose clean and your mouth shut while I try to clean this up and save your badge," McKee said while visiting him in the hospital the day he and Bobby shot Chizik dead.

Not much McKee or Doggett could do for Rhonda Mae, but they did manage to keep Charlie out of the Texas Child Protective Services system, reaching out to Consuela Ruiz, sister of Armando Ruiz, the boy's dead father, to take him in. Charlie would be safe, surrounded by Armando's formidable family.

Rhonda Mae was Colorado-bound to face murder charges that would shine a spotlight on her that any cartel killer could see. Deputy U.S. Marshal Gabe Cucinotta, terminal dumbass, showed up at Doggett's office again, licking his chops about hauling her back to Cortez, acting like he was the one who tracked her down.

Hard to kill arrogance and stupidity. Good to get one over on the blustery Fed blowhard, though. Burch kept Big Russett, the CAR-15, and the big brick of cash, triple-wrapping the money in plastic before putting it in a footlocker and burying it in the barn, right where he always parked the cherry '68 Four-Four-Two that Carla Sue gave him. The money would stay there until he could figure a way to get it to Rhonda Mae or her attorney that wouldn't get him arrested.

Turtle Wax the white-knight armor again, bubba. Gotta rescue the damsel in distress one more time.

He also reached out to a Houston defense attorney named Barton Phillips, a protege of the late and legendary Racehorse Haynes who once got Burch and a client out of a jam with a homicide cop who kept trying to hang a murder rap around his neck.

Phillips put him in touch with W.C. Porter, a semi-retired defense attorney living in Durango after running rings around prosecutors in Oklahoma City for a quarter century. He agreed to represent Rhonda Mae for a cut of that money hiding under his Four-Four-Two, $30,000 up front, full amount to be named later. Sold American.

Burch knew the strong undercurrent flowing between Rhonda Mae and himself was more than the mutual love they had for her grandmother. They had twice killed people together to survive. And he had twice rescued her. She returned the favor, shooting an old friend who was about to put a bullet in his brain. That formed a bond tempered by violence. Didn't know if it was love. Didn't look like they'd ever find out. Hell, he was twenty years older than her. But they knew the attraction was there, and they both danced around it, dropping hints now and then, skittering away if the other rose to the bait.

Hadn't seen or heard from Carla Sue, his lethal inamorata, in more than two months. Didn't know if she was alive or dead. When he got the carnal itch, he'd dial up Carmen or Alma. He even scored the Fat Man's Perfecta, a big chicken-fried steak with peppery milk gravy and fried okra, cooked and served up by Alma in the kitchen of her cafe after closing. Then a short ride over to her twenty-six-foot Flying Cloud to make the bed springs squeal.

"I like to keep a man fed and fucked. It's the key to his heart."

"Can't argue with that."

"But I know your heart's not mine. Not yet."

"Keep treating me this way and that might just change."

Alma, slender, long-legged, small-breasted, and naked, arched an eyebrow, pursed her lips, and wagged a finger at him. She didn't buy the lie.

Carmen, with her thick black curls, fleshy curves, and wicked mouth, liked to play their carnal games on the road as much as she did at home. Despite the distance, she would drive out to Burch's place, staying as long as she could before she had to drive back to town to start prepping her food truck for the day ahead.

Since he wasn't slammed with new cases, he cooked her dinner. Simple stuff. Steaks, pork chops, smoked brisket, Italian sausage and peppers, chili. Then they'd strip the clothes off each other and try to wreck his rickety bed, two large-bodied lovers eating up every square inch of mattress.

"Getting shot didn't damage your cock or tongue. Both are still running strong, baby."

"We've also managed to stress test my stitches. Haven't busted anything open yet."

"Care to try again?"

"Give me a minute."

Burch knew he couldn't keep stringing them along much longer. He also knew that neither one of them was a substitute for the woman who already claimed his heart. Not that his battered old heart was that much of a prize. More like a fractured lump of coal.

His longing for Carla Sue wasn't constant. He could lose himself in ranch chores or a book and whenever he was with Carmen or Alma. Or talking to Bobby Quintero, who occasionally showed up with a six pack of Pearl in bottles and the latest gossip from the Cuervo County Sheriff's Office and the greater Faver metroplex.

"Doggett's got a new main squeeze—Gabriella Martinez, branch manager at First Bank of West Texas. Good lookin' woman. Don't know what she sees in our sad-eyed fearless leader."

"Has she brightened his mood, caused him to smile more often?"

"Let's just say he's a little less dark and doesn't walk around pissed off all the time."

"Well, hell Bobby—that might not have a damn thing to do with her and everything to do with my absence."

But when he was alone and parked in a front porch rocker with his morning coffee or his Maker's sundowner, he kept hoping to see a plume of dust rising from the road that ran past his gate, signaling the arrival of a rocket red '72 Olds Cutlass Supreme convertible with Carla Sue at the wheel. Not every morning or evening, but often enough.

Long hikes deeper into the box canyon that cupped his house with a rock-faced U also helped blunt the heartache and tamp down his rising restlessness. He carried the M1 with him, slung over his shoulder with the butt end up, six clips of 30.06 in a cloth bandolier slipped over his neck and a surplus aluminum canteen with a canvas cover hung on a web belt cinched around his waist. He usually toted a canvas bag stuffed with tin cans and beer bottles for plinking. Other times, he hid in the brush and tried to nail a coyote or, if it was cold enough, one of the rattlers warming themselves in the sun on a ledge halfway up the south wall of the canyon.

Some days, he carried Rhonda Mae's CAR-15, a Vietnam-era favorite with a select group of elite troops. Not that often. Just enough to get friendly with the gun and its loud, short-barreled ways. The damn thing could lay down some fire. And he learned to control that jacketed bullet stream, running thirty-round clips on full auto and figuring out how to keep the muzzle on target instead of climbing toward the sky.

He got competent and comfortable, appreciating the gun's close-range handiness and potency. But he preferred the heavier, more powerful M1 Garand, a rifle he qualified with during Army basic training in 1968 and still shot well. It could reach out and touch bad guys the CAR-15 couldn't but didn't match the smaller gun's ability to chop them up in tight quarters.

Not that he needed the prompt, but after-midnight visitors gave him a jolt of fresh motivation to keep his shooting eye sharp and his guns always handy. Valentina Garza and her praetorian guard of top *sicarios* came calling in two black Suburbans with smokey-gray tinted windows.

Burch, restless and hounded by ancient loss and fresh regret, was already wide awake and rocking on the front porch with a Winchester twelve-gauge across his lap, keeping him company. When he heard the squeal of his roadside gate and tires rumbling over the cattle guard, he jacked a round of buckshot into the pipe and stuffed fresh Levi Garrett leaf into his jaw.

The Suburbans stopped about ten yards from his front porch. The *sicarios* stepped into the dust then fanned out in an arc, focused on him with pistols held low along their legs. Burch kept his hands very still and very visible. Valentina Garza stepped through the apex of the arc to stand at the bottom of his porch steps.

"*Buenas noches*, Detective Burch. I hope you don't mind the intrusion, but I wanted to thank you personally for killing that *diablo bastardo* Chizik."

"That devil bastard needed killin', Doña Valentina, and I was happy to do it. While I appreciate your thanks, it was my duty to take him down."

"Of course. Chizik killed someone dear to me, and I swore I'd personally avenge that death. My men were searching for him, but you found him first and fulfilled my wish, whether you knew that or not. To close the circle, I felt it was necessary to give you my thanks. Face to face."

"To honor your oath to avenge your friend."

"*Sí*. I knew you would understand. Although we've never met before, I knew of you through things my father said. He told me you are a hard man, a worthy adversary, but also a man of honor."

"I'm nobody's hero, Doña Valentina. I'm also a piss-poor host. Can I offer you a drink? All I have is bourbon but I can pour you a glass so we can toast your friend."

She nodded and whispered to a *sicario* standing by her side. The gunsel climbed the porch steps and stood in front of Burch. With a polite, "*Con su permiso,*" he lifted the shotgun from Burch's lap and followed him into the kitchen. Burch poured three fingers of Maker's in two rocks glasses and carried them outside to stand in front of Valentina Garza. He handed her a glass.

"To Santiago Cruz," he said, raising his glass.

"*Sí*. To Santiago." she said, clinking her glass against his.

They left. Burch locked and bolted his front door and climbed back into bed, shotgun next to him for cold comfort, pretty damn sure he'd never fall asleep.

Silence from Doggett and McKee. Then again, he didn't expect to hear from either of them until the Rangers handed in their final report. And that conversation would be very short. Either, *Come in Monday, pick up your badge, and get back to work.* Or, *Adios, motherfucker. Come clean out your desk and pick up your severance check.*

If he got the chop, he'd probably slink back to Dallas and hang out his shamus shingle one more time. See if he could rent digs on Marquita Street again. Snag an office on Mockingbird. Again. Hook a boot on the bar rail at Louie's once more for an endless pour of Maker's, neat, with an ice water back. Tool around town in that sweet '68 Four-Four-Two, rap the pipes now and again, peel some rubber, watch the needle climb toward the century mark on a dark and lonely stretch of I-35 near the Oklahoma line.

Forget about his noble, gold-shield fantasy once and for all. And bury the ghost of Carla Sue Cantrell in the blue exhaust and four-barreled roar of the badass ride she gave him.

Burch knew he didn't have to wait until he returned to Dallas to grab a dose of therapy from his fine piece of Big American Iron. He could get that high-speed rush right now.

Don't dick around, pendejo. Grab your Colt, your Ray-Bans, a windbreaker, and that Resistol straw. Rip the tarp off that Four-Four-Two. Fire her up. Get gone.

Before he could blink and change his mind, he was booming up U.S. 67 northeast of Alpine, listening to the roar of the 455 Rocket engine and four-barrel QuadraJet, downshifting the Muncie four-speed to pick up I-10 west of Fort Stockton and ripping up asphalt on U.S. 190 east of Iraan, rocketing toward El Dorado.

All before sunset.

The speed soothed his jangled nerves, smothered the longing in his heart and gave him a free-falling peace he hadn't felt in a very long time. The scenery rolling by—the jagged peaks, the sudden dip and roll of the lowlands, the long sand-and-rock desert flats—reminded him why he fell in love with West Texas.

Looked like the bones of the earth ripped open for all to see, a sun-blasted land where nobody could hide. Not even the nightmare demons that once tortured his days and nights.

He didn't brood about Carla Sue or Sudden Doggett. Or those demons. He didn't fret about Rhonda Mae. He didn't cling to his gold-shield fantasy. He smoked Luckies and sang along to hard honky-tonk songs from an all-night trucker's program he picked up on KOKC-AM, a clear-channel station out of Oklahoma City.

... Thanks for sending something I can't use/Received your invitation to the blues ...

Nothing better than a Ray Price classic. He had a short stack, eggs up, and country ham for dinner at an IHOP on the I-10 service road near Sonora. Flirted with the waitress while washing down his meal with watery coffee you could see clear through.

For a delayed dessert, he picked up a pint of Maker's at a liquor store. Continued his high-speed run down U.S. 277. Dove into a cheap motel on the outskirts of Loma Alto, locking the anti-theft bar to the steering wheel of the Olds and tripping the battery kill switch.

Breakfast was a ham-and-cheese omelet and hash browns at a Denny's in Del Rio. And then a long, gas-guzzling run on U.S. 90 through Dryden, Sanderson, and Marathon before taking a hard left on U.S. 67 in Alpine and rattling over the cattle guard at his front gate.

As he slowly bumped his way up the caliche trail to his house, he got a double vision of himself. Rocking by his lonesome on the front porch, searching for a plume of dust from a tomato-red Cutlass Supreme ragtop, waiting on a ghostly love who never showed. Watching a nocturne blue Olds muscle car on the road running past his place, trailing dust he could see and taste. Right here. Right now.

Sumbitch. Been waitin' on my own damn self. Tyin' my own self up in knots. Waitin' for the axe to fall. Waitin' for Carla Sue. Waitin' just to wait.

Fuck that noise. Dial up Doggett right now. Tell him to keep his motherfuckin' badge. Tell him "I quit. And you can go fuck yourself."

A voice in his ear. Wynn Moore, his dead partner: *I see that road trip blew the cobwebs out of your brain, Sport Model. Clearest thinkin' you done in a long damn time. Don't wait, though. Follow through. Right now.*

Good idea, Wynn.

He climbed the porch steps and saw a note tacked to the front door. It was from Dub McKee: *Stopped by to talk. Call me soonest. Dub.*

He stepped through the door, snatched the cordless phone out of its charger, grabbed a bottle of Maker's, and plopped down in the closest front porch rocker to dial up Dub.

"Just rolled in and saw your note. Had a revelation on the road, signs and portents I won't bore you with. Here's the short version: I quit. You can tell Doggett to stick that badge up his ass."

"Now wait a minute, Ed Earl. I just about got everything smoothed out."

"No, you wait a minute, Dub. I appreciate everything you done for me. But my mind's made up. Doggett ain't ever gonna change. And I'm sick unto death of bein' a whippin' boy for a man who can't be thankful for some saving grace."

He cut the connection and took a long pull of Maker's straight from the bottle, enjoying the burn of the bourbon and the sweet bliss of having nothing to do and nobody pulling his tail. Nothing and nobody felt mighty fine. So did his view of the sun sliding down on his blasted patch of desert heaven. The tight coil of tension in his chest loosened up another notch. His brain slipped into neutral.

He lit a Lucky and let his eyes roam where they pleased, mind blank, soul at ease. No demons. No heartache.

No bullets to dodge. No worries. It wouldn't last, but it was as close to happy as he ever got.

Happy—what the hell is happy anyway, Wynn?

Dunno, Sport Model. Let's ask Jake Gittes.

Nicholson in Chinatown?

Nah, The Two Jakes. Khan the butler asks Jake whether success has made him happy. Jake dodges the question: "Who can answer that question off the top of their head?" Khan nails him: "Anyone who's happy."

That's a good 'un, Wynn. Right here, right now, I'm with Khan. All is right with my world, and I am content.

But are you happy, Sport Model?

Who can answer that question off the top of their head?

Burch shook his head, chuckled and speared a random thought. *Wonder what the neighbors are up to?* He spotted a trio of javelinas rooting in the dirt on the far side of the trail running past his front door and caught a coyote staring at him while slinking along in the eternal quest for the next rabbit, snake, or mouse to kill.

Maybe I won't move back to Dallas. Maybe I'll stay here with the four-legged folks next door. Might get me a dog. One of those blue heelers. Call him Max. Or Buster.

And tell him to never ask me whether I'm happy.

About the Author

Jim Nesbitt is a lapsed horseman, pilot, hunter, and saloon sport with a keen appreciation of old guns, vintage cars and trucks, good cigars, aged whisky without an 'e', and a well-told story. He is the award-winning author of five hard-boiled Texas crime thrillers that feature battered but relentless Dallas PI Ed Earl Burch—THE LAST SECOND CHANCE, THE RIGHT WRONG NUMBER, THE BEST LOUSY CHOICE, THE DEAD CERTAIN DOUBT. and THE FATAL SAVING GRACE. For more than 30 years, Nesbitt was a journalist chasing hurricanes, earthquakes, plane wrecks, presidential candidates, wildfires, rodeo cowboys, neo-Nazis, and nuns with an eye for the telling detail and an ear for the voice of the people who give life to a story. A diehard Tennessee Vols fan, he now lives in enemy territory—Athens, Alabama—with his wife, Pam, and is working on his next novel.

www.ingramcontent.com/pod-product-compliance
Lightning Source LLC
Chambersburg PA
CBHW020331120726
47904CB00002B/371